IN HIS EMBRACE

Books by

TERESA SMYSER

Heaven Help Us!

The Warrior & Lady Rebel

In His Embrace

Capture A Heart of Stone

IN
HIS
EMBRACE

Warrior Bride Series, Book 2

Teresa Smyser

ACKNOWLEDGMENTS

I am so thankful for all the encouragement I receive from my family. If it weren't for my husband, Keith, my daughter, Whitney, and my daughter-in-law, Samantha, this book would still be on my computer. Thank you for prodding me to the finish line.

After the completion of each chapter, I have my "critique" girls who offer excellent suggestions on how to improve the storyline. Thank you, Whitney Kroh and Lynne Brown, for your valuable time spent reading my rough draft.

Next, I place my novel in the hands of my capable editor Joan Orman. I truly appreciate each red mark and comments on the pages of my manuscript. Red has become my new favorite color.

During the editing process Whitley Fleming works on a suitable book cover that will reflect the heart of my story. I put her graphic design degree to the test, and she never disappoints.

Lastly, I want to thank you, my readers. I greatly appreciate your enthusiasm for my novels. Your eagerness for each new story keeps me on target.

As you can see, it takes a team to get my novel from my first idea to a finished product. None of it would be possible without my Lord and Savior, Jesus Christ who gave me my vivid imagination and provides me spiritual guidance through His Word. To Him be the glory!

Chapter One

1612 England

Tormented screams pierced the air. Brigette held her breath. The cold from the stone wall seeped through her dress as she edged farther into the dark corner of her hiding place. How much longer would she have to endure those dreadful shrieks and cries of torture?

Footsteps pounded past her within inches of her feet. Darkness became her friend, almost comforting, as she tucked her feet under her dress and squeezed her eyes shut.

Another scream tore through the air. Her fingers jammed into her ears. Could no one stop those ear-splitting screeches that bled through the closed door? Oh, how she wished she resided anywhere but trapped near the horrifying sound. The nasty dungeon offered a more peaceful respite than the dark alcove where she now hid.

"Thomas, find her!" Nicolas bellowed.

Brigette squirmed. Which was worse, facing what was behind the closed door or suffering from her brother's fury? At one time she influenced him with her tears and childish spectacles, but no more. Her methods didn't work against his hardened heart.

Unless she wanted to be on the receiving end of Nicolas's wrath, she must emerge from her shadowed location. He was the brother in charge of selecting her future husband. If she infuriated him, he might choose a hideous old man as her mate. *Sigh!*

Crawling from behind the large urn, her eyes met scuffed boots. Without looking up she knew they belonged to Thomas, her other brother. When he grabbed her arm, his strong fingers tangled in her braid. The entanglement yanked her hair as he jerked her to stand.

"Come with me." He snarled. "You should expect I would find you." With a brusque hand, he dragged her toward the closed door unmindful of her pain. "You know what is expected of you, and hiding has done nothing but increase Nicolas's anger. You would have been better served to come when first summoned."

"Thomas, you are hurting me."

"That's the least of your problems, little sister. You must do what's required of you or risk the fury of our brother." Pausing, he smirked. "Mayhap a flogging is what you need to mold you into a more pleasing woman. Come." Her feet skidded and slipped as she resisted his pull.

As a child, Thomas had been her fun-loving brother. Time erased his kindness toward her and replaced it with hostility and bitterness. Would she ever see a glimpse of who he used to be? His present resolve allowed her no time to contemplate that question.

Within seconds, she stood before Nicolas who paced outside the closed door.

"Where have you been? You knew I commanded you to aid Isabelle in this gruesome task, yet you hid like a child." His face burned red.

Thomas shoved her down at Nicolas's feet. "Her behavior is despicable."

"Thomas, stop this at once! Go see to your tasks."

From her position on the floor, Brigette watched as he stomped through the passageway. Good riddance. She and Thomas had been at odds since he found out about her role in Lady Fairwick's unfortunate accident. Even though she admitted remorse for her part, the past stuck to her like tar. No one cared to hear from her penitent heart. Well, no one except Isabelle.

"Get up, Brigette." Nicolas gripped her arm and hauled her to her feet.

"Please, Nicolas, I will do anything but this."

"Your pleas are lost on me ever since you tried to harm my wife." He shoved her through the open doorway. "Now, help my wife or be on the receiving end of my hot temper." He closed the door, leaving her inside the room.

With her body plastered against the closed door, she scanned the chaotic room. Her sister-in-law, Abigail, sprawled in the bed writhing with pain. Agnes, the village healer, stood close by waiting for the inevitable. Unperturbed, Isabelle sat at Abigail's head and smoothed back her hair while whispering reassuring words until she saw Brigette.

"Where were you? I've needed you!" Isabelle rose from the bed just as Abigail launched another panic-stricken cry when her body lurched.

"I'm going to be sick," Abigail wailed.

"Here, use this pail." Isabelle held a bucket next to Abigail's head as she lost her meal. Brigette pressed her eyes shut. Bile rose in her throat from the sound and smell coming from the bed. *Oh, Dear Jesus, get me out of this mess, I pray You.* She peeked to see Isabelle headed her way. Oh no!

"Come, Brigette." Isabelle rubbed her hands together. "I want you to feel the babe move." Isabelle grabbed for her hand that remained fisted behind her back. "It is a precious miracle from God, and I want you to experience it, too."

Isabelle possessed a warrior's grip. Given no choice, Brigette stumbled toward the bed and Abigail. She tried hard to resist the tight grasp, but to no avail. Isabelle placed her hand on the hard, protruding stomach.

Isabelle rambled on about how the stomach contracted and became hard in order to help push the babe into the world. All she wanted to do was avoid Abigail and escape the dreadful room. She and Abigail rubbed together like silk over a rough plank.

With no mother to offer guidance, her brothers, Phillip, Nicolas, and Thomas had raised her. Phillip, the one married brother, attempted to get his wife to oversee her training. It had gone poorly. With a condescending attitude, Abigail spent much time complaining how she was denied the coveted *lady of the castle* position. What a fiasco growing up surrounded by three brothers who tried to pawn her off on a woman who hated her.

Without warning, Isabelle released her hand.

"'Tis time."

Brigette stepped away from the bed and watched Agnes stand ready with clean cloths, and Isabelle climb onto the end of the bed.

"Brigette, you will assist Agnes in cleaning the babe once it's born."

Horrified, Brigette looked at Abigail, her hair plastered to her sweat-dripping brow. For once Abigail refrained from ranting at her, too entrenched in the birthing process to give her a glance. She thought to take a couple of backward steps toward the door but stood frozen as she watched. Who was louder, Isabelle yelling for Abigail to push, or was it Abigail screaming in anguish? Either way, she made a vow never to marry and produce children. Birthing was a disgusting and painful process she planned to prevent.

After much coaxing, pushing, and crying, the babe launched into Isabelle's waiting hands.

"'Tis a girl," Isabelle exclaimed with glee. After cutting the cord, she thrust the baby into Agnes' expectant hands and then sat waiting … for what Brigette didn't know. Without turning her head Isabelle said, "Help Agnes. Take care to watch all she does. You need to know these things for the future."

She followed Agnes to a table containing warm water and more clean cloths. Somehow, she obeyed Agnes' instructions, all the while promising herself to remain free from this type of predicament. At one point she looked over her shoulder to see Abigail deliver again. If it was another babe, there was too much blood for it to survive. With a rapid hand, she crossed herself at the notion, yet strained to hear the conversation between her sisters-in-law.

Isabelle explained to Abigail that she delivered the afterbirth—

the part that kept the baby alive and growing inside of her during those long nine months. *Ewe!* Brigette didn't care what they called it, it looked repulsive.

The time dragged by as Isabelle issued more duties for her to perform. The last task? Holding the red, wrinkled mess of a babe—one might even say ugly babe.

Gazing at the baby's face, she whispered, "A hard life is in front of you unless you develop into a comelier little lady. Trust me, I know."

"Oh, Abigail, she's already whispering love words to her niece," Isabelle said.

Her eyes grew round when she looked at the two on the bed and found Abigail smiling at her for the first time in her life! She blinked hard to see they still grinned.

"Bring her to me," Abigail said with a soft voice.

Her knees wobbled at the endearment in Abigail's voice. Walking with careful steps, she lowered the baby into waiting arms. No longer was Abigail's face twisted in agony. She appeared peaceful and content. Could the birth of a baby change a person in an instant? Even an unattractive baby? If that were the case, then a true miracle happened today.

At last, her future at Fairwick Castle grew hopeful.

"Oh, Nicolas, wasn't it a delightful day?" Isabelle asked.

In bed, Nicolas rested on his back with hands behind his head while watching his wife brush her long, brown hair. He offered a lopsided grin. "If you say so, my love. It didn't seem all that delightful from where I sat."

Distracted from her brushing, she stared wide-eyed at him. "Nicolas! What a preposterous comment. All you men did was wait while Abigail performed the hard work."

"Now, wife. I meant no harm by my words. You don't understand what was required to keep Phillip from passing out or worse, from running headfirst into the confinement room. He acted like a cat in water. 'Twas a pitiful sight to see. But I don't wish to discuss the birthing process with ye at this time. Come. 'Tis time to be in bed by your husband." He smiled and patted the bed.

Isabelle laid aside her brush and shuffled over to her side of the bed. As usual, she fell into the high mattress and rolled to the center until she butted against his side. He snuggled her close and let out a contented sigh.

"Now this is more to my liking."

"I must say, I am a bit weary from the day."

"'Tis no wonder," he said with a gentle reprimand. He laid his hand upon her stomach. "Ye must have a care for our own babe."

She nestled a bit closer at his words. "Yes, but that doesn't mean I'm feeble. 'Tis early yet. There are five more months of waiting with much preparations to do." With a slight twist, she peered into his face. Her brow wrinkled. "You haven't told anyone, have you?"

"No, my sweet. I'm abiding your word on this and awaiting your consent."

"Good. I want Phillip and Abigail to be the center of attention for now. They waited so long for this sweet babe, and I want nothing to diminish their pleasure."

Nicolas's finger removed a lock of hair from her cheek. He leaned down and placed a quick kiss on the end of her nose. "There will be more than one day to rejoice over the birth of young Philippa. I invited our neighbors to Philippa's christening followed by a feast of celebration. What think ye of that, my wife?"

She raised on her elbow. "Oh, Nicolas, that sounds delightful. You are such a thoughtful man."

"'Twill also give me time to evaluate Brigette's possible suitors."

She lowered her brows. "What mean you?"

"Now, wife, don't get all flustered like a mother hen protecting her chick. 'Tis past time for my sister to marry and create a little one of her own. Today was a good beginning for her to witness the wonder of a babe being born."

"But she is still young and has much to learn. Growing up without a woman's influence left her at a disadvantage. I'm concerned her new husband won't be understanding of her ways."

Nicolas snorted. "What you mean to say is he wouldn't understand her selfishness and immaturity." He rubbed her arm. "To please you I even invited Laird McKinnon."

"Does that mean you forgave him for kidnapping me?"

"It means he will be included, nothing more. Daniel never could resist a pretty face, and she does have that going for her."

"Nicolas!" She nudged his leg with her foot. "She boasts many wonderful qualities to recommend her, but can we not delay this until a later date? I have yet to teach her the ways of a woman with a man or how to run a castle or …"

"Stop trying to coddle my sister. There's no better way to learn than on the battlefield. Mayhap a husband will succeed where I failed—purge her self-regard and dramatic acts."

"Husband, there is much sweetness buried beneath her performances."

He placed a finger to his wife's lips. "No more discussion on the matter. 'Tis already decided. Phillip and I will assess her potential husbands at the christening."

Chapter Two

One month later ...

"Rider approaches," Duncan shouted from the gatehouse.

Daniel strode to the keep steps and waited. He never knew what to expect with an uninvited guest. Sometimes it was a pleasant interruption from his daily grind of running a castle at the border of Scotland and England, while other occasions proved distasteful confrontations. With arms crossed and feet apart he wore his best intimidating scowl.

The scruffy rider rode straight to the steps producing a dust cloud that encompassed the man. Daniel remained stoic until he knew the man's intentions.

From atop his horse the man asked, "Are ye Lord McKinnon?"

"Aye."

A big grin flashed across the man's face as he slid to the ground. Holding the bridle to his mount, he said, "Me name is Warrick, and I've a message to deliver to ye from Lord Nicolas Fairwick of Fairwick Castle. I'm to await yer answer."

Daniel cringed noting the messenger acted too cheerful for his taste. Something was amiss. Nothing good ever came from his old friend, Nicolas Fairwick. Resigned, he flung his arms down. "Come inside where we can talk in private. Kenneth, see to his horse." He spun on his heel and strode inside the keep. Warrick

9

bounded up the steps to follow.

Daniel led the courier into the empty grand hall where he ordered a repast for his visitor. Undoubtedly, the man was thirsty as well as hungry after his ride across the border. He offered Warrick a seat on the bench at one of the tables while he stood with one foot on the opposite bench. He leaned on his knee and waited.

After the man pulled a long drag on his ale, he wiped the dribble on his sleeve and grinned. "Are ye ready to hear me message?"

Expecting the worst from his nemesis, Daniel forced himself to remain indifferent.

"Aye. Get on with it."

Warrick stood and rummaged through his pocket to produce a crunched parchment.

"Ye'll need to read it for yerself 'cause I can't read."

He hesitated for a moment not sure he wanted to read the missive sent from his childhood friend. His foot thumped to the floor as he snatched the paper from Warrick's hand. Warrick didn't seem to notice his agitation as he plopped down and dove into the meal placed before him.

While Daniel perused the note, the tension in his shoulders rinsed away like dirt under a spring rain. It announced a happy occasion for Lord Phillip Fairwick, the oldest of the Fairwick brothers and his wife, Lady Abigail. Lord Nicolas Fairwick planned a feast at the christening of his new niece, Philippa. After many years of doubt, his brother produced an offspring—the first one for the Fairwick brothers.

A spontaneous smile spread across his face. Nicolas had refrained from mischief this time. Their last altercation resounded anew in his mind when months ago, Nicolas tainted the well water at his castle. His jaw clinched at the recollection. 'Twas best not to revisit the details of his memory.

"Enjoy your meal, my friend." He gave a hearty slap to the man's shoulder. "And tell your *lord* I am pleased to accept his invitation to the feast. Of course, I'll have my guard in tow, as well as young William. Tell him I'll expect grand accommodations for my group."

"Yea, m' lord," he said with a mouthful.

"Now, don't forget to notify Lord Fairwick of my housing needs. I'll be expecting the best lodging since we are such close companions." He imagined the expression on Nicolas's face when he received that bit of news. "In fact, I'll write a response for you to take with you." Rubbing his hands together, he began to plot what trouble to stir up against Nicolas.

Ever since Nicolas wed Isabelle, his friend's life had spiraled out of control. He acted as if he ruled as the head of Fairwick castle when in fact his wife was the neck that turned the head. He lived to please his wife and to do her bidding.

Pondering how much Nicolas had changed, Daniel realized he had been spared. At one point he considered keeping Isabelle for himself. He was grateful Nicolas had been the victor. From where Daniel stood, he arose triumphant with that skirmish. His friend would be an easy target since his bride consumed his thoughts.

On that happy note, he left Warrick to finish his meal while he went to write his response.

Brigette sat by the fire in her room twisting her nightclothes into a knot and then releasing it. Nicolas informed her that during the feast tomorrow, he and Phillip would hunt for her a spouse. She was to be the hostess at one of the tables filled with prospective husbands. She leaned her head against the chair as a lone tear slipped down her cheek. Her life was over.

Tap, tap, tap.

"Bridgette, may I come in?"

She groaned. Isabelle. Maybe if she ignored her sister-in-law, she would leave.

The door creaked open, and Isabelle's head poked in. "Brigette, didn't you hear me? I need to talk with you before tomorrow

11

arrives." Without waiting on an answer, she walked in and sat on the stool at Brigette's feet. Taking Brigette's hand into her own, she rubbed gentle circles on the back of her hand.

"Please don't be angry with me. I could do nothing to sway your brother's mind. You know how he gets when he and Phillip connive together."

She gazed at Isabelle through misty eyes. How could she be mad at the one who mothered her this past year? In fact, she shuddered to think how she had plotted to have Isabelle slain when she first arrived at the castle and how close the scheme came to fulfillment.

With a gentle pull, she extracted her hand from Isabelle's grasp. "'Tis alright, Isabelle. I'm not at odds with you. 'Tis my two brothers who have me out of sorts." Her bitterness gnawed a hole in her stomach. "They knew I wished not to wed, yet I'm being forced against my will. 'Tis Nicolas enacting vengeance for my earlier treatment of you. He refuses to accept my apology as if he never made an unwise choice." Her lips pressed tight.

"Oh, my sweet. I'm sorry ye are wounded from Nicolas's decision, but 'tis the way for women. We are to wed and produce heirs for our men."

Brigette jerked upright. Her hands grasped the chair arms.

"He may force me to marry, but he can't compel me to create a child. I'm telling you right now, I will not reproduce for a man. Nicolas will have no say in that part of my life."

She lurched from her seat and tramped over to the window.

"Oh, dear. I didn't come to upset you further. There are some things you need to understand about marriage—happenings between a husband and wife. I don't want you to enter the marital bed unaware."

She whirled around to face her sister-in-law. "Please, Isabelle, no more. It is enough for me to grasp the fact that I have no control over my life. After witnessing Abigail give birth, I can't bear to hear what happens in the marital bed." Her dress bunched in her fists. "Please spare me a repugnant scene that will forever play in my mind. Please," she begged, "cease this line of discussion."

12

Isabelle lowered her head. Brigette hated to rebuke her, but she couldn't tolerate another word on the subject. She predicted if word got back to Nicolas about her treatment of his beloved wife, she would reside in the dungeon for the duration of her stay.

Isabelle lifted her head wearing a tight smile. "As you wish. Let's talk about tomorrow. I commissioned an exquisite new gown made for you to wear. Collette will style your flowing golden hair in the latest fashion with jewels woven through it. You will be the most beautiful woman in attendance. The guests will have a hard time focusing on sweet Philippa with you in the room."

And so, it went. She listened half-heartedly to Isabelle explain Brigette's role at the feast. She was to sit at a long table full of nasty men who would vie for her hand in marriage. It sounded like she might have a small say in who the brothers considered if she stayed in Nicolas's good grace—a near impossibility.

At a younger age, she controlled all three brothers with tears. After the death of her parents, when Abigail refused to help, the brothers turned her care over to servants with minor interference from those three selfish brutes. Her manipulation of her brothers had been easy to accomplish since none of them wanted to deal with her theatrics. Not anymore. Now, Thomas loathed her, and Nicolas tolerated her. Phillip stayed preoccupied with his own family dynamics that captured his attentions.

After Isabelle and Nicolas wed, Isabelle tried to reform her. In the beginning that proved futile. Today, however, she loved and respected her brother's wife. Isabelle had her best interests at heart, but she failed to save Brigette from her destiny. Marriage. Foul, horrible marriage.

Isabelle's voice droned in the background as her mind danced with disgusting likelihoods. If she angered Nicolas, her husband might be old, smelly, and fat. So, to please Nicolas, she must play her part.

Tomorrow she planned to shine brighter than a star in a cloudless night sky. She intended to waltz into the grand hall with a pleasant demeanor using her best acting skills to the fullest. She refused to wed an offensive, old man for all eternity. The toughest test of her sixteen years would unfold on the morrow.

"God help me," she whispered.

Chapter Three

As Lord and Lady of the castle, Nicolas and Isabelle stood at the keep entrance welcoming their guests. Lord Sherwood and Lord Mathias, from neighboring estates, brought their wives for the special event. Maids showed them to the rooms they would occupy for the duration of their visit. When called for, men spent one night and returned home, however, traveling with their wives meant an extended stay.

The castle buzzed with activity and chatter. Servants scurried to and from the kitchens while visitors mingled in the grand hall. A heavy guard patrolled inside and outside of the castle. Opening his home to visitors often proved risky. Even as Nicolas talked with two men, he scanned for trouble.

And trouble walked through the doorway—Clan Elliot. Laird Fergus Elliot was the head of the clan that he had encountered raiding cattle on English soil. It had not ended well for the Elliot reivers. In fact, the young man accompanying Fergus Elliot looked like the one he had allowed to live and return with a message to his Clan.

"Welcome, Laird Elliot," he said without emotion. "Please allow me to introduce my lovely wife, Isabelle."

"Weel, now, arna ye bonny." Elliot took her hand and kissed it.

15

Nicolas watched as Isabelle extracted her hand and discreetly rubbed it on her gown. He wished he could spare her the offense.

"This laddie is me son, Brodie."

Nicolas wanted to remind Brodie that they had met, but from his countenance, he didn't recall their encounter. In fact, his face appeared daft. "Please join in the festivities in the grand hall."

"Weel, Lord Fairwick, I would like a ward with ye in private," Laird Elliot said behind his hand.

"I have guests to attend. Can it not wait?"

"It weel but take a moment."

"Very well. Come this way." He gnashed his teeth as he led Fergus Elliot into a small room next to his war room. Brodie failed to follow.

Without delay Nicolas turned to face the despicable man. "What is it ye wish to discuss?"

"I understand ye might need to lift a burden from ye shoulders."

"What riddles do you speak?" He didn't have time to play a guessing game with Fergus Elliot while Brodie roamed unattended.

"Ye sister. She's in need of a hoosband. Me Brodie is in need of a wife. I would be willin' to take her off yer hands for the right price."

It took great effort to keep from ramming his fist into Fergus's throat. Yes, he wanted to find Brigette a husband, but never would he consider Clan Elliot. Never! Knowing how it would displease Isabelle to create a ruckus before the feast even began held him in check. "Thank you for your kind offer. I will take it under advisement."

"Dinna tarry long. Others weel be after his affections."

"I must get back to my guests. Phillip and I shall discuss your proposal. Today is our day of celebration for Phillip and Abigail. Brigette's betrothal must wait, but I won't forget your proposition."

Fergus Elliot's eyes narrowed. "Make sure ye dinna." He turned on his heel and stalked from the room.

As he watched the back of Laird Elliot, his stomach soured. He was angry with his irksome sister, but not enough to subject her to the torture of being forever linked to Brodie Elliot. Death offered a better option. In addition, the idea of the Fairwicks tied to the Elliot clan through marriage was not to be borne.

He loosened his fist and took a couple of long, deep breaths before joining his wife. As he exited the room, there stood his old friend, Daniel—in a kilt! His night was shaping up to be miserable.

"Oh, Brigette, you are beautiful," Isabelle gushed. "I know this feast is to celebrate precious Philippa, but for many, you will capture their focus."

Brigette stood motionless as Collette put the finishing touches to her hair. She admitted, her reflection in the mirror was striking.

Isabelle had chosen a dark, rose-colored taffeta for her gown with a white, lace overlaid bodice. The straight taffeta sleeves reached her wrist. To add flare, a flowing, pale rose silk over-sleeve banded above each elbow with the tips reaching her fingertips. The elegance included a lace V-shaped insert reaching from her waist to the floor. To complete her elegant gown, a silk cape attached at the shoulders draping her back. Her silk-covered slippers peeped from under her majestic gown.

Her joy fizzled when she remembered why her lordly brother allowed such a stunning dress. He was determined to parade her in front of the men he hoped might take her for a bride.

Isabelle clapped her hands when Collette finished. "Splendid. Let me go ahead of you and take my place with Nicolas. Thomas will escort you to the dining hall where you will be announced to our guests. Please pause at the archway and wait until all the applause diminishes. Then he will lead you to the head of the table you are to hostess."

She grabbed Isabelle's arm. "Please, not Thomas!"

"Now, now. He agreed to put your differences aside for this special occasion. I have his word not to cause a scene. I'm asking the same from you as well. Please?"

She peered into Isabelle's expectant eyes and melted. Her mind flashed back to when her sister-in-law hovered between life and death because of the arrow she all but put there herself. How could she deny her anything?

"Of course. I will do it for you."

No doubt, Thomas would spew nasty remarks all the way from her room to the grand hall. She closed her eyes at the thought. His words could slice like a knife. With no one hearing the exchange, he would remain safe from accusation. Her chest constricted at the mere prospect of his presence. There was no hope for it. She must perform or be on the receiving end of Nicolas's wrath.

Isabelle reached for her hands and held them tight. "I'm so proud to call you my sister. You have grown and matured this past year in many respects. In other ways, I feel I'm releasing my baby bird from the nest to soar to new heights. Have no worries for your future. God has a plan." On those final words, she gave a quick kiss to her cheek and floated out the door. Collette soon followed leaving her alone.

She practiced walking from the window to the door and back again. Gorgeous, full gowns were fun to wear until you walked in them. She prayed Thomas would lend his arm when she came to the stairs, or she might tumble to her death. What a fitting end to her life. Without a doubt, he would be pleased with her demise.

Standing at the window, she watched as guests arrived. Nicolas had invited neighboring English families and a few from across the border in Scotland. He tried hard to keep the peace between the countries during these unstable times. King James still worked on bringing Scotland and England to co-exist as neighbors instead of enemies. Right now, all remained peaceful, but for how long?

Before she turned from the window, her eyes latched onto hairy knees. A Scotsman in a kilt rode tall and proud. Oh, dear. Nicolas hated men to wear those in his presence. Why he had such a distaste for kilts mattered not. Smiling to herself, she felt certain the night would provide some entertainment watching her brother's reaction to the kilt-wearing man. Just the thought brightened what might prove to be a gloomy evening.

With her gaze fixated on the landscape, she mulled over the morning. All the family rose at dawn to meet in the chapel for Philippa's christening. So precious in her white gown and cap with her toes poking out when she kicked. Brigette's brother, Phillip, flashed resplendent in his military finery, but his wife held her attention.

Abigail, who antagonized her most of her life, held her new baby with such joy radiating from her face that she appeared angelic. She had smiled at everyone as she floated around the room. The transformation of her astonished Brigette. Abigail spoke kind words to all the family, including her. Unbelievable!

With sweet memories meandering through her mind, she jumped when the knock came at her door. She turned to see her escort frozen in place.

She watched her brother as he watched her but couldn't fathom his thoughts from his blank face. "Is it time?"

He shook his head as if coming out of a stupor. He stiffened as his hand went to the hilt of his sword strapped to his waist. "Yea. I have come to escort you to the festivities."

She wanted to refuse but instead walked over and laid her hand upon his arm. "Onward to the slaughter," she murmured.

He frowned. "What say you?"

"'Tis nothing. I'm ready."

Before taking a step, his eyes swept her form. "Ye look fetching tonight. I'm sure ye will garner much attention."

Surprised, her eyes grew wide before she masked her reaction. "Thank you, Thomas."

"This doesn't mean I have forgiven ye for what ye did to Isabelle last year. 'Tis naught but an observation."

Of course, leave it to sir aggravation to offer a compliment only to stab it to death in the next breath. "It doesn't matter. I'll soon be out of your life once Nicolas marries me off to the highest bidder."

When he remained silent, it relieved her of small talk. He conducted himself a gentleman as he led her along the stony passageway and held her steady as she navigated the winding stairway. After reaching the bottom of the stairs, she squared her shoulders before facing the crowd gathered in the great hall.

Thomas stopped under the archway waiting for their announcement. All eyes swiveled toward her when they broadcast her name loud and clear. A few gasps echoed around the room.

Brigette pinned a smile and held her head high. Her regal entrance would make Isabelle proud, and that's the only person she cared to impress.

Chapter Four

Brigette glided across the floor of sweet-smelling rushes as Thomas guided her to the proper table. Once they reached the head of the table, he made the introductions.

"To your left we have Lord Donald Armstrong and his son, Adam. Sitting next to Adam are Laird Fergus Elliot and his son, Brodie." Each of them stood when introduced except Brodie. His father dragged him up.

"Ye leuk bonny tonight," Brodie drawled as his eyes raked over her figure.

Brigette gave a slight shudder at his forwardness. She turned toward Thomas and noticed his ferocious frown directed at Brodie. It seemed Thomas disliked the interruption or mayhap Brodie's disrespectful stare. For once it relieved her to have Thomas by her side.

After an awkward moment of silence, her brother continued as if Brodie hadn't spoken. "At the end of the table, on your right, is Lord Walter Kerr and his son, Martin. Finally, here to your immediate right is Laird Daniel McKinnon and his son, William. To each of you I present the ever lovely, Lady Brigette Isolde Fairwick, sister of Lord Nicolas Fairwick." The men extended a slight bow to acknowledge her beauty and status as the only sister of the Fairwick brothers.

After she settled in the high-backed chair at her end of the table, shuffling feet and scraping of benches ensued as the men sat. Thomas relaxed at the opposite end facing his sister.

With her back ramrod straight, her clinched hands lay hidden in her lap. She drew on her many years of acting abilities she used on her brothers when she wanted to get her way. This performance, however, was of high import. She expected Nicolas to see her wed to one of the men at her table before the year ended. Not one woman resided at her table to offer aid in the conversation. Resigned, she allowed her deep sigh to escape. *Let it begin.*

"Ye ar' quite comely," William said.

She looked down into the precious face of a little boy. "Why thank you, young sir." She could tell her answer pleased him. His chest puffed out and his smile grew. No doubt he learned that inflated chest business from his father. "I'm so glad you are dining at my table, William."

"I'm almost six. Dost ye like little boys?"

A smile crept across her face at his straightforwardness. Tilting her head, she reached out and clasped his pudgy hand. "I most certainly do. Little boys are among my favorite people." She glanced to see his father studying her with an unreadable expression. At that moment, servants interrupted as they placed food on the table and poured drinks into their goblets.

Since her back faced the head table, she didn't notice Nicolas stand to propose a toast. William took note and jumped to assist her to her feet. His chivalry enchanted her. Too bad he was too young to marry.

"Thank you all for coming to the special feast honoring our newest family member, Philippa Emma Gail Fairwick, daughter of Lord Phillip and Lady Abigail Fairwick. Let us toast for a long and healthy life."

"Here, here," all responded with raised goblets.

After a sip, Brigette grimaced. She hated the taste of ale and preferred water or diluted wine.

"Is the ale not to yer liking?" Laird McKinnon asked.

She dabbed her lips with a napkin. "No, I prefer water. I also don't like what ale does to people when they drink too much."

"Ha. Ye've mayhap not met the mon who could handle 'is ale," Brodie boasted. His father elbowed his side, but it made no difference. He continued with his obnoxious banter. She turned a deaf ear to his unpleasant chatter by giving her attention to the men closest to her side.

"Lord Armstrong, I hear you had a great hunting adventure. Pray, tell us about it."

Adam needed no further encouragement. He launched into a spirited discussion about the boar they killed. Her insides tremored at the details involving spears, swords, and rivers of blood.

"Mayhap less detail is better suited for our dining conversation," Daniel said.

Adam stopped mid-sentence and stared at him. His father, Lord Armstrong, intervened. "Please excuse our manners, Lady Fairwick. Adam didn't mean to be insensitive to your delicate nature."

Brigette watched as Adam's face turned multiple colors unsure if from anger or embarrassment. There was much for her to learn about men in general. "Apology accepted, kind sir. The fault is mine for suggesting such a topic." Looking at each man around the table, she smiled. "Does anyone know a less frightening tale to share for our entertainment? Perhaps one about kittens or puppies?"

"I 'ave a new puppy!" William exclaimed. Laughter erupted at the table as the awkward moment diffused.

"Now, William, tell it aright."

"I'm sairy, fither." William ducked his head and peered up at her with big brown eyes. "Weel, I'll git a puppy soon."

"That sounds exciting. What kind of puppy do you wish to have?"

She watched as the men lost interest in the conversation when William proceeded to give details about the perfect puppy. His childish chatter was more to her liking than that of the grown men vying for her attention. It was a joy to watch him talk with his hands and fidget on the bench from his excitement. A slow smile formed as she listened to his sweet voice.

His father laid a hand on William's arm and spoke a gentle reprimand. "Ye may talk more with Lady Fairwick after ye've eaten more of yer meal."

"Aye, fither."

The men at her end of the table fell silent as they ate their meal with an occasional exchange. However, Thomas had a challenge keeping peace between Brodie Elliot and Martin Kerr. The free-flowing ale affected the sons. Their loud voices carried around the room. It proved impossible to ignore their hot-headed exchanges. If she listened to them boast about their far-fetched exploits much longer, she might go mad. She shot them a quelling stare, but it did no good. Beasts! If these were all Nicolas offered in the way of a husband, she was in deep waters tied to a sinking bolder.

"It seems that a specific strategy by your brother played a part in our seating arrangement," Daniel said.

She frowned. "What mean you?"

"Last year your brother interrupted an attempt by some reivers to steal Lord Kerr's cattle."

She tried to remember the incident but couldn't recall the specifics. "Explain."

He leaned over William while she bent close to hear his soft answer. "The reivers were from Clan Elliot."

Gasp! She jerked upright in her seat as her gaze flew to the end of the table. "Oh, my. That explains much." Her nostrils flared. "Leave it to Nicolas to agitate a rattlers nest and expect me to keep all safe from their venomous poison."

She stood with hands on the table and leaned forward. "Gentlemen, gentlemen, let's not come to blows. 'Twould disrupt my evening." All heads turned her way. "Please, conduct yourselves in a noble manner. We are all here to rejoice with Phillip and Abigail over my precious niece, Philippa. Remember it!"

As she eased into her seat, Brodie laughed out loud. With both elbows on the table, he angled around his father. "Weel, now. Act noble indeed. Have ye forgotten yer own less than noble act?"

Concentrating, his meaning escaped her. This past year she stayed invisible in her own home to allow Isabelle and Nicolas the needed time for the newly married couple. As her mind raced to think of what he stated, he enlightened her.

"I dinna call it noble when ye tried to kill another!"

Her hand flew to her throat with a quick intake of breath. The other men were stunned into silence at his declaration. Mortified that he brought up her tainted past at the dinner table, her anger bubbled from deep within as she contemplated a response. Her eyes narrowed. "He that is without sin, cast the first stone."

Daniel grinned. "Well said."

She acknowledged his comment with a slight nod, but her anger smoldered.

Brodie's ignorance shone forth when he countered. "'Twasn't a stone, but an arrow."

His father yanked his son's beard and uttered harsh words that blistered her ears. Laird Elliot's words didn't affect her as much as the knowledge of Nicolas's intentional act that made her blood boil. *I'm going to strangle my brother!*

Daniel had observed Nicolas's sister the moment she first entered the room. Her beauty breathtaking. Adorned with jewels and ribbons, her golden curls shimmered in the candlelight. The modest dress she wore was fitting for a young woman of her stature with just enough lace at the neckline to invite a man's mind to wander. Her regal walk depicted a spirit gliding across the floor to her destination.

After the death of his wife, he hunted for a mother for his young son, William. At one time, he envisioned another love match as he experienced with William's mother, but that idea vanished long ago. Nonetheless, having a wife that was pleasing in face and form would ease the sorrow of lost love. Brigette's loveliness drew his attention, but he had to be mindful of how she reacted to his son.

The moment she acknowledged William by the touch of her hand gave Daniel hope that his search might soon end. Up to this point, she had conducted herself in a manner worthy of a royal position.

"Laird. Tell me of your home."

Brigette's request redirected his thoughts.

"My castle lies a stone's throw across the border in Scotland where I possess great land holdings. I inherited the title and land from my Scottish father and English mother upon their deaths." He leaned closer to her. "My properties and wealth have grown under my rule."

All he lacked was a wife. Attending this celebration opened a possibility to gain a wife and a strategic alliance with Lord Nicolas Fairwick, his childhood friend and sometimes rival. However, he needed the full accounting of her part in Lady Isabelle Fairwick's near death experience before offering marriage.

His son's next move seized his attention. William tugged on Brigette's sleeve and whispered with urgency, "I need ta go."

"You need to use the necessary, sweet one?"

Without delay, Daniel rose to his feet. "Please excuse us, Lady Fairwick. If ye will but point us in the right direction, I will assist William."

She ignored his request. Pushing back her chair, she grabbed William's hand. "Come, William. I will take you where you need to go." With her nose in the air, she left the grand hall without a backward glance.

He followed to persuade her to let him handle William's dilemma. Once Brigette cleared the archway, she attempted to pick William up in her arms.

Daniel pushed her arms aside. "I will carry him. He is too heavy for you."

"Certainly. Follow me." On that short command, she grabbed a handful of her dress and moved at a fast clip toward the stairs that lead to the upper level.

He trailed behind her. Her sashay on the stairs afforded him a nice view as her dress swished back and forth with each step. He gauged her height a bit over five feet in stature. If they were to

26

embrace, she would fit snug under his chin. As his mind darted to forbidden places, William tightened his hold around his neck.

"Hurry, papa."

After reaching the second floor, she stepped aside and pointed right toward the end of the long passageway. "There at the lighted torch on the wall. The door beside it is the one to the necessary. You will make better time without me."

"Thank you."

A guard stood at the door of Nicolas and Isabelle's room. "Gilbert, let them pass," she yelled.

Daniel ran the length of the stone corridor. He didn't want William embarrassed with an accident in his breeches. As his kilt swayed, he wondered how she viewed his clothing. He already knew what her brother thought of the Scottish attire. Upon reaching the end, he and William disappeared inside with a quick slam of the door.

She stopped in front of the guard. "Anything to report?"

"No, m' lady. All is quiet. 'Twould seem the festivities are keeping everyone in the grand hall tonight except for your friend that ran past."

"Oh, he is not my friend. He is one of the men sitting at my table this evening. His son needed to go …"

"He wore a kilt."

"Yes."

The two emerged from the privy. William broke from his father and ran to meet her. "Whew. I made it," William announced.

She stooped to his level and took his hands into her own. "I'm so happy an accident was averted." He reached to hug her neck. "Do you wish to see the nursery where I used to play as a young girl?"

William turned to his father. "What say ye, papa?"

Daniel considered the two who held such hopeful expressions. "We dinna want to keep ye from yer guests."

She stood to her full height. "Actually, William spared me an embarrassing moment, and I have no wish for a hasty return to more of the same unless you desire it?"

"I suppose a bit of time can be spared."

"Excellent." Taking William's hand, she led them to another hallway. She pointed out the door to her room on her left as they continued to the end of the passageway. There on the right was a closed door.

She let go of William's hand and pushed open the door to reveal a dark room. Reaching up, she removed the lighted torch on the wall and proceeded into the room. She lit several candles scattered around the chamber while he and William waited just inside the doorway.

Brigette circled back and put the torch in a holder by the door. She swept her arm outward. "What do you think, William?"

"'Tis a fine room."

"Come with me." She led him to a closed trunk and knelt upon her knees. With a grunt, she pushed open the top and pulled out several items of interest: a horse, four soldiers, a doll, and a bag of marbles. "You may play with these for a few moments, if you wish it."

William's head swiveled to Daniel. "Papa?"

He walked over to the trunk. "Ye may play for a bit if it pleases ye."

"Och, aye!" he exclaimed with childish exuberance.

Daniel presented his open palm to help her stand. Her soft hand felt cool to the touch. "Are ye cold?"

She withdrew her hand. "No." She walked away from him and stopped by a window.

He moved behind her. "Are ye troubled?"

She turned to face him. "This room brings back unsettling memories."

Standing close to her, was her skin as soft and as smooth as he imagined? Her blue eyes shone as bright as a cloudless summer sky yet distressed. "Why dinna ye tell me whit troubles ye? Mayhap I can offer assistance."

Walking away, her finger trailed across the chair back. "I'm afraid no one can erase the hurt from my past."

"Are ye referring to whit Brodie spoke aboot?"

Without a word, she watched William for a brief time before sitting in one of the two chairs by the fireplace. She hid her hands in the folds of her dress. "Yes. My reputation is forever spoiled. I'm sure you have heard all the rumors."

Daniel sat opposite her. "Aye, but I much prefer to hear the truth from ye." He watched as her eyes darted around the room while she twisted her hands. She made one last glance toward William who played with the soldiers before her tormented eyes met his.

"It's a sorry tale. Are you sure you want to hear it?"

He smiled. "I'm a mon who wears a kilt in England and survives it. I can listen to ye're sairy tale and endure." His words brought a sad smile to her face.

She took a deep breath before beginning. "Last year, Isabelle came to our home. Beautiful. Intelligent. My brother, Nicolas, was quite taken with her. Until that point, I had been led to believe that I wasn't Nicolas's sister. Growing up without parents, servants told me tales for their own amusement never realizing how it might twist my thinking."

He had no trouble envisioning an impressionable little girl with no parental guidance, one who didn't know her place in the family while her brothers ignored her upbringing. His anger flared toward Nicolas who ignored the harm the servants executed against his young sister.

"Anyway, I believed I could marry Nicolas and remain at my only home as the *Lady* of the castle. When Nicolas told me he planned to wed this stranger, I became furious. My plans were being torn asunder. In a panic of losing all, I intentionally calculated her demise. 'Tis quite unforgiveable…" She trailed off as her lids closed.

Daniel had obtained the story from her unforgiving brother. Of course, Nicolas's story came from a man in love with his bride. Now, he very much wanted to hear how Brigette's tale played out. "Have ye continued to harbor such feelings?"

29

After a deep breath she opened her dewy eyes. "Absolutely not. After a short time spent with Isabelle, I too grew to love her. She gathered me close as a child to a mother's bosom. For once in my life, I experienced the tender touch of a mother's love, and I yearned for more of it. My focus shifted from her destruction to one of admiration and affection. In my childish exuberance, I failed to remember the agreement made with Eugene." She shook her head. "While I basked in her attention, Eugene calculated his strike."

"How old were ye?"

"I turned fifteen summers last year," she whispered as her head sunk to her chest.

She had been more than young in age. Because of a lack of nurturing from her brothers, she was intellectually immature. Despicable! He observed William happily playing, secure in his surroundings because he was well loved and cared for. Brigette's next words jolted his attention back to her.

"He shot her with an arrow, you know. If accurate, she would be dead." She shuddered at the telling. "All because of a selfish, hateful girl." She stood and looked at William who played far enough away not to hear her shameful tale.

"Ah, lass, many things hampered yer development. Ye can't carry all the blame on yer shoulders. Three irresponsible brothers are partially to blame for the fiasco. They should have seen to yer care with more deliberation. It sounds like ye're verra sairy for the hurt ye caused which should go a long way in healing the rift in yer family."

She slowly turned toward him wearing an unhappy smile. "You're kind to say so, but I think not. When it comes to Isabell, Nicolas is not very forgiving. 'Tis alright. He will soon marry me off to some poor soul, and I will no longer be his concern."

Daniel detected the maturity in her voice as he looked upon her gloomy countenance. He gauged that she had grown much from her terrible ordeal. A sad young woman with no hope stood before him, not a young selfish girl out to do harm.

With a sudden jerk, she looked at the closed door. "Thomas is calling my name. You must stay here until I get back to the grand dining hall. If Thomas catches us together unchaperoned, Nicolas will see that you are shackled to me for all eternity. I must hurry."

Daniel followed her to the door and placed his hand upon the latch. "Dinna fash yerself. Nicolas scares me not."

He was glad when her sparkling eyes met his. "You know, Nicolas hates kilts."

He winked. "Aye."

She gave a mischievous smile. "I like you, Lord Daniel McKinnon. You have spirit." She ran from the room leaving her giggle ringing in his ears.

Chapter Five

Nicolas lightly kissed his wife's lips. "Ye are more beautiful than I could ever imagine. Being with child has enhanced your loveliness." He gathered her into his embrace by the open door a step inside their room.

"Oh, my husband, you are blinded." She laid her head on his chest and wrapped her arms partially around his body. "My rounded belly is getting harder to hide. I'm as big as a sack of apples. There's nothing beautiful about that!"

"Suffice it to say, you are wrong again." He smiled. "But enough of this chatter, I am away."

She reared her head back and viewed his face. "What are you about so early this morn?"

"Daniel asked for an audience." He wiggled his brows. "I believe he is enamored with Brigette. At least I hope so. I knew if I dressed her up and paraded her around, someone would take the bait."

She punched him in the chest. "What a dreadful thing to say!"

He had the decency to appear sheepish as he released his hold and reached for his sword to slide into his scabbard. "Last night was beastly long. I want you to stay here and rest all day. I hope to run most of our guests to their homes afore the sun sets." He brushed the tip of her nose with his finger and then high-tailed it out before she could strike again.

33

She yelled down the hallway. "You are impossible."

He whistled all the way down the winding staircase. Once reaching the entrance to the great hall, he surveyed the area. Daniel and his son were finishing their morning meal. He strolled over and settled on the bench across from the two. "Greetings, young William. Did ye sleep well?"

"Oh, aye," he replied with a full mouth.

"William, please answer once ye've swallowed yer bite." Looking at Nicolas, Daniel shook his head. "Manners are slow in coming." Then he ruffled Williams's hair.

"I received word ye wish to speak with me this morning."

"Aye. 'Tis something of import. I wish to discuss it before I take my leave."

"Oh? Leaving so soon?"

"Aye. I have matters to attend. May I have a private audience with ye this morn?"

"As ye wish. Once you complete your meal, meet me in the war room there." Nicolas pointed across the passageway.

He nodded in agreement as Nicolas stood to leave. "Thank ye."

Daniel watched Nicolas talk with other guests as he made his way around the room—ever the charmer. However, his treatment of his sister sickened him. In his opinion, no amount of charm could replace his lack of attention to Brigette's upbringing. With the title of Lord of the castle, it made him solely responsible for decisions regarding his sister. In Daniel's opinion, he had failed on a grand scale nearly costing him Isabelle's life. The more he reasoned, the clearer his choice.

He assigned one of his men to watch over William while he talked with Lord Fairwick. He stood and straightened his kilt with delight. Knowing how his *friend* hated men wearing kilts added to his pleasure of wearing one under Nicolas's nose. He wore a wide grin as he walked to the war room. The door stood ajar, so he walked in and clicked the door shut behind him.

Nicolas sat at the round table tracing the hilt of his sword where it lay atop the table. His booted feet crossed at the ankle as they rested next to his sword. Thin rays of sun filtered through the two small windows with dust particles swirling in the sunbeam. Though shrouded in darkness, the filtered sunlight illuminated his face. To Daniel, he appeared quite relaxed.

"I see you wore that wretched kilt again this fine day. Are ye trying to start a brawl with men who find kilts womanish?"

He ignored Nicolas's attempt to draw him into a verbal altercation. They had business to discuss, and he wanted to waste no time. With feet spread apart and arms crossed at his chest, he said, "I wish to ask for Brigette's hand in marriage."

Nicolas's eyes grew large, but he couldn't interpret his expression. Surprise or delight? His feet hit the floor with a thud as he leaned forward. "Isn't this a bit sudden, even for you? Ye just met her last eventide."

"If she is free to wed, I'm happy to offer a bride price we both can agree upon."

Nicolas squinted. "Are ye aware of her tainted past?" He paused for a moment. "She attempted to murder Isabelle."

Daniel dropped his arms and clasped them behind his back. "I've heard the sordid tale from your sister's own lips, and it coincides with the rumors floating aboot. It matters not."

He watched as Nicolas rubbed his chin. Perhaps it was his desire to leave for home or his anger toward his friend, but he couldn't quite read Nicolas's mood—an unusual occurrence for him. Ever since they were young boys, Daniel understood him without a word spoken. Not today.

Nicolas leaned back in his chair and regained a relaxed posture. "I must discuss this unexpected offer with Phillip. I value his opinion on such matters and decisions concerning our sister. We will wait to discuss a bride price once Phillip and I reach an agreement."

"As ye wish. Don't tarry. I plan to obtain a wife and a mother for William soon. It can be the lass or another. With Scotland and

England at peace, I believed 'twould be strategic for us to join forces sealed by marriage."

Nicolas's eyes narrowed. "As I said, I will confer with my brother. I will not be rushed on the matter."

Daniel walked to the door. With his hand on the latch, he turned back. "If ye haven't sent word in a fortnight, I will press on with my search for a wife." He left the door open as he walked out leaving Nicolas to stew over his parting words. The Fairwick brothers would not likely receive another desirable offer for their sister's hand given her murky past. If the men who gathered at his dining table the previous night were the best prospects they found, the brothers should chase him down and accept his offer. None of the other families represented had the manpower or the wisdom that Clan McKinnon brought to the table. The Fairwick brothers would be wise to accept his proposal.

In time past, the two men were close friends. Even when their fathers battled as enemies, that fact had added intrigue to the boys' secret meetings for mischief making. Now they were men who had put away their childish behavior. They both carried the burden of managing a castle and all the responsibility that duty entailed.

Each of them had increased their land holdings after their fathers' deaths. With Nicolas on the border of northern England and him on the border of southern Scotland, it stood to reason that they should join forces to keep the peace. However, it all depended on the brothers' decision about Brigette.

He stepped outside the castle doors to see William playing chase with a group of boys. Going down the keep steps, he called out. "William, come. We are away."

"Sairy, but I have to go," William said to the ragtag group while scuffing his foot in the dry dirt. "Fare thee well."

William followed his father to their waiting horses. Daniel boosted him into his saddle and then mounted his own horse. When he raised his eyes, Brigette stood on the top step of the keep. Her blond curls danced in the slight breeze as she looked around the courtyard. Did she search for him? He nudged his horse toward the keep and noticed her faint smile when she spied him.

"Are ye leaving so soon?"

"Aye. There are important matters to attend."

"I'm sorry to see you and William go. Who will help with the conversation tonight?" A weak laugh escaped her. "You both rescued me more than once when I faltered, and I won't soon forget it."

"'Twas our pleasure." With eyes fixed on hers, he felt torn about leaving her with the likes of Brodie, but she wasn't his concern. She remained Nicolas's, and he would do well to remember that.

William's horse now stood beside his father's stallion. "Ye ar' verra bonnie this fine morn."

Her face softened at William's words. "Oh, William, you are such a sweet boy. One day you will make some girl extremely happy."

"Weel ye coom to see me?"

Daniel watched her countenance fall. She swallowed hard as she blinked fast. "Thank you, William. Nothing would make me happier. Mayhap one day." Her lips tipped up. "Go with God."

With a nod of his head in her direction Daniel turned his horse and trotted across the courtyard. He allowed his men encircling William to proceed him through the outer gate. He glanced back. She raised her hand in a final farewell before letting it drop to her side. The sun glistened off her wet cheek. His hands tightened on the reins as he forced himself to turn from the sight. *Nicolas, ye swine!*

Brigette wiped the wetness from her face not wanting others to ask why she cried. They might deem her smitten with Lord McKinnon. She would miss the McKinnon pair, but they weren't the reason for her tears. Lord McKinnon and William had provided a slight reprieve from her dire situation. Just the thought of what awaited her in the near future caused her great anguish. How would she survive?

She went back inside and straight toward her room. Mayhap if she stayed out of sight, her brother wouldn't make her perform for their guests. What she said or did would have no bearing on who he chose for her to marry, so why bother?

Her suggestion of becoming a nun he dismissed without consideration. In fact, Nicolas and Thomas had burst out with laughter at her idea. Hopeless … plain hopeless. She descended deeper into the miry pit where she had no control over her life's outcome.

Why was she born a woman instead of a man? Men got to choose the direction of their destiny while her fate lay in her brothers' hands. Life wasn't fair.

The longer she contemplated her lot in life, the more depressed she became. If she knew anything about survival in the wild, she would take to the forest and disappear, but that was never going to happen. The fear of little spiders sends her into a frenzy.

Assuredly, far worse awaited her in the woods. The servants had told her disturbing tales of what lurked deep in the woods. Of course, they had lied to her about her heritage, mayhap the forest was not so scary. With that glimmer of hope, she put her mind to other alternatives for escaping her dismal future.

Chapter Six

Phillip jostled his young daughter on his shoulder as he walked around the solar. Isabelle sat lounging on the settee gazing out the window while Nicolas leaned against the fireplace and looked around the room

"Is Abigail coming?" Nicolas asked as he fidgeted with his knife.

"No. She is resting. I don't think she wanted to be a part of our discussion. You know how she feels about Brigette."

Nicolas glanced up. "I thought they had mended their differences."

"Yes, what you say is true, but Abigail didn't want to upset their fragile truce."

"Nicolas, please. May we get on with this distasteful chat?" Isabelle asked. "The anticipation causes me great torment."

"Of course, my love. I will make it as painless as possible."

Now that Philippa slept, Phillip eased in a chair flanking the fireplace and nodded for his brother to proceed. Nicolas took a deep breath. "Our little sister made a fine impression on the men at her table. Three of the fathers approached me with a marriage proposal which is surprising given her sordid past."

Isabelle gasped. "Husband! Not another word about incidents well past."

"Now, wife, 'twas but truth. Whether ye want to remember it or not, the fact that her reputation is forever stained doesn't change. I'm just thankful there were three willing to take a chance on marrying their sons to a would-be-assassin."

"Enough!" She rose from her place by the window. "I must join Abigail. I can't bear to hear another disparaging word about Brigette."

"Isabelle." Nicolas reached for her arm, but she side stepped on her way out the door.

Phillip grinned. "'Twould seem you have some reparation to do tonight."

He huffed as he plopped into the chair facing his brother. "My wife is quite volatile in her present state. I seem to say nothing that pleases her when it comes to our little sister."

"Ah, brother. You have much to learn about the fairer gender. But enough idle words, Philippa will not sleep overlong. What do you wish to share with me?"

"One offer we can disregard without discussion."

"Laird Elliot?"

"Precisely. Even though I still harbor animosity toward Brigette for her actions against my wife, I would not give my dog to the Elliot clan. As you know, Brodie was one of the reivers who challenged me and is too senseless to even remember me." Shaking his head in disbelief, he continued. "I'm convinced that Lord Kerr only offered his son, Martin, when he got wind of the Elliot proposition. Walter was not to be routed by the likes of Fergus Elliot. He's still entertaining the idea of retaliation against the clan for the loss of cattle the night of the attack."

"I agree with ye brother. Those two don't sound too promising. Who was the third?"

Nicolas beamed. "'Tis my old friend, Lord Daniel McKinnon." He rubbed his hands together. "Daniel can't resist a comely face which is what I counted on."

"Ye wished for The McKinnon to wed Brigette?"

"'Twould be poetic justice for all the times Daniel created skirmishes between our families. Not the least being when he kidnapped Isabelle. He is fortunate I didn't kill every person at his castle. With that in mind, I think it best if we had him as an ally instead of an enemy and what better way to keep an eye on him than for him to live as part of the family. With blood ties, we wouldn't be concerned about a day of reckoning from when I poisoned his well water."

"Why must we marry her off in such haste? Should we not withhold our decision until more are presented as possible suitors?"

"No. I don't wish to delay. Isabelle will give birth this year, and I don't want our sister's future still unsettled. Selfishly, I want to enjoy my first child without her lurking about. Think about it. Her reputation precedes her in our realm. We are blessed to acquire one advantageous proposal."

"Brother! Lurking about? What nonsense. She is no longer a threat to anyone." Phillip rubbed circles on his daughter's back.

"'Twasn't your wife she tried to kill. Anyway, Daniel granted us a fortnight to consider his offer. We don't want to tarry and miss this opportunity to see her wed. He is a civilized Scot to be sure."

"Since I don't know him as you do, I will defer to your knowledge on the man. What about his holdings?"

"Like us, he increased his properties when he claimed control after his father's death. There should be no trouble with him providing the bride price we agree upon. In addition, he can offer Brigette all she needs to live a comfortable life if she behaves herself."

"Nicolas, ye must desist with this harmful speech. 'Twill not change the past but might damage relations with our sister."

Both men sat in silence for a brief time listening to the sweet sounds made by the sleeping babe. Each lost in his own thoughts until Nicolas broke the quiet. "Are we in agreement that Daniel is Brigette's best selection for a husband?" He locked eyes with Phillip as he awaited his reply.

"Lord McKinnon satisfies me. However, I believe your urgency is misplaced. Nevertheless, you are Lord of this castle, and I will relent to your judgment."

Brigette returned after a short walk to clear her head. She expected to devise a strategy of escaping her dilemma, but that was not the case. Rubbing her head, she almost collided with Isabelle barreling down the passageway. She grabbed both of Isabelle's arms to keep her from stumbling. "What is the trouble?"

Her sister-in-law's eyes danced around without making contact. "'Tis nothing. I'm on my way to check on Abigail."

Brigette's gaze narrowed as she observed her sister-in-law's agitated movements. Something was amiss. "Where is Nicolas?"

"He and Phillip are in our room."

"Discussing my future, no doubt."

"Why don't you come with me to see Abigail?"

Brigette tilted her head and smirked. "Truly? Me and Abigail? Together?"

With a light touch, Isabelle patted her arm. "Come now, Brigette, have not you and Abigail got along remarkably well since Philippa's birth?"

"Yes. But I don't expect it to continue based on our past history together. So, go on with you. I'm off to talk with my brothers."

"You'll need to knock hard before entering. You know how they become high-spirited when they discuss matters."

Now she was convinced her brothers were up to mischief. Isabelle tried too hard to keep her away from the two schemers. Perhaps she feared Brigette might overhear them without their knowledge of her presence. Hmm.

"Don't concern yourself. I'll make my presence known."

"Off I go," Isabelle said. She walked part way down the hallway and turned back. After a short pause, she continued on her way.

She watched until Isabelle waddled out of sight and then sprinted toward Nicolas's room. She hoped her sister-in-law had left the door ajar so she might listen to her brothers without their awareness.

Before reaching his doorway, she removed her shoes and tip-toed the rest of the way. If the door stood ajar, she desired to listen a moment before knocking. She took a second glance to make sure no one saw her creeping about.

It was easy to hear Nicolas's booming voice. He talked loud even when he tried to whisper. In fact, he issued a disparaging remark about her reputation. As she stood there listening, more hurtful comments drifted through the cracked door. Nicolas wanted her gone while Phillip tried to sway his thinking. Should she barge in or sneak away?

Frozen with uncertainty, she gasped when Thomas grabbed her arm. He kicked the door open and pulled her into the center of the room. All the commotion woke the baby who burst out crying.

"Thomas, what are you about?" Phillip demanded as he juggled his screaming baby. "You scared young Philippa."

"Look who I found lingering outside the door," Thomas announced with a tight grip on her arm.

"Release me at once," she said through clinched teeth. She jerked her arm free which caused her to stumble. After a scathing stare at Thomas, she turned her flashing glare toward her middle brother. "So, you plan to marry me to the highest bidder?"

Nicolas stood as a thundercloud formed on his face. "Sister, eavesdropping never turns out well."

"Stop avoiding my question. You should have consulted me before deciding to wed me to one of those dolts I had dinner with last night," she said with a raised voice. Philippa's cry grew in intensity.

"Phillip, take your daughter to her mother. I can't even think," Nicolas shouted.

"No! I want Phillip to hear what I have to say," she said with authority. The three stunned faces staring back at her almost made her smile. Phillip bounced his daughter and patted her back. Thomas wore his perpetual frown and Nicolas … well he looked as if he could run her through with his sword if clutched in his hand. Good. They were mad but listening.

"All of my life the three of you thrust me aside while you pursued your own objectives. Never once did you care where I was or what I did until now. Raised by disgruntled servants, I had a variety of wrong beliefs. Those mistaken convictions triggered my behavior that nearly cost Isabelle her life."

"Precisely!" Nicolas roared.

Turning her full anger on him, she raised her arm and pointed at his heart. "You," she snarled, "the one who parades around the castle as if you were God himself. Telling all who will listen how God is so important to you and how He saved your wife from certain death. How you rely on God to direct your path. Ludicrous!"

Though tears filled her eyes, she continued with a strong voice. "Even though you say Jesus was a master at forgiveness when He forgave the thief on the cross, you can't bring yourself to forgive your sister. I asked, no begged, for your forgiveness, yet you withhold it. You are no better than the Pharisees the Bible talks about."

"Now, Brigette," Phillip said above Philippa's cries. "Let's discuss this once we have all calmed."

She kept her eyes locked on Nicolas when she answered him. "I think not, Phillip. From what I garnered, there is no discussion. The almighty Lord Nicolas Fairwick has ruled in his own favor." Her harsh laugh escaped. "I will be relieved to be away from here. My chances are better with another family." She whirled around and bumped into Thomas. After a hearty shove against his chest, she stalked out of the room.

For a few minutes the lone sound in the room was the leftover crying hiccups of Philippa. All eyes stared at the empty portal. Thomas turned to his brothers. "Are you going to let her escape punishment for her defiant attitude and disrespect?"

Nicolas rubbed his hand over his face and then the back of his neck. "Ample words were voiced for one night. I will sleep on it

44

and make a decision tomorrow."

"I, for one, have heard enough. Did I not tell you we should not be hasty?" Phillip admonished. "Her argument has merit. We failed her."

"Failed her?" Thomas exploded. "We are not to blame. She almost killed Isabelle!"

"The outcome of her life might have been altered if we had nurtured her. Instead, we each trained hard, fought wars, and went about our business as if no sister existed. The fault lies with each of us."

"That is pure speculation, Phillip. Only God knows if her mindset would have turned out differently," Nicolas said.

"Well, I still think she should be disciplined," Thomas said.

"That's always your answer," Nicolas said. "It's a good thing I didn't punish you each time I deemed it necessary. You would not have survived. Now, everyone out. I need to think."

He paced the length of the room with hands behind his back. Phillip left the room in haste while the youngest brother remained behind for one last stab. "Punish her!" he snarled and departed before Nicolas responded.

Chapter Seven

Days later with her head against the cold stone encasing her window, a stirring in the courtyard caught Brigette's attention. Right before dawn, Nicolas and a few men headed out while the dew still clung to the ground. The briskness of the breeze caused the horses to prance and fling their heads with anticipation of a fast ride. Carried torches lighted their way.

For two long days, she pled illness to escape further exchange with those horrid men and their sons. Last night she cried until exhausted which left her with gritty eyes and a headache. Unable to sleep, she tried to figure a way out of her quandary, but to no avail.

Now she stood at her window and watched as the group rode under the raised portcullis and thundered across the drawbridge. Without a doubt, her brother rode to secure an agreement with her soon-to-be husband. Who had he chosen?

Rubbing her eyes, she breathed deep and long. Her shoulders sagged as she blew out her frustration. She shuffled her way toward the bed. There she flopped face down with arms sprawled. Weariness of the soul weighed on her like a heavy stone. Movement? Impossible.

Tap, tap, tap.

She groaned into her comforter. Who dared knock at her door at dawn? She remained quiet in hopes the person left.

Tap, tap.

"Brigette? Are ye awake? 'Tis me, Isabelle."

If it had been anyone but Isabelle … She rolled to her back. "Come in, I'm awake."

"I'm sorry to come at such an early hour, but I feel the need to speak with you while I have time. There's something of greatest import we must discuss."

She sat up and patted the bed for Isabelle to join her. Her pregnant sister-in-law settled on the bed facing Brigette. "I fear Nicolas left this morning to secure a marriage covenant for you."

Unfazed, she asked, "Do you know who he chose?"

"He withheld the information for fear I wouldn't keep a secret from you … said it was for my protection."

Brigette flopped to her back and stared at the ceiling. "It matters not. I will soon be gone from here, and your lives will carry on."

Isabelle scooted closer and grasped her hand. "Please don't say it. I love you like a sister and will sorely miss you. I pray you will live close enough to allow visiting between us."

"Don't count on it. Knowing my brother, he will choose the man farthest from Fairwick Castle to ensure we are kept apart."

"Now, lovey, he isn't vindictive. He's just doing his duty to procure you a husband."

Brigette pulled her hand from the loose grip and rolled off the bed. Poor Isabelle. She wanted to believe the best of her husband, but she knew her brother well. He had no intentions of letting her remain nearby.

"'Twill be a wonderful adventure."

She frowned at Isabelle over the remark. A grand adventure indeed. She had grown into a master at manipulation and recognized a fellow manipulator. Isabelle tried too hard to paint an enchanting future. No doubt her forthcoming marriage fell far short of grand. Not wanting to hurt Isabelle, she said, "I'm sure your assessment is true."

She watched as her sister-in-law smiled in relief. "Of course, it is. Marriage is simply delightful. I never realized two people could have so much pleasure together—even in bed!"

Brigette threw her hand up to stop her from further details. "Please, Isabelle. I've told you before, I don't wish to hear about you and my brother." She walked over to the dwindling fire and grabbed the poker. "Was there any other reason for your visit before the sun awoke?"

Isabelle scooted off the bed and walked to where she knelt at the fireplace. Brigette jabbed the logs wishing they were her infuriating brother's backside. She leaned on her haunches when the fire came alive and was surprised when Isabelle grabbed the poker from her hand.

"Sit with me a moment by the fire?"

Her lips pressed tight. Isabelle wasn't leaving anytime soon. Prepared to endure a lecture, she dusted off her hands before nestling in one of the oversized chairs.

"Please hear me out before making any comment."

Brigette declined a response.

"Please?"

"As you wish."

"I know when I first came, we had a shaky start. However, it didn't take long before I imagined us the best of friends, if not sisters." Isabelle beamed.

"Was that before or after I tried to have you assassinated?" she asked deadpan.

"Brigette! You promised."

"Forgive me … proceed," she said with a flip of her hand. Realizing she imitated a move much like her brother, Nicolas, she snatched her hand from the air and tucked it in the folds of her robe.

"As I stated there is much I need to say before time escapes us. The incident you talk of is in our past. I want us both to leave it there and focus on the future. I know beyond a shadow of a doubt that God has a plan for your life just as He did for me to marry Nicolas …"

She stopped listening when Isabelle mentioned God having a plan for her life. God didn't care about her. Where was God when her mother died? Where was God when she fended for herself? And where was God when servants misled her while in their care? He wasn't concerned about her then, and He sure didn't care about her now. If He did, He would stop Nicolas from making a marriage covenant for her. No, God had abandoned her long ago.

"… so, you see, God will direct your paths and keep you safe if you but place your trust in Him alone. Have you ever made a commitment to our Lord and Savior Jesus Christ?"

"I go to mass and confess my sins as required. Don't fret about me, Isabelle. I am not afraid of my future. Now enough of this talk. I'm famished. Shall we break our fast together?"

Brigette offered Isabelle no option but to agree with her suggestion as she walked behind the changing screen to ready for the day. She bit her finger to hold back her cry of despair.

"Of course. I'll meet you downstairs when you are ready," Isabelle whispered.

When the door clicked, she buried her face in her hands allowing her tears to fall. She wasn't sure what distressed her more: the notion of leaving Fairwick Castle or how she wounded the one who loved her most. Who would help her now?

Daniel supervised the mixing of the mortar required to repair loose stones in the wall near the postern gate. It seemed the castle required constant maintenance to keep it in good order. Even though the rising sun just began to warm the day, he already broke a sweat.

"Papa, might I stir."

"If Gilly will allow it," Daniel said as he squeezed William's shoulder. He watched as the lad's eyes brightened when Gilly nodded his approval. To see the exuberance of his young son granted him great joy. Not having a mother to guide him, William stayed by his father's side. It amused Daniel when William imitated him in mannerisms and speech which caused him to fill with pride.

50

"Riders," yelled Adair from the guard post.

Daniel wiped his hands on a rag as his determined steps ate up ground. It didn't take long before he arrived at the keep steps to await his unexpected guests. He showed no emotion as Lord Fairwick and two knights rode through the gate. The rest of his men remained outside the gates. It wasn't lost on him that Nicolas made a strategic move when he left most of his men outside the castle walls. It was to be a pleasant encounter.

"Might I have a word with you?"

Daniel stood with his hands clasped behind his back. Leave it to Nicolas to project a demanding tone even when in Scotland. Arrogant man. "Of course. Please tell all of your men they may come inside the walls and receive refreshments after their journey."

He waited for Nicolas to dismount before leading the way inside. Daniel clapped his hands, and two servants scurried to do his bidding. He waved his arm in front of him. "Please, sit while you await your ale."

After Nicolas spoke to his two knights, they walked over to the long tables and rested on the benches. Looking at Daniel, he said, "I wish to talk with you alone. Is there somewhere more favorable for a private meeting?"

One brow rose as Daniel stared back. He paused but a moment. "Follow me." They walked through the grand hall and exited a door on the other side into a passageway. There they climbed a stone stairway to the second floor where he guided them into a library. "Make yourself comfortable while I see to our sustenance."

It didn't take long before he returned carrying a tray of cheese, bread, apples, and ale. After setting the tray on his desk, he shut and bolted the door. This caused Nicolas to raise questioning eyes.

"I don't wish for us to be interrupted," he explained.

He sat behind his desk while offering Nicolas a chair on the other side. A strategic move on his part. He planned to hold the upper hand in their conversation. He poured them a drink and leaned back in his chair. "Now, what brought you to Scotland this fine morn?"

Nicolas consumed much of his drink before plopping the mug on the desk. Without any preamble, he said, "I wish to discuss Brigette."

Daniel forced a courtesy smile as he placed his mug on the desk. He watched as Lord Fairwick rubbed his hands on his pants in a jerky motion. "And …?"

"The last time we spoke, you indicated that you wished to contract a marriage covenant between our families. Does that offer still stand?"

Daniel sat still for several moments. He wanted to give Nicolas time to simmer while he contemplated his response. It was doubtful the Fairwick's had received any other offers or none acceptable. He leaned his elbows on his desk and steepled his fingers. Nicolas's knee jiggled up and down.

"Do you wish to wed Brigette or not?"

"If I agree to wed your sister, 'twill be on my terms."

"Wha—? Your terms?"

"Ye heard me aright."

Nicolas's brows pulled together. "It depends on what your terms might be."

"As we both know, your sister's reputation became polluted by her own hand. I dare say there are no other men who wish their sons to bond with her. 'Twould not be beneficial for them to do so."

Nicolas jumped to his feet and placed his hands flat on the desk. "I am well aware of my sister's ruined reputation. If you remember, you are the one who approached me about an alliance, not the other way around."

With a snarling face inches away, Daniel remained stationary. Muscles grew taut. "That is true. However, as I specified, it will be on my terms or not at all." He held the upper hand in the conversation which allowed him patience. "Why don't you sit and hear my terms? You have the right to refuse them."

Nicolas backed away from the desk. "As you wish." He plopped into the chair and folded his arms across his chest. "Proceed."

Daniel let out the breath he held and leaned back in his chair. "First, the wedding will take place here in full Scottish tradition. You will have the honor of throwing out your coins to the village people on our way to the church. Unlike your wedding, the Banns will be published three consecutive Sundays. I want no surprises. Second, I will determine her dowry."

He held up his hand when Nicolas started to interrupt. "In conclusion, you will provide the funds for the wedding feast in Brigette's honor, and your family will depart for home before the day is out."

Nicolas's face turned dark red as his eyes narrowed. "This is preposterous. Isabelle will never agree to all you suggested."

"It matters not what Isabelle wants." He paused to let that register while he watched the tic in his friend's cheek. "This is your sister's wedding, and you are her guardian. The way I see it, you have few options available."

Nicolas shot to his feet and pounded his fist on the desk. "You do not lesson me on Brigette's possibilities. There are other choices."

Daniel rose and bumped his chair back with his legs. "Then our conversation has ended. I will see you out." Nicolas's eyes grew wide as his head jerked as if slapped. Daniel wore a mask of indifference. He had him right where he wanted him—desperate.

"Wait," Nicolas said.

Inwardly, Daniel smiled. Victory tasted sweet!

Chapter Eight

"Oh, fiddlesticks. Brigette, please stand still." Isabelle grumbled from under the heavy fabric. "I can't seem to get this plaid pinned straight. I'm afraid we might have to enlist the help of Daniel."

Brigette twisted around to see her sister-in-law's head hidden under a mountain of material. "Isabelle, come out from under there. Your hair will be a mess. Just leave it off. If my future husband wants me to wear this for the ceremony, he can attach the confounded thing himself." After Isabelle surfaced, Brigette whipped around and pulled the plaid to the floor with one jerk.

"Oh, dear. You mustn't move so fast, or your hair will fall. Remember, he made a point to ask that your hair be swept off your neck with curls framing your face."

After weeks of preparation, today was the day.

"Why does he have the say in everything?" She stamped her foot. "It's not fair. I didn't even want to wed anyone. Now I have to do as Lord McKinnon wishes, and we haven't even repeated our vows yet! This doesn't bode well for our future." She stepped away from the mirror dragging the plaid behind her while her chin sunk to her chest.

Isabelle glided up beside her and linked arms. "Oh, my sweet Brigette. All will be well. You will see. You gain so much by marrying Lord McKinnon. Don't forget you get a precious son in the agreement."

55

Her tense body relaxed. "Yes. At this point he is the one positive to this upheaval. Let me show you what my beloved William presented to me." She pulled her arm free and draped the tartan over her left arm. From inside the front of her dress, she withdrew a tiny pouch. Inside she extracted a smooth, round stone.

"Look. He entrusted me with his most prized possession." She held it out to for Isabelle to see. "I promised to wear it close to my heart during the ceremony. He hugged me tight and kissed me as if I gave him a treasure worth keeping."

With one finger, Isabelle turned Brigette's face toward her. "You are giving him a treasure worth keeping ... you."

The tartan slid to the floor as her arms went slack. Moisture filled her eyes. "Thank you," she whispered. "You seem to know the words I need to hear. Perhaps one day I will gain wisdom like you."

Isabelle shook her head. "Any wisdom I possess comes from God. I'm nothing more than an imperfect woman when left to my own devises."

Brigette clinched her teeth. She didn't want to say words to offend, but she didn't want to hear more talk about God. "I suppose you better fetch Daniel or a maid if we are to get this plaid attached before the wedding. Such a bother." She huffed as she picked it up.

Being big with child left Isabelle a bit scattered and easily distracted. "Oh, yea ... of course. I'll be but a moment." Away she waddled leaving her alone.

Brigette made her way back to the looking glass with the plaid in tow. She couldn't fault him on her dress. He spared no expense. It was beautiful. She stood properly attired for a Scottish wedding all the way to the six pence in her shoe. Feeling the coin under her foot made her smile.

Her betrothed insisted that Nicolas toss his own coins with an open hand to the village people as they made their way to the church. For sure, every peasant within the McKinnon realm would line the road. She chuckled. Nicolas hated parting with his money, especially for her.

"It's good to see you can smile and chuckle on our wedding day," Daniel said from the doorway.

She jumped from surprise. "I didn't hear you approach."

"That 'tis obvious by the way you are holding our clan plaid."

Her eyes grew large. She jerked the plaid off the floor and dangled it before her. "Please forgive me," she whispered. "My mind wandered."

"It matters not. Let me assist you."

She perused his wedding attire as he sauntered over to where she stood. His kilt, fastened with straps and buckles, reached the top of his knees. A broach attached his plaid at the shoulder. Her gaze traveled downward to see some type of pouch hanging from an apron in the front. A smile formed on her lips.

He removed the tartan from her hand. "Dare I venture to hope your smile is for me?"

Her eyes darted back to his. With a grin, she said, "I'm but thinking of Nicolas's reaction to your kilt, and it brings me pleasure."

"Ah, yes. It brings me great satisfaction to know it annoys him."

His touch on her waist warmed her through the dress. Her heart doubled in time as she held her arms out from her side. "I thought of Nicolas throwing his coins during the processional. Mayhap I will need to pry his hand open," she rushed to say.

This brought laughter from Daniel. He made quick work of her sash and then took her outstretched hands and brought them between them. With eyes locked together, he said, "I wanted him to suffer some pain and his purse strings provided an excellent solution."

"You are a devious man, Daniel McKinnon," she said on a quick indrawn breath.

Still clutching her hands, he said, "I know this is not what you wanted for your life, but in time, I hope you will be content. And for no reason should you ever fear me. Even though I am not a perfect man, I am reasonable." Without losing eye contact, he tilted his head. "Do you trust me?"

Swimming with unknown emotion, his brown eyes held her captive. Before she had time to think, her lips moved. "Yes."

A wide smile broke across his face. He raised her hands to his lips with slow deliberate, progress. Lost in the moment, the warmth of his breath and gentleness of his kiss nearly made her swoon.

"Come. Let us enjoy our wedding day."

His comment snapped her from a near faint. Like a lamb led to slaughter, he guided her out the door.

Lord McKinnon provided a decorative, two seated, enclosed carriage for Brigette and Lady Fairwick to ride to the church. Beside them Nicolas rode on horseback throwing coins along the way. If Brigette didn't see children scrambling to retrieve the money, she had threatened to yell at Nicolas to increase the amount. For once in her life, she held the power to tell her brother what to do. It was a small recompense for all the trauma he had caused her, but a reward none the less.

Isabelle squeezed her hand. "This is such a beautiful wedding day. The carriage is grand. You are stunning in your bridal dress. Not to mention, his people are rejoicing over this union. 'Tis a wonderful start for you."

She mumbled some type of reply while observing hundreds of people lining the path. Some dressed in finery while others wore tattered clothing, but each of them sported the colorful clan plaid and a wide smile. The flutters in her stomach increased in vigor the closer they came to the church. In desperation, she tried to calm her rapid breathing. 'Twould be mortifying if she fainted at Daniel's feet on the church steps.

All too soon, the carriage halted, and Nicolas flung the door open to retrieve Isabelle. When she turned toward Brigette, Isabelle's face paled and fear shone from her eyes.

Brigette clutched her sister-in-law's cold hand with concern.

"Are you ill?"

Isabelle's features softened. "No, sweet girl. For a brief moment I was transported back to my wedding day, and my stomach lurched at the memory. I didn't mean to alarm you." She patted Brigette's knee before taking Nicolas's hand to descend the carriage steps.

Panic choked her until she saw Phillip's smile in the crowd. He was her one brother who held some affection for her. Most days he came to her defense when Nicolas or Thomas riled against her. Her feeling of safety soon vanished when Thomas's face blocked her view. As the unwed brother, he was to escort her to her betrothed. Phillip needed to assist Abigail and Philippa.

Moisture gathered above her lip and along her hairline even though a cool, crisp breeze skimmed her neck. Her heart raced and her stomach ached as if she ingested a heavy rock with shards of glass sticking out. She would surely die from the effects.

"Brigette, take my hand," Thomas commanded.

Without a word, his battle roughened fingers swallowed her clammy hand. Her free hand gathered up her dress to keep from falling headlong to the ground. Thomas's firm hold provided her confidence.

Nodding heads and smiling faces greeted her at every turn. Could they see the swift beating of her heart? Would she spew her meal at their feet before reaching the church steps? Oh dear, what an ultimate humiliation!

Within ten paces she reached the foot of the church steps. Daniel stood at the top awaiting his young bride. His expressionless face left her unsettled. Did he regret his bride choice?

"Ye ar bonny!" William exclaimed. He clapped his small hands for emphasis.

Her eyes darted toward little William as he stood at attention next to his father. His bright countenance brought a shy smile to her face. His mere presence lightened her heart for an instant.

Noise abounded as the crowd pressed closer to the couple. With slow deliberate steps Laird McKinnon descended the stairs. Her eyes grew wider and her breathing faster with each step he took. Thomas placed her shaking hand upon Daniel's arm. He covered her trembling fingers with his and led her to the church doors.

"Ye ar' breathtakingly beautiful," he whispered.

Instead of soothing her jangled nerves, his words increased her apprehension. It made her mind dash straight to what might happen in the bedroom tonight. Drat Isabelle for even mentioning that aspect of marriage. Brigette feared what she knew nothing about.

Without time to dawdle on the thought, the couple turned to face the crowd as the priest began the first part of the ceremony. She didn't know what the priest uttered because all she heard was the rushing of water and her own chant inside her mind. *Don't' swoon. Don't swoon. Don't swoon.* At one point she closed her eyes when she noticed the cluster of people swaying before her face. *Breathe!*

"Brigette, are ye aboot to swoon?" Daniel asked.

Her eyes popped open and zoomed to his face. "Oh … I am fine. Is something amiss?"

"Ye swayed with yer eyes closed, and ye failed to answer the priest."

Her lips formed an 'O' but no words came out. "What do I need to say?" she whispered.

He smiled. "Juist say aye."

"Aye," she said to the priest. Upon her one word, the peasants erupted into cheers. She jumped from surprise.

"Is she me mither now?" William asked.

"Aye," his father replied. He picked William up and allowed him to give his new mother a kiss on the cheek. That one act increased the volume of the gathering twofold which startled her even further. Could she withstand more unexpected uproars?

Daniel tugged her hand, but she held fast. "Come. We ar' to go straight inside far the rest of the service."

"I supposed it was over," she said in exasperation.

"Try to hold on for a wee bit. It weel be over soon. None but the families go inside."

"Will you always talk with this thick accent?" she fumed. "Understanding you is difficult."

A thundercloud formed on his face. "I'll try to speak more to yer liking in the future. However, ye are now the bride of a distinguished Scottish Laird and would do well to remember it. It might behoove ye to learn the Scottish way of speaking."

Her eyes narrowed at his quiet determination. "I'll try to remember my station," she said through tight lips.

As they glared at each other, the priest cleared his throat. Their heads whipped around to the priest and then around to see a silent crowd watching the couple. With a stiff back and tight shoulders, she said, "Shall we proceed?"

Chapter Nine

Daniel watched as Brigette fiddled with her meal. She had failed to make eye contact with him since their quarrel on the church steps. He recognized how her condescending tone about his Scottish brogue had annoyed him. Their disagreement in front of his people aggravated him, but she needed to know who ruled, and it wasn't her.

"Is the food not to your liking?" he asked in perfect English pronunciation. He wanted to kick himself for succumbing to her demands already.

She turned her head halfway but never raised her eyes to meet his. "I fear my appetite has waned."

Daniel placed a finger under her chin forcing her to lift her head. When she lifted her face, her eyes swam with unshed tears. His irritation washed away like a leaf in a rushing river. How could he stay angry at his new wife when she seemed terrified? "I'm sorry we experienced our first disagreement. Let us put it aside and enjoy the festivities. Shall we?"

She blinked. With swift action Daniel caught and wiped away her tears. He didn't want others to witness her distress and misunderstand. His people loved to a fault unless they believed their laird dishonored.

"I will try."

"Can you give a smile for the guests to see? It would go a long way to endear you to them," he said with kindness. He watched as she struggled to allow her smile to form. He envisioned a long battle to reach the heart of his bride. Nevertheless, he wasn't a successful warrior by chance.

William sat on the other side of Brigette. He must have sensed her sadness for he reached over and took her hand into his. "Ye ar' so bonnie, and ye ar' me mither." He grinned and tried to wink at her.

"William, you are the most precious boy I know." She hugged him close. "I can't wait for us to get better acquainted."

"How aboot we go outside? I want ta shew ye something."

Daniel noticed his wife struggling to decipher his son's question. He leaned close and whispered in her ear. "William wants to show you something outside."

He placed his hand on her back and peered past her to speak to William. "Nay, William. She will not be playing with ye today. Yer mother and I are the honorees at this banquet and must remain until our guests depart."

William's eyes grew large. "Do I have ta stay at the table?"

"Nay, son. Ye may be excused to play."

Without delay, William stood on his chair. His short arms wrapped around his mother's neck and pulled her to him for a sweet kiss on the cheek. After releasing her he said, "I loue ye." Then he scampered off to play. His bodyguards rose from their seats and followed him out the door.

Daniel noticed how William's embrace loosened some of her hair from its pins, but she didn't seem to care. The fondness she expressed toward his son helped to soften his earlier judgment of his young bride. He reminded himself of her inexperience as a wife and a mother, both roles thrust upon her without a choice.

When he rubbed her back, she turned anguished eyes upon him. *Now what's the matter?* "What troubles ye, wife?"

After a couple of sniffs, she clinched her hands in her lap and hung her head. "I fear William is my one friend in this room who accepts me as I am. I know I will disappoint everyone and don't know how to stop it."

He covered her fists with his hand. "Do not add such a burden to yer shoulders. Each of us disappoint others at times. Be yourself. The people will grow to love you even as little William loves you … and … as I will grow to love you if you allow it." He hoped his words held true. "Now where hides that feisty young woman who rejoiced when I wore a kilt to aggravate Nicolas at Philippa's christening?"

Her lips trembled with the makings of a smile. "'Twas delightful, was it not?"

"Aye." About that time, the bagpipes played for the Traditional Grand March led by the newly married couple. "Come, 'tis time for our dance."

Her bewilderment didn't faze him. Grabbing her hand, he drew her to her feet. He presented no choice but to comply as he pulled her along. Between the bagpipes and the loud cheers from the guests, it was impossible to explain the dance to his wife. No doubt, she would catch on.

As they began the march, the maid of honor and the best man Daniel chose for the wedding joined in the dance. Then her relatives were coaxed into the line of dancers. The infectious happiness of the guests soon had Brigette laughing as she stumbled along.

Once others engaged in the dance, he led his wife to their seats to watch in amusement. "What dance is this?" she all but shouted.

"The Grand March."

"I see how it got the name," she commented as she watched them march around the room in some semblance of order. "I'm a bit confused. Why two ceremonies?"

"The villagers and guests witness and understand the first ceremony on the church steps since it is done in our local dialect. Even I don't understand all of the Latin Mass the priest performed inside the church. I once spoke Latin verra well but stopped studying it after my father's death."

"Oh? Were you too sad at his passing that further study pained you?" Her eyes shone with innocence.

65

Picturing his father's displeasure and constant badgering for Daniel to improve didn't set well with him. He didn't wish to discuss his father whom he never pleased. However, he was so delighted that his wife talked with him that he refused to dwell on his deceased father.

"Nay. I had no need to know it fluently. Plus, at his passing, I had a castle to run and important decisions to make. Therefore, no time for studies."

"I never knew my father. He died when I was quite young."

He noticed she replied matter of fact without a trace of sadness. Maybe she was the fortunate one. In his later years, her father had developed a terrible reputation. Hopefully, she would not press him about his knowledge of her father. He watched as she tilted her head and tapped her chin.

"Why did we cut a ribbon when we exited the church?"

He smiled as he welcomed the change in the topic. Neither of their fathers did he wish to intrude on their wedding day. "It's a Scottish tradition called *creeled.* The ribbons held a fishing basket. To allow the basket to fall to the ground brings good fortune for the married couple."

"What was the purpose of ripping the tartans and tying the strips together?"

"That represents the unity of our families. Since you are from England and don't have a clan color, both of the plaids were my colors. 'Tis customary to see two different tartans tied together as two clans unite."

"Oh. I see."

What raced through her mind as he witnessed her first real smile of the day? It reached all the way to her eyes.

"I must say. Seeing Nicolas's reaction to your full clan dress delighted me. When he spied the feathers in your cap, I feared he might collapse on the spot," she said with laughter ringing in her tone.

Again, another person he did not want to discuss—Nicolas, his childhood nemesis. Nevertheless, her relaxed mood pleased him.

"Tell me about your costume," she continued.

He bit his jaw to refrain from lashing out. Costume, indeed. "'Tis more than a costume. 'Tis the clothing befitting a Clan Chief."

"Oh." Her head ducked. "Excuse me. I didn't mean any disrespect."

"No offense taken." He lied. "The three eagle feathers tucked behind the crest badge indicate I am the Clan Chief. The clan badge is my family crest encircled by a strap-and-buckle worn on a kilt or shawls to show loyalty. I wield the power to withdraw the badge from anyone I deem disloyal or unworthy to wear it."

"Oh, my." Her eyes widened. "I hope I'm never deemed unworthy. I don't know all of your customs, and without consideration, I might make a blunder."

He took her hand in his. "I will be lenient with my new wife. Dinna fash yerself." When he noticed her perplexed expression, he clarified. "Do not worry yourself."

Her confusion cleared. "Continue with your explanation. I find it fascinating."

He described his Scottish attire in great detail. If it kept her attention focused on him, then so be it. It pleased him she wanted to know more of his heritage. They had the whole night to become acquainted.

Lord McKinnon's description of his clan and some of their customs, fascinated Brigette. It was all new to her since her brothers forbade her to venture far from home and never into Scotland. She even enjoyed the lilt in his voice which reminded her of her curt words on the church steps about his speech. She blamed it on her fury and fatigue. Months ago, Isabelle informed her of his volatile temper. She best refrain from angering him.

Earlier her stomach had rolled and churned like an ocean in a storm. However, as her husband talked to her, it calmed enough for her to eat a few bites of the delicious wedding meal. The noise from the celebrating guests was deafening which resulted in her and Daniel touching heads to hear one another. Their closeness proved pleasing. He even smelled nice.

As the day wore on, Lady Fairwick came to the head table. "Lord McKinnon, might I speak a private word with your bride?"

Brigette noticed his eyes narrowed before answering. "Of course. Don't keep her from the banquet overlong."

Isabelle nodded.

Brigette's husband rose when she stood. Stiff from the long hours watching the merrymakers, she said, "Please, excuse me." She used proper etiquette to make sure she didn't offend him. Like the touch of a feather, she placed her hand on his arm. "I will return soon. Where might we go for privacy?"

He indicated a door behind their chairs. "That door will lead into a hallway. Take the stairs to the second floor and my study is at the top of the steps. A servant will show you the way." He motioned to a young girl. "Please take them to my study and wait outside the door until they are ready to return."

She curtsied. "Aye, m' laird."

Brigette hid her smile behind her hand at the girl's thick accent. At least she understood what the servant spoke. She assisted her pregnant sister-in-law to prevent a fall on the stone stairs.

Once inside the study, she helped the expectant mother into the chair behind the desk since it appeared softer than the one opposite. After closing the door, she walked to the middle of the room. With many books arranged on shelves, the room resembled a library. Delightful!

"Please, sit." Isabelle pointed to the chair.

Brigette needed a moment to fluff her dress in order to be comfortable. "What is so important?"

"I failed to tell you some essential points about tonight."

It took great restraint not to roll her eyes. "All will be well. You needn't worry."

"Cease," Isabelle said with force. "Hear me out."

"As you wish." She didn't want their brief time together strained. It might be the last time she saw Isabelle for quite a spell.

Nicolas wouldn't allow his wife to travel after today. The question remained, would Daniel permit her to visit Fairwick castle? It reminded her once again of how circumstances twisted out of her control which rekindled her anger.

"I do not want you shocked tonight. This is a most meaningful night to your husband, and you must see that it proceeds without discord. First, don't be alarmed when he asks you to remove all of your clothing."

"What?" Brigette exclaimed. "He sees me without a night dress?"

"Yes."

Her face heated as her heart tripped. She gripped her trembling hands to hide the effect Isabelle's words created.

"Whatever he asks of you, do it without question."

This grew worse by the minute. Why hadn't she listened to Isabelle earlier? When Isabelle attempted to explain about the intimacy that would transpire between her and Daniel, she feared she might vomit out her dinner. She swallowed hard to hold it in. Shutting out Isabelle, her imagination tormented her with terrible pictures. Death surely awaited her.

"Do you have any questions?" Isabelle whispered.

With wild eyes Brigette looked at Isabelle's face—pale as flour. "How can you say this will be enjoyable? It sounds horrific. No woman should have to endure such!"

"Oh, my sweet. I wish you had the opportunity to grow fond of Daniel before speaking vows as I did with Nicolas. My heart belonged to him, so the night of consummation proved blissful," she said in wonder.

"Please, say no more!" She closed her eyes and covered her face with her hands. "My life is over."

Isabelle stood and leaned forward with her hands flat on the desk. "Stop this at once! You are not a little girl any longer, so do not try your theatrics on your husband. It will not go well for you if you do. This is God's plan for women. If you embrace the role of wife and mother, your days will be pleasing."

Brigette hopped out of her chair and paced the room. How could this be happening to her? All she wanted was solitude to live out her days, yet now a wife to a stranger. *Trapped!*

Isabelle gentled her reply. "William needs a mother."

Her pacing slowed as those words stirred her protective senses. The image of precious William caused her heart to soften. Too bad his father had to come with the contract. She wiped away her tears and faced Isabelle. "I've heard enough. Let's return."

"That's it? No other questions?"

She walked around the desk and wrapped Isabelle's hands with her own. "Daniel needs to see that I can be trusted. I gave my word we would not tarry. However, I want you to know how your love and concern for me bolsters my resolve. I'm Fairwick born. I will survive." The two embraced. "Come. Let me help you on the stairs."

I will endure for William. I must.

Chapter Ten

After returning to the grand hall, Brigette tried to act pleasant and agreeable with Daniel. She didn't want him to find fault with her on their wedding day. However, she became anxious when her kinsman rose to make their departure. Even though she wasn't speaking to Nicolas and had no desire to converse with Thomas, it saddened her to see Phillip leave. Phillip, her anchor in times of trouble and uncertainty. Now her last line of stability was about to withdraw from her. Her heart sped up as they each approached the high table for their farewells.

"'Tis early. Are you leaving?" she asked Isabelle.

Isabelle glanced at her husband. "Yes. We need to return before my wife becomes too tired to travel," Nicolas said.

"You aren't staying a few days here?" Brigette asked in a high-pitched voice. She looked at Daniel for his approval, but his scowl silenced her.

He placed his hand atop her hand that lay on the table. "Wife, allow them the privilege to take their leave. It's been a long morning for Isabelle. She needs her rest."

Brigette looked between her husband and Nicolas. Something was amiss but she didn't know who to blame. Either way, she was about to be left in Scotland forever with a man she barely knew. Her eyes welled up as she stood to her feet and walked around the table to embrace the woman who acted like her mother. "Oh,

Isabelle," she whispered in her ear. "I'm going to miss you terribly. I do love you so."

Likewise, was all Isabelle uttered. Both women cried in silence as they held one another until Nicolas drew them apart.

"We must be away." Nicolas nodded at Daniel. "Until we meet again."

Brigette hugged Phillip and kissed baby Philippa in his arms. She even managed an awkward embrace with Abigail. However, she made no attempt to engage Thomas or Nicolas. Though she could skewer her two brothers for their part in creating this mess, she would miss their cantankerous ways. There was comfort in the familiar.

Daniel joined her as they walked her family to their waiting horses. Her husband held fast to her hand making it impossible for her to follow them down the steps. One final touch from her kinfolk was not to be. She began to tremble, and her stomach stirred. When the last rider cleared the gate, her tears fell in earnest. Left all alone, she feared the long night ahead.

"Wife, you seem shaken." He put his hands on her shoulders and gently turned her to face him. When their eyes met, his features softened. "Do not fear. I will guard you well. My people are now your people." He wiped away her tears with the pad of his thumb. "Come. Let us return inside to enjoy our guests. There is much celebrating left to do."

Brigette walked on rigid legs as if marching toward a fatal encounter. Questions raced through her mind. *How long will we stay downstairs? What happens to me when I'm alone with Daniel? Will he be disappointed? Will I?*

As her family rode away, Daniel noticed the terror in his bride's expression. No doubt she felt abandoned by her people as she faced isolation in Scotland. In his opinion, her youth and inexperience in the role as wife, mother, and lady of his castle provoked additional fears. Her apathetic brothers were to blame for it. They left her ill equipped for the task. In this situation he needed patience which he held in abundance, or so he imagined.

Once inside, he tried to engage Brigette in conversation, but it fell flat. Her stilted and awkward answers fluttered out with little or no eye contact. She was even less interested in dancing with him and wore her anxiety like a woolen cape on bare skin.

As the shadows lengthened, he noticed her shoulders slumped either from weariness or sadness—unsure which. It was past time for them to depart to their living quarters while their guests' merrymaking continued into the wee hours of the morn.

He stood and offered his hand to his bride. "Come, wife. 'Tis time we depart upstairs." He watched her eyes grow wide with alarm. Leaning down he whispered near her ear. "Try not to appear fearful or the guests might take offense."

With haste Brigette masked her emotions as she stood. "I'm sorry," she whispered. She tried to duck her head, but Daniel allowed it not.

He touched under her chin. "Head high as we leave the room. Try to act pleased with the situation," he warned. Astonished at her transformation, he admitted he married a talented actress. She smiled and talked with people as they made their way around the large room. Without a doubt, her acting abilities carried her through tough times at Fairwick castle.

The loud, rowdy group shouted their lewd comments to the couple with enthusiasm. He kept a tight hold on her hand as they circled the room. He didn't want her to bolt from fright. "We will make a discreet exit, so no one follows us to our room. I wished to spare you the traditional stripping of the husband and wife in front of a group of intoxicated and undisciplined men," he murmured in her ear.

Her head whipped around toward him as she gasped. "Oh, yes! Thank you."

Daniel tried to act nonchalant as they circled the room and visited with their guests. Thankfully, most of his friends relaxed deep in their cups and wouldn't notice when the two slipped out through the back door of the grand hall. They weaved back and forth as if they had no intentions of leaving the festivities. Brigette's decorum pleased him. Her polite voice exuded kindness as she interacted with strangers. She floated through the crowd with the dignity of a queen. He hoped once she settled into a routine, she would do well in Scotland.

After working their way through the room, they ended behind the head table. With the suddenness of a cat springing at its prey, Daniel pulled her through the doorway and bolted for the stairs.

"What are you about?" she asked in alarm.

He laughed. "We are escaping the thunderous crowd that is sure to follow if they comprehend where we are headed. Hurry."

"Wait!" She paused long enough to grab her dress and pull it above her ankles. "I don't want to meet my death at the bottom of these winding stairs."

When he looked at her, her face shone bright with mischief. Her radiant smile transported him back to the time they shared at Fairwick Castle in her childhood room. Now, her face mirrored that day when she was gleeful over his kilt, and how it irritated her brother.

The two raced up the stairs with Brigette giggling like a schoolgirl. At the top of the steps, she stopped and bent over. "I must catch my breath." She straightened with haste when pounding footsteps echoed from the bottom of the stairs. She turned startled eyes toward him. "How much farther?"

"Too far for you to run in those slippers." He scooped her into his arms and sprinted left around a corner and through another passageway. It delighted him the way she clung to his neck as she watched behind them. The sweet fragrance from her skin caused him to falter. It had been many years since he held a woman close, and he relished it. He noticed a calm settled over her once she rested secure in his arms. But would that calm endure through their night together?

"Oh, dear. I see them coming," she squealed.

"Do not fear." He rounded one more turn and within a few strides he reached a closed door. The guard standing outside the room opened the door, and then pulled it closed after the couple slipped inside.

Daniel released her and spun around to bolt the door. Once secure, he turned to find her laughing behind her hand.

"That was exhilarating. I'm impressed you ran that fast while you carried me, and grateful you didn't stumble." Her eyes sparkled with amusement.

Thankful that her previous aloofness had vanished and left the mischievous woman he desired in her place, he leaned against the door gazing at her. To watch her animation was refreshing and enjoyable. "I can rise to the occasion when called upon."

Pounding fists on the closed portal along with loud cries for entrance caused her to jump. "Open the door, m'lord. We'll assist ye and yer bride."

While resting against the door, he watched his young wife turn numerous shades of red. Her eyes grew to full moons with each rowdy word that seeped under the door. "Dinna fash yerself. They will not gain entrance this night. Ye are safe with me." He used his tranquil horse voice in hopes to soothe her. No man wanted a skittish wife on their wedding night.

She wrapped her arms around her waist, but when he pushed away from the door, one hand raised to her throat. He stopped without taking a step. "Brigette, 'tis me, Daniel. There is no need for distress." When she didn't show signs of relief, he took a different tactic. He walked around her and knelt to stoke the fire.

"Ye didn't seem to eat much at the feast. Was it not to yer liking?"

Her feet shuffle as she crept closer to where he knelt.

"Oh, no. Nothing like that. The food appeared delicious. I suppose I didn't have much of an appetite with the excitement of the day."

He laid aside the poker but remained on his knees as he turned to speak to his wife. "I'll send for a bit of cheese and bread to hold you over till the morn. Is that to yer liking?"

"I don't want to cause you any trouble."

If he hadn't been watching her when she spoke, he might not have understood her. As she stood before him with head bowed low, he envisioned an innocent lamb. Her quiet words caused his heart to wrench with pain. His uncertain bride was afraid and at his mercy.

"'Twill be no trouble." He rose to his feet but didn't make a move toward her. "Ye look as if ye might collapse. Why don't ye sit here by the fire while I speak to the kitchen maid?" He held out his hand. After a moment, she reached for his hand and allowed him to guide her to the chair. "Get comfortable, and I'll return straight away."

She fretted. "Is it safe to open the door?"

"I'm the lord of this castle. Each mon will heed my word or suffer the consequences. Rest here, and I'll return soon. We have all night to get acquainted."

As Daniel lifted the latch on the door, he saw his wife's panicked expression.

Chapter Eleven

For a while, Brigette fidgeted in her chair twisting her dress into a mess. Her stomach knotted—tighter than a fisherman's rope. What did Daniel mean get acquainted? Oh, why had she ignored Isabelle and missed important details?

After a few agonizing minutes, she distracted herself by scanning the room shared with her husband. At least she believed they shared his room. Perhaps as Lady McKinnon she earned her own room. A place to escape and be alone?

She stood and considered the elaborate furnishings. One thing for certain, her new husband surrounded himself with elegant items. Large portraits hung on the wall. She recognized Daniel and William in the painting above the hearth. The woman beside Daniel must have been William's mother.

Oh dear. Would he leave the massive likeness of a dead woman above the fireside? She certainly hoped not. As the new lady of the castle such a thing was not to be borne!

Not wanting to linger over those thoughts, she strolled around the enormous space. To the right of the fireplace, four windows boasted colorful stained-glass inserts. The open shutters allowed the light to cast an array of colors around the room. Even though the light diminished as darkness crept in, the colors still glistened.

Stopping at a table containing a full chess set ready for play, she picked up the queen. "Will you survive in your new place little queen?" she whispered. "I think you will." She kissed the queen and used her to knock the king piece flying off the board. "Well done, my queen." She giggled.

At that moment, Daniel came through the door with a tray of food in hand. His unexpected entrance startled her which caused her to drop the queen. "Oh. You surprised me, and I dropped the chess pieces." She stooped to retrieve them, but the king had skittered under the table. On her knees, she grasped the queen and ran her hand along the floor for the king. His black color made it difficult to find.

"Here. I will get the missing piece. Kneeling in your wedding attire might soil it."

In haste, she pushed to her feet with the help of holding onto the chair. She replaced the queen and brushed a bit of dust off the dress with her hand.

"'Tis alright. No harm done."

When she looked up, he stood by her side. His body radiated heat better than any roaring fire. He made quick work of finding the chess piece and set it back on the board.

"Let us eat our meager meal together." As his arm wrapped around her waist, his warm touch inflamed her. His nearness stirred her stomach all aflutter.

"Thank you for your thoughtfulness." Her senseless chatter caused an inward groan. At sixteen, her obvious inexperience burned bright. She couldn't even make intelligent conversation. *What would Isabelle say?*

"Will you tell me about your fine home while we dine?" That sounded better to her ears and appeared to please her new husband because she swore his chest puffed out a smidgen.

"Of course, I am delighted to tell you about *your* new home." They stopped before reaching the chairs. He took both of her hands into his and pulled her against his chest. "We have much to share this evening." His breath skimmed her face. He quieted her trembling with a kiss.

Releasing her, he waved his hand for her to sit. Even as he

spoke, her rapid heartbeat drowned out his voice. Why was she unsettled? She didn't want him close at hand, yet his nearness pleased her. A puzzling contradiction.

How could she partake of the food he brought when her stomach crawled with spiders? She shuttered at the notion for she despised spiders. Nibbling on a piece of cheese, she struggled to understand her emotional sways. One minute she wanted to run out of the room and back to England. Then her husband kissed her, and she liked it. Was this what Isabelle tried to explain? Oh bother!

"The castle has remained in my family for many years. First, it belonged to my grandfather and then to my father. One day wee William will rule. With a castle of this magnitude, I spend much time seeing to the repairs and daily maintenance of my home. My grandfather started replacing all the wooden structures with stone. I continue with that process today. The keep is almost completed. However, there are a few wooden buildings susceptible to fire. My goal is to prevent my enemies from burning us out."

He devoured his repast as he boasted about his holdings. She tried to stay alert to the conversation. However, the lack of sleep from past days, coupled with her absence of appetite, left her weak and weary. She placed her cup and platter on the nearby table while his voice faded to a murmur.

"Brigette?"

Her eyes popped open to see his face within inches of her own. Did she doze off? How long had he watched her sleep?

"Oh, my." Heat rose from her neck to her face. He must judge her no better than a babe-in-arms who can't stay awake as the evening wanes. "I'm sorry."

He placed both hands on the arms of her chair and smiled. "'Tis alright. You endured a long and exhausting day. Let us retire to our bed."

That one word, *bed*, jolted her alert. She swallowed hard. "Oh, no. That's not necessary. You may continue sharing about your home. There's no need to hurry to bed. For certain, I'm not even tired."

He straightened and towered over her. His smile grew even wider. "No. 'Tis time." He took her hand and drew her into his arms. With her body flush against his own, he said, "Trust me, wife. All will be well." He placed a soft kiss on her cheek before leading her to their grand platform bed.

"There are some last instructions I need to explain to my guards. I will leave you alone while you prepare. Notice I purchased a special night dress for you to wear. Please, have it on when I return."

He exited the room, and a maid entered. Brigette dared a peek at the bed. Atop the feather mattress laid an ornate white gown decorated with satin ribbons and jewels bordering the plunging neckline. Her heart pounded as her breath came in quick gasps. How could a night dress bring her such fear? *Oh, Isabelle, I want to come home.*

"I'm here to assist ye."

Brigette allowed the girl access to her ties. She made quick work of removing the wedding attire and donning the white gown. With a quick flourish, the girl tied a fluffy bow in the front. The maid hung the bridal dress on a wall peg and placed her shoes underneath.

"Is there anything else ye be needing, miss?"

Brigette's smile quivered. "No. Thank you for your help."

The maid curtsied and left the room without a sound.

Brigette's hands trembled as she closed the front of the gown with a tight knot instead of a bow. Perhaps it was childish, but it did make her feel a bit secure.

Uncertain what to do next, she stirred the fire with a hardy poke to the logs. With no immediate plan, she curled up in the fireside chair and watched the flames dance in the night. Her thoughts swirled as her eyes drooped shut.

"Brigette? It's time to come to bed."

She jerked awake to see her new husband standing over her. "What did you say?"

"'Tis time for us to retire. Come."

Her eyes widened. Had he waited long? Craning her neck, she

glanced back at the huge bed. "Are you sure there is enough room for both of us? I can always sleep elsewhere."

Her response brought a hearty laugh. "I think not, wife. Tonight, we sleep together."

She unfolded her shaky legs and stood. Trying to act mature, she threw her shoulders back and proceeded to walk to the far side of the bed.

"Wait," he said. "There is one thing I desire to do before turning in." With Brigette facing him, he proceeded to remove her hair pins one at a time. As each curl fell from its place, he twirled it around his finger. It was a slow, distressing deed for her, but he seemed to take great pleasure in the act. Once her long locks were free from their tight hold, he ran his fingers through her tresses massaging her scalp in the process. He inhaled the aroma of her hair and groaned.

"This fragrance pleases me."

His hands produced a most delightful sensation making it difficult to concentrate on his words. "Mm," was her one reply. However, when he cuddled her in his arms, her mind engaged. Her body stiffened with fright.

He exhaled with a loud puff and leaned his head against hers. "Wife, you have no idea how desirable you are to me. Ease your mind and follow my lead. We will weather this night together and build on our relationship. Trust me."

He released her and walked around to the other side of the massive bed. Her eyes grew wide with alarm as he disrobed. It shocked her when he showed no embarrassment about his nakedness as he crawled under the covers.

"Weel ye stand thar all night hiding yer eyes?"

Still standing by the bed with her face covered, she peeped through her fingers at her husband. Why had he resorted to speaking thusly? He knew she had a hard time understanding the Scottish dialect. It aggravated her.

"No." She crawled up the steps beside the bed and fidgeted with the coverlet trying to get under it without touching him. With her back to her husband, she had no idea what he was about. When something touched her uncovered neck, she screamed and went into action.

Her body lurched forward as her elbow flew backwards connecting with his face. Daniel let out a yelp.
Landing close to the edge of the mattress, she fell off headfirst.

One foot intertwined with the covers causing her to land halfway off the bed. "Help me," she squealed. "There's a spider crawling on me!" She thrashed about trying to free her foot.

"Stop this at once," he bellowed. "'Twas no spider. 'Twas my hand, ye foolish woman."

By now she had broken free from the hold of the bed covers and stood next to the rumpled bed. Her breath came fast and hard from her struggle and her fright. The once beautiful locks of hair were now a disheveled mess. She shoved her wild mane out of her face to see him holding his face and moaning.

"Are you sure it wasn't a spider on my neck?"

He released his face. "Yes!"

When she saw his angry face, her jangled nerves got the best of her. She burst into uncontained, hysterical laughter. By the light of the fire, a discoloration formed on his face. "I believe you will have a blackened eye in the morn," she said between gasps of laughter. "I delivered quite a wallop." Covering her mouth with her hand, her eyes danced with amusement.

After a few moments, he chuckled. "What a pair we make, Brigette Isolde McKinnon."

Hearing him say her married name subdued her merriment. She was no longer the little sister of the Fairwick brothers who did as she pleased. Now, she was the wife of a powerful Scottish Laird and with that came responsibilities. Her first duty was to please her husband and everything that entailed.

"I'm sorry for our bit of misunderstanding," she whispered.

"'Tis alright." He straightened the coverlet and propped himself on the pillow facing her. "I do recall you mentioning your fear of spiders. Believe me, I will not repeat my mistake. This is but one small hurdle as we discover about each other."

There was no escaping her purpose. She adjusted her twisted gown, loosened the knot and formed a bow instead. She smiled. "Beware, I'm coming back to bed." She nestled under the sheets. "Let the education begin."

Chapter Twelve

The next morning Brigette soaked in a steaming bath ordered by her husband. It delighted her that he anticipated her body's need to recover. After the first night with him, she dreaded for darkness to fall. Would it be pleasing if she loved her husband as Isabelle suggested? Doubtful.

Daniel indicated that this bed sport might transpire every night unless she professed *unclean*. Oh, dear ... the mention of that particular word caused her immediate mortification. Speaking thusly just wasn't done.

As if the horrors of the night hadn't been enough, this morning he informed her everyone in the castle knew what transpired between them. Straightaway she wept. He erupted into laughter as he buckled on his sword. Her lone consolation had been when he allowed her to remain in their room while he accepted the taunting over his black eye. He was sure to receive harassment by his men followed by their offensive gestures. She had witnessed the likes of it often at Fairwick Castle.

Grateful to escape the unpleasant teasing, she savored the theory of her husband's humiliation. The idea soothed her wounded dignity even though a paltry victory. He need not think she planned to stay in their room all day as he suggested. Exploration awaited her, and she planned to venture far from this room.

Upon exiting the tub and peeking around the partition, she spied her clothing trunk right inside the door. Her brow rose. "I wonder when that arrived?" Not wanting to be caught bare as a newborn babe, she rummaged through her trunk and found a nondescript day dress. In order to dodge undue notice, the dull, brown dress was ideal. With her unadorned, wet hair plaited down her back, she stood in front of a floor mirror. "Well, Brigette, ole girl, you can pass as an ordinary maid." She smiled. "Perfect!"

Easing open the heavy door, it relieved her to find the hallway empty of guards. At least her new husband hadn't dishonored her with a constant guard by her side like her brother, Nicolas. Turning right led to the stairs which directed her to the grand hall. Wishing to evade her husband, she chose left.

She tip-toed to prevent the loud clicking noise of her walking boots on the stone floor. Acting the spy brought back childhood memories of hiding from her brothers. When they wanted her to practice sewing or entertain dinner guests, she remained hidden until they gave up the hunt. Somehow her small triumph of outwitting them had made her feel clever. Now, the memory just reminded her of their lack of interest in her at all.

Not wanting to dwell on gloomy recollections, she used her crafty ways to see how long she could go undetected in the McKinnon castle. Maybe her skills would prove helpful to Daniel sometime in the future. Staying close to the wall in the shadows, she maneuvered down another passageway until voices slipped through a half-closed door. To elude detection, she slid into the darkness of an alcove next to the room from whence the voices emitted. Holding her breath, Brigette listened.

"Dinna fash yerself. The mon weel nae suspect ye. Visions of his bonnie wife weel keep his mind all a dither."

Laughter.

"Ye grab her and hold tight. I weel nook her in her head. Then we drag her oot the back straight to the horse. Mayhap we can have some sport with 'er before turning 'er over ..."

Shh. "I heard a sound."

Brigette wanted to pinch herself for shuffling her feet when she thought a spider crawled on her dress. The darkness didn't permit her to verify her suspicion. Unfortunately, those men reacted when she kicked the vase.

When it sounded as if they were coming near the doorway, she slipped from her hiding place and walked at a rapid pace down the corridor. Her escape was thwarted. One man grabbed her braid and yanked hard. She lost her footing and fell backwards into his arms. Twisting, she fought but was unable to break free from the foul man's grip.

"Whit have we here?"

"I believe we have a bonnie lass to entertain us," the second man said as he sauntered up to the duo.

"Let me go at once," she said in her haughtiest voice.

"Weel now. I think not. Ye ne'er listen to anither mon's tale. It's a verra sairy thin' to do."

She jerked hard against the hold. "Do you know who I am?"

The men snickered at her discomfort while they slid their hands over her face and form. "Me thinks yer a scullery maid," the first man said.

"One in sore need of some loovin'," the other man replied.

Brigette had tolerated enough of their improper actions. She hadn't lived with three brothers not to know a few moves to escape unwanted attention. Much to her relief, the wretched men left her hands free. With a tight fist she punched the first man straight in the throat. He released her at once as he gasped for air and grabbed his throat.

Taken by surprise, the second man lunged and managed to seize the sleeve of her dress but wasn't prepared for the swift kick to his knee from her boot. He howled with fury but held fast to her clothing. Her sleeve ripped when she bounded off at a run back the way she had come, screaming for help with each step.

When she turned at the end of the corridor, she ran into the solid chest of a guard. "Whoa, lassie. Whit seems to be the trooble?" He held her arm to steady her.

Out of breath, she pointed backwards. "There are two men

down that hallway who tried to accost me."

"Whit are ye doin' here?"

"Stop asking me questions while those two galoots get away!"

"Ye'll need to coom with me." He held fast to her arm and dragged her toward the stairway.

Her heels dug in, but his brute strength caused her to skid along on the stones. "Let me go. Do you know who I am?" She expected him to remember her from the celebration. However, her words bounced off his broad back with no effect.

"I'm the laird's wife."

Her declaration didn't even cause the giant to pause in his mission. When they reached the circular stairway, she decided it in her best interest to cooperate. A tumble on the stairs presented a terrible ending to her first day. She huffed all the way down the steps. After the tussle with the two ruffians, she knew she looked a fright. Her frayed braid fell in her eyes, her torn dress flapped in the breeze, and she fumed. A dreadful combination.

The guard tugged her to the great hall. He stopped inside the archway to the room holding her arm as if she were a hostage. The talking began to cease as each person turned to see the bedraggled woman in their midst. At this point, she was beyond humiliation. She was livid!

One by one, all heads swiveled to their laird to see his reaction to the intruder.

"Brigette? What are ye doin'?"

At the mention of her name, she turned fiery eyes upon the guard and jerked her arm free as his grip loosened. She stomped her way through the people until she stood in front of her husband. "As I tried to explain to *your* guard, two men attacked me in the passageway. He could have apprehended them if he hadn't insisted that I was an intruder whom you needed to handle!"

She glared as her husband's face grew red. No doubt her words angered him, but at this point, she didn't care.

"Come with me, wife. We will straighten out this misunderstanding in private."

"Misunderstanding? Two wicked men got away because your

guard didn't believe me."

"Silence!" he bellowed.

He turned and walked toward the door at the back of the room. The same door they used as their escape from the wedding celebrations the night before. Her eyes narrowed as she drilled her gaze into his back. Without glancing right or left, she stalked behind him even though it chaffed to do so.

On the other side of the doorway, Daniel waited by the stairway. After she cleared the threshold, he slammed the door leading from the great hall. "What is the meaning of this scene?"

"How dare you take that tone with me? I am your wife and should be treated with respect which your guards and your servants don't seem to understand."

His frown grew deeper by the second. "We will discuss this in the privacy of our room." He spun around and jumped the steps two at a time leaving her to find her own way.

"Arrogant man," she murmured. She raised her dress and clomped up the stairs. Her face burned hotter than a lighted torch. How dare he act like she was somehow to blame for this debacle? What infuriated her more was how the wicked men had escaped.

The two walked in tense silence until they reached their room. At that point, Daniel stopped and swept his arm for her to proceed him through the doorway. He followed by banging the security bar in place. She came to the middle of the room and whipped around to face her husband.

With arms folded across his chest and feet spread apart, he repeated his question through tight lips. "What is the meaning of this?"

Ignoring his irritating manner, she launched into her tale. "I started on a stroll to familiarize myself with my new home when two brawny men confronted me. Thinking I was a maid, one grabbed my braid while another ran his hands over my face and body. After I escaped, I ran to get help. And you know the rest. The guard didn't believe who I claimed to be and allowed those men to flee in another direction! What are you going to do about this?"

After her ultimatum his face became a thundercloud. He threw his hands down in disgust. "No wonder the men thought you were a maid. This dress belongs on one of lesser status than the lady of the house. You should have stayed in our room like I instructed you to do for the day, and this wouldn't have happened."

Furious did not begin to define her temperament. She seethed. "You will not lay the blame at my door." Walking to within inches of his face, she said, "You mean to tell me that it's acceptable for a servant to be molested in *your* castle as long as the culprit leaves me alone?"

"That's not what I said, and well you know it."

Brigette failed to comprehend the tic in his cheek as a warning. She kept on with her argument. "Even if a woman wore naught but a smile, she should know that she is protected from nasty men with evil on their minds. Did you not tell me to trust you? That all would be well?"

The veins in his neck bulged.

After a deep breath he said, "Tell me what these men look like."

Without breaking eye contact, she delivered a physical description which included that one man owned a bruised throat, and the other man exhibited a distinct limp after her well-placed fist and foot.

"Wait here. I will return. Bolt the door once I am clear."

She watched him leave. After she thumped the bar secure, she tramped around the room, fuming with every breath. If this was what she could expect, the vision of Fairwick Castle's dungeon appealed to her. The longer Daniel delayed, she wondered if he went to finish his meal, or, if perchance, he was trying to find her assailants.

In one half of a day as the lady of the McKinnon Castle, her reason for not wanting to marry multiplied. Not only did she fear getting with child, the trauma of living with an arrogant man distressed her. Those troubling reflections whirled around like a windstorm as she continued to pace. All the while she pondered how Isabelle accepted her lot in life and flourished in the midst of it.

Following what she deemed hours of waiting, Daniel tapped on the door and identified himself. With reluctance, she permitted his entrance before securing the bar. The time alone had calmed her jangled nerves, but his presence caused some to resurface.

"Well? What did you learn?"

"No one saw either of the men you described—not in the castle or outside on the grounds." He paused for a moment with his glare pinning her to the spot. "Did you make this whole incident up to get attention or to punish me in some way? Nicolas repeated childhood tales about you, but I hoped you had outgrown your theatrics."

She couldn't believe what he spoke! How was she to respond to those accusations? Could she ever become the woman she desired to be with her past haunting her every move?

"If you believe I invented this whole story ... you truly don't know me at all." She turned away from his judgmental stare. Reaching up, she yanked her torn sleeve until it came off in her hand. She walked over to the low burning flame in the hearth and threw the shredded sleeve into the fire.

"What are you doing?"

She stripped off her outer clothing and pitched the whole dress into the blaze. Standing in her undergarments, she turned to her stunned husband and asked without emotion, "Since your mind is already made up about me, to defend myself is pointless. What would you have me wear?"

Her actions must have shocked him. He stood unmoving with his lips parted.

"The draft is cool. I need an answer." She allowed her irritation to flow through her words.

He shook his head before approaching her with slow steps. When she was within his reach, he stopped. He rubbed his forehead and wiped his face as if to erase the debacle. "Brigette, I fear we have gotten off to a poor beginning. Why don't you get dressed, and we will stroll the castle together? I will introduce you to my people while making it clear you belong to me. Then we can circumvent future misunderstandings."

Her mouth twisted while trying to make sense of her husband's statement. Unbelievable! She blinked several times. Her uncaring husband would not cause her to cry today.

Chapter Thirteen

When Daniel failed to give an answer about her dress, Brigette paraded across the room to her clothing trunk. He watched as she threw one dress after another over her shoulder to the floor. Each one suitable in his estimation. Was she trying to further provoke his anger?

"Wife, anyone of those dresses is suitable for you to wear. What are you about?"

While still on her knees, she turned her head. "Since I am the interloper here and not familiar with your customs, you should choose." After her blunt statement, she resumed her task.

Refusing to be drawn back into the fray, Daniel stooped and picked a simple, yet beautiful forest green dress. It had a modest neckline decorated with ribbon and lace. The color would showcase his wife's golden hair and snowy complexion.

"This dress is appropriate for our outing today." He stood close by her side and offered his hand to help her rise.

He watched as emotions played across her face while she contemplated whether to accept his hand or not. Common sense won out as she grasped his hand and stood. He pulled her close and wrapped his arms around her waist. At first, she stiffened and remained aloof. His thumb moved back and forth on her back.

"Let us put this disagreement behind us and enjoy our day together. My men will continue to search for your attackers, but we

93

mustn't allow them to steal the joy of our day. What say you, wife?" He noticed the longer she stood in his embrace, the more yielding her body became.

"Even though you never acknowledged my story as truth, I am encouraged your men are hunting for my assailants. For this, I thank you."

Again, he held back his aggravation with her need to stab him for his lack of believing her. He made a great effort to relax his clinched jaw. "In our future, there will be many things we disagree about, but we will muddle through them to form a closer bond." He placed a light kiss on her parted lips. "Do you require my assistance with your dress?"

"I think not."

When she looked down at naught but undergarments, her face heated. With his arms still holding her, he whispered next to her ear. "I will return for you in a moment." He gave her hips a light squeeze before leaving her to prepare.

After meeting with two guards and allowing ample time to pass, he entered the room and caught his wife twirling around in circles while her dress danced in the air.

"There's the amusing young woman who captured my attention many months ago."

She gasped at his sudden arrival as she wobbled to a stop. Wearing the dress he chose, she had added a green ribbon through her hair. Her blue eyes shone bright against her pale complexion which also enhanced her pink lips.

A small grin graced her lips. "I used to challenge Thomas to a spinning contest. It was one competition I won every time."

He smiled. "Now that is something I would relish watching, except I wish to see Nicolas spin. Did you ever challenge him?"

"Yes, but only once. He fell in the dirt after staggering about which made him appear foolish but provided me great satisfaction knowing I bested him at something."

"Mayhap you will dare me to this game of rotation. One I will gladly accept," He tapped her up-turned nose. "But for now, let us be away. I need to properly introduce you to my people." She slid her hand through the crook of his elbow as he led her into her new battlefield—the hearts of his people.

"Look there. He leads her around like a prize."

"A bonnie lass to be sure. Whit is to be done aboot 'er?"

"Weel now, I know not whit the master plans. 'Tis a shame we dinna recognize 'er in the passageway. For now, ye do naught. Ye watch and wait."

"Dost ye think 'e will share the bounty with us?"

"Perchance. We can hope," he laughed and punched his cohort in the arm.

The two men had changed their disguises after their encounter with Brigette before resurfacing among the peasants. The one with the limp dragged his leg as if lame, and the other hid his bruises with a dirty scarf. The horse dung smeared on their cloaks created such a foul smell, no one came nearby.

It was not uncommon for Daniel to allow poor vagrants to work in the stables. To protect the castle, they remained under the watchful eye of a guard while working. Of course, too much ale had reduced their guard to a more amiable nature allowing the abductors to escape without notice.

All beggars worked during the daylight hours but were required to leave the castle grounds before nightfall.

"Tonight, we 'ide in the 'ay until all are abed. We can assess the best way to do what the master demanded."

"The handsome reward is all that motivates me to agree to such a dangerous scheme."

While Daniel introduced his wife to the blacksmith, Hamish, William ran into the shed. "There ye be," William exclaimed. "I've been looking for me mither." He ran and hugged Brigette's leg.

95

She stooped to cuddle his precious son. "I'm so happy you came to join us. What have you been about this fine morn?'

Daniel watched as they carried on a sweet conversation. While he observed their exchange, he grew more confident that he made a wise choice in a new mother for his young son. She was attentive to William's every word as if he were a king. Their eyes locked together, and all others vanished from their view.

The scene before him caused his focus to shift to memories of his first wife. Young and in love, they never dreamt of not growing old together. Now, he was twenty-six years old with a sixteen-year-old bride. Love was not the reason for his second marriage, but one of convenience—to provide a mother for his son and to get a wife in the process.

She looked at him while still kneeling before William. "Is that acceptable to you?"

Caught unaware, he said, "I'm sairy, what did ye say?"

"For us ta show mither our secret place and mayhap eat there."

Daniel beheld two expectant faces and couldn't refuse them. Somehow his son had accomplished more with Brigette in a few minutes than he achieved in the last twenty-four hours. As the scripture says, *let the little children lead them.* He could learn much from his son's innocence.

"William, ye go ahead and tell the cook what ye need. We will be along. Make sure to ask for sweet cakes."

"Yea, papa." He gave his mother a quick peck and ran from the shed to do his father's bidding.

Still on her knees, she said, "He's such a precious boy."

He watched his son half run and half jump his way to the castle steps. "Aye." While his eyes centered on William, she grabbed his arm. "Here, allow me." With a firm grip, he helped her stand.

She dusted dirt from her dress. Upon completion of her task, she turned questioning eyes upon him. "Why do you talk like an Englishman and switch to a Scottish brogue? It can be a bit confusing as to what you are saying."

"Remember, before you came, I spoke what my people understand. I will switch back and forth as I deem necessary. Don't worry. Ye will git the hing of it."

She pursed her lips in a pout. "I hope you will speak where I can understand you while I learn this new accent."

Her pronouncement angered him. It seemed selfish of her to expect him to bow to her wishes. Then remembering the treatment she had received from her brothers, softened his attitude. She suffered much growing up at Fairwick castle. He desired her to find peace and happiness at her new home. "I will do my best. Know at times, I will offer a hurried response and can't guarantee how my speech might come out."

Her pout turned into a smile. "It is enough that you will try."

It pleased him that she didn't stay angered for long. Arm in arm, the two strolled to the center of the courtyard to wait.

"Should I go see about William? He might need some help."

"He is fine. Fiona will pack all we need for our outing and provide a servant to help him carry out our repast."

Daniel's feet shuffled while they both stood in silence. Neither produced the right words to say to the other. He was as awkward as a young man with his first desire for a woman. It aggravated him that he was not more in command of the situation with his young bride. He felt like an old man in her presence.

Disengaging her arm, he said, "I'll go check. Wait here." With those curt words, he strode off at a fast clip up the steps.

He disappeared inside the keep leaving her with mouth open and eyes wide.

"Daniel McKinnon, you are quite rude at times," she said to no one.

She glanced up to see worker men and guards watching their new lady with curiosity. Left alone in the middle of the courtyard, it didn't take long before she started for the keep steps. An exuberant little boy burst from within followed by his father.

"Mither, I git ta ride me pony!"

"That's nice. Are we going far?"

"Och, yea."

She backed up. "I'm not accomplished at riding a horse."

"No worries," Daniel said. "You will ride with me. You two wait here with the basket of food, and I'll retrieve our horses." Off he strode without a backward glance.

She wrung her hands until a small, warm hand caught hold of her finger. "Dinna be a feared. Papa will see ta yer care."

She sat on the step and wrapped her arm around his tiny waist. "You are such a charming boy. I'm most delighted to be your mother. We will get along magnificently."

He smiled bright.

The laird exited the barn with William's pony and a huge, black stallion. A stableman held them while he walked over to gather his family.

"Oh, dear," she moaned. "Your horse is quite large."

"Of course, he is my war horse. We travel everywhere together. I ride no other if he is available." He hoisted William into his saddle. "Be sure you don't make sudden moves near his head. He's known to bite strangers." He secured the food basket to his saddle not recognizing the fear in his wife.

When he turned to help her onto the horse, she stepped back several paces. Sighing, he realized his mistake. He had added to her fright, and now she seemed panicked. With the guard holding fast to his horse, Daniel took hold of her hand. "Come, wife. I will give you a boost up, and then mount behind you."

When he gave a slight tug on her hand, she remained rooted. "Perhaps we might take a wagon?"

"Nay, mither. Then ye wouldn't be able ta see me secret place. Ye must coom."

William's words were effective. Brigette ambled a little closer at his persistent pull. "I'll keep you safe today, my dove."

She stopped. The appearance of wonder bathed her face. "What did you call me?" she whispered.

He surmised his words of endearment sounded foreign to her. It delighted him that the expression pleased her. However, his irritation with Nicolas surfaced. In his opinion, it exposed the lack of approval or praise from her brother.

Daniel's protectiveness reared like a stallion with his mare— ready to wrap her in his arms and expound on her value. At this point, after their morning disagreement, 'twas doubtful she'd believe him. For now, he just repeated his words.

"Ye are my sweet dove." Her whole demeanor relaxed.

"Thank you," she said with awe. He placed her in the saddle and joined her atop his great horse. A multitude of guards surrounded them as they trotted across the drawbridge and into the open field. She relaxed against his chest and gripped his forearm.

He peeked to see a contented face. How long would the serenity last?

Chapter Fourteen

Safe in her husband's arms, Brigette enjoyed the ride on his war horse. She never imagined it could be so exhilarating. The gentle rolling hills dotted with sheep were breathtaking. When she turned to observe the scenery, the wind grabbed her braid. At one point it smacked her husband in the face. The wind snatched away her carefree laughter as Daniel sputtered to remove her hair from his mouth.

Nicolas never allowed her horseback riding lessons. He preferred her to learn more womanly tasks. In her estimation, it meant he didn't want the blame on his head if she got hurt. Thinking on her brother riled her. Therefore, she pushed his memory away for today … perhaps forever.

"Might I learn to ride a horse by myself?"

"Your brothers never taught such an essential task?"

She huffed. "No, I'm afraid not."

"Of course. I will teach you myself, but first, I must find you the perfect horse to serve you."

She twisted around to face him. "You mean I'll have a horse to call my own?"

"Naturally. We will search together to find one that suits you and that I find serviceable."

"Oh, how wonderful!" She planted a quick kiss on his cheek before turning forward. Unbelievable! Her own horse! Even though her morning had a dreadful beginning, it was getting better by the minute.

"I enjoyed that reward." He nuzzled her ear. "Tonight, I welcome more than a kiss."

Chills raced down her neck. To be desired by him thrilled her. She appreciated a few benefits to marriage but thinking of the night's activity dug up her fears like digging for turnips. Fears she pushed aside. Not wanting to dampen her fun outing, she buried those thoughts under her forget-about-it rock.

"Hurry, Papa." William trotted ahead of his parents when they slowed to talk. When he stopped near a group of trees, he announced, "I'm hungry."

"According to William, he is always hungry," Niall said with a grin. Niall, Lord McKinnon's first in command, assigned orders to the group of protectors. Laughter rang out as the guards dispersed into the forest to allow the three privacy. The men remained ever watchful of the noble family—close yet unseen.

Iain grabbed William's pony when he jumped off. Each man loved the young boy and would sacrifice their life for his if called upon. Because of the great attention given him by his protectors, he played oblivious of any danger.

"William, have a care," Brigette called out. She pushed against Daniel's hold. "Let me down. I need to corral him before he is hurt."

"Ah, sweet wife. He is safe enough. My men always keep a close watch on him. Even though my adventurous son might appear at risk, I assure you, he is not."

Once again, his small compliment made her feel treasured. Sweet wife indeed. Living under her brothers' restrictions and without a mother to guide her had stunted her progress as a woman. Not to mention how being nurtured by vindictive and jealous servants had stunted her emotional development. She soaked in those words that refreshed as rain to a parched land.

Iain held the stallion while Daniel slid off and reached for his wife. With her chin tucked and her eyes averted, she said, "Thank you for those kind words."

102

His hands stilled. Not understanding why he delayed, she glanced to see him staring at her. "Is something amiss?" she asked.

"There are many reasons to compliment you, but sometimes I might fail in that husbandly duty. But know this, Brigette McKinnon, you are a beautiful woman with a kind heart who is already showing signs of a devoted and caring mother. Whether I say the words or not, you are worthy of them. I hold onto hope, in our near future, you will grow to love and care for William's father." Wearing a crooked grin, he pulled her from the horse to stand in front of him.

Unsure of what to do, she grabbed his shoulders to steady herself. Her face almost touched his chest. His finger stroked her cheek bringing her eyes to meet his. "I have confidence that our future together will be verra guid." He slid his hand down her arm and secured her hand in his own. "Come, before that rascal eats all of our food."

Brigette traipsed behind her hungry husband while warm sensations swirled in her stomach. Starved for praise, she savored each affectionate word. Is this the type of bond Isabelle spoke of so often? Could she grow to love her husband, content with her portion in life? Oh dear, if only their union wouldn't produce a child. She decided she must resist his charm for her own wellbeing.

The wee McKinnon selected a sunny spot in the middle of a group of trees. The low limbs and bushes concealed them from the guards. Hidden from sight, it was as if they were the sole people for miles around. To add to the atmosphere of secrecy, he told them to whisper.

Daniel stretched out on their blanket and leaned on his elbow awaiting the meal. She tucked her dress around her outstretched legs and leaned back on her hands as William handed out the food. She smiled at his childish ways all the while listening to the calming sounds from the breeze. Leaves rustled and birds sang a lilting tune.

The time spent in their secret spot proved peaceful and relaxing for Brigette. She enjoyed watching the interplay between father and son. The strong laird showed genuine love for his young son. He answered every question as if it were the most important thing of his day even when William shot them in rapid succession. Daniel scarcely had time to eat his repast, but he didn't seem concerned.

"Fither, can I show mither me secret crossing?"

"Oh, there's another secret I get to share?"

Daniel rubbed his whiskered face as he considered the request. "Weel, she'll have to be sworn to secrecy first. Do ye think she can keep our secret?"

William's eyes grew wide. "Can ye?"

She looked from father to son. "Wel-l, I suppose I can honor your wishes on the subject."

He looked at his father. "Is that an aye?"

Daniel sat up. "Aye."

He hopped on his father with excitement and tussled a moment before rolling on the blanket to his mother. Crawling into her open lap, he trapped her face with his pudgy little hands. "Ye are the best of mithers." After placing a moist kiss on her cheek, he threw items into the basket.

"Here, sweet boy. Since you were so gallant to serve our meal, I'll pack it away." No sooner had she voiced her words, he jumped up and ran off.

"William?" she hollered. She glanced at Daniel. "Do you need to go after him?"

He brushed off his hands. "No. My men are there to keep in step with my son. They are used to his swift movements." He chuckled. "He takes them on a merry chase most days."

Brigette had to trust that her husband spoke truth. She didn't dare go after the boy since he said no, and she was unsure of which direction he ran. Even with her limited knowledge, she understood to become a good mother, she needed to anticipate the child's actions. After placing the last item inside the basket, she stood. Daniel folded the blanket, grabbed the basket, and offered her his arm.

The couple walked into the clearing to find William on his pony surrounded by the mounted guards. Off to the side, Niall held Daniel's horse. She tried to act unafraid as he placed her in the saddle even though her heart performed a pirouette inside her chest.

"Is this surprise far from here?"

"Nay, follow me," William said.

Several men encircled him as he kicked his pony into a trot followed by the couple. The rest of the guard fanned out around the couple.

"The countryside is quite beautiful in Scotland," she said.

"I have to agree with your opinion. The lush rolling hills and expansive grasslands are spectacular. Even though I spent much time in England with my mother's family, Scotland is my home."

"What is that pretty purple flower I see?"

"That is thistle. 'Tis our national flower."

"Breathtaking. Its splendor is showcased by the green grasslands."

"There are many scenic places bordering our home that are pleasing on the eye. One day we will go exploring." He spoke near her ear. "Alone."

Her body quivered as his breath tickled her neck. There were moments like this when she anticipated her future with enthusiasm. The thrill of having a handsome laird as her husband excited her until she remembered their morning quarrel. Mayhap it was normal for them to squabble and then reconcile. Many unanswered questions plagued her that only Isabelle might answer, but would she be allowed to speak with her again? Not if Nicolas stepped in. *Sigh.*

"I hope that sigh expressed contentment." Daniel murmured in her hair.

Unsure of how he might respond, she dared not expose her thoughts. Best to keep some things to herself.

"Yes."

It wasn't long before the tiny laird in training brought them to a halt. Several men dispersed into their surroundings while the remainder of the guards stood close at hand. "Are we still on your land?"

"Aye. My holdings are quite expansive." With no further comment, he lifted her to the grassland and ensnared her hand as he led her to where his impatient son waited.

"Son, one thing a man must do when a lady is present is to check the area for unsavory creatures."

"Och, aye, papa." William and his guards scurried about the area hunting for any animals that presented a threat to his new mother.

She did her own surveillance of their location. "Is this a dangerous place?" she asked in a hushed tone.

"Nay. I'm training him in the art of safeguarding his lady. It's never too soon to begin this type of education."

"Oh. That eases my mind."

William returned with a big smile. "All is safe, papa."

"Well done, my son." He picked William up. "Let's show your mother our secret crossing. Shall we?"

"Aye." He squirmed with eagerness. His bright eyes focused on Brigette.

Daniel warned his son. "Now remember, ye must proceed with caution. When I place ye on the ground, stay with us and don't run ahead."

"Aye, papa."

He gripped his mother's right hand and his father's left hand. After his father gave a nod of approval, he pulled them through a group of trees until he came into a small clearing near a cliff.

"Oh, dear! Stay back from the rocky ledge. You might fall." Her breaths came quick.

Laughing, William edged closer to the edge. "Not too close, son," Daniel warned. "You don't wish to send your mother into a swoon."

"What is the meaning of this?" Brigette asked a bit agitated.

"Papa is making a rope bridge! We will be able ta cross ta the other side soon."

Her brow creased as she squinted at Daniel. The memory of a servant's young child falling to his death off a cliff flashed vivid in her mind.

"Surely, you jest?"

"Now, wife. This is a grand idea. There is not a bridge within many miles. The other side is still our land, and we wish to reach it from here."

William bobbed his approval.

She held Daniel's gaze as he spouted off his nonsense about why they needed to build a suspended bridge. Of course, he knew she wouldn't criticize the idea if it came from her new son, but he would get an earful on their ride back to the castle. What a preposterous idea with which to include such a small boy.

"Let me shew ye what we built so far," William said.

She ooed and ahhed over the part of the bridge he had constructed not wishing to hurt his feelings. On the other hand, his father was about to find out what it meant when she made her wishes known.

William tugged on her hand. "Come take a luek over the edge. I'll show ye whit ta do."

Imitating her new son, she got on her hands and knees to crawl the last few feet to the ridge, but dizziness claimed her when she peeped over. The sides of the canyon rose three times as high as the castle walls back home with a meandering river at the bottom.

She watched as he pushed a rock over, but from their great distance, she never heard it splash. When he started to throw another rock, she grabbed his hand. "I've seen enough. Let's move away from the ledge."

A loud gasp escaped her when he hopped up and ran to his father a few feet behind them. She scooted backwards until she deemed it safe enough to stand.

"William, ye must have a care. This is a perilous place. One wrong move and ye could fall to your death."

"Now, Brigette, let's not scare him. He knows to proceed with caution." Daniel eased closer to her and held her shaky hand.

107

"Come sit over here while you catch your breath."

William hopped from foot to foot with excitement. He even talked his father into taking a few minutes to work on the bridge. Daniel tied tight knots through the pre-cut wood planks made just for their secret venture.

"Luek, mither. When the bridge is done, I will walk ta the other side over the deep canyon. Did ye see the river far below?" He crept closer to the overhang.

"Yes, I did see it." Perched on a tree stump far from the edge of the bluff, she chewed on a fingernail. Concealed under the hem of her dress, a foot tapped a fast staccato. "Come. Stand by me."

"I canna. I'm working with me fither."

Hair tendrils danced as she released a puff of air. There was no help for it. Called to watch this preposterous undertaking caused her stomach to toss. She was thankful the bridge seemed far from completion. Mayhap time remained to destroy their outrageous plan and save William from certain death.

Chapter Fifteen

Daniel had no idea one small woman could raise such a ruckus. In the beginning, she encouraged William in his rope-bridge project. But when his son coaxed her to peer over the cliff while lying on her stomach, her horrified face was enough to quell most men. The words she reserved for Daniel, however, cut deeper. If her tongue were a sword, he would have drowned in his own blood before reaching his horse.

He was relieved William remained unscathed by the remarks she directed at him alone. Once the two mounted, she persisted with her scorching comments. She fell short of calling him a blithering idiot. His forceful, commanding voice terminated her tirade. Now they rode with blessed quiet, yet her rigid body spoke volumes. He expected further heated exchange once they reached the castle; of this, he was sure.

With nothing but the sound of hooves beating the earth, Daniel reflected on recent events. Had he been too quick to wed Lady Fairwick? At present, she acted more childish than his first opinion. Had Nicolas somehow tricked him into this marriage contract expecting his sister to bring the mighty Lord McKinnon to his knees? No doubt, her ornery brother broke into hysterical laughter when the vows were exchanged knowing he had bested Daniel leaving him no recourse.

As his mind drifted from one question to the next, he

remembered his first wife, Anna. Young and in love, the impending birth of their second child brought them blissful joy. Not long afterwards events took a horrible turn. He blamed himself. Desiring not to revisit the dreadful night of her death, he changed course.

"You may speak." His voice sounded gruff to his ears.

"Humph."

The response irritated him. With her, he endured as a rolling cloud on a stormy day. Submissive and agreeable described his Anna. One who never questioned or denied him. Yet his new wife accomplished both with ease.

"I might have been a bit brusque earlier."

No answer.

Perhaps groveling was required if he wanted a compliant wife for the rest of the day. "I'm sorry if I offended you." There, that should suffice.

She twisted her upper body to face him. Her eyes, mere slits. "Offended? Brusque? I say a mean-spirited ogre who holds no idea how to speak to a lady when she disagrees with you is more accurate."

Daniel bit the side of his jaw. Heaven preserve him, she could kill with one swipe of her razor-sharp tongue. "I apologized for my earlier comments. What say you?"

She turned back to face the road. "I beg your pardon. I didn't recognize your apology. If that's what you did, I suppose I'm obligated to accept it. But," she said as she whipped her head around, "I do so under protest." Her hair smacked his face with each twist of her head.

He swallowed his chuckle. "I accept your surrender even though offered under protest."

When she gave him a withering scowl, he grinned. Her eyes moved to his mouth when he saw a slight facial twitch as she suppressed a smile.

"Come now, my bride. Let us talk this over at another time. I understand much was thrust upon you, and William's bridge might have been too much. It's just …" He glanced away. "It's just that he wants to earn your love by impressing you."

She gasped. With her legs astride, to turn her whole body about in the saddle involved much twisting, pulling, and grimacing. There was a bit of elbow throwing before she straddled the horse backwards. She didn't seem troubled that her dress hiked above her boot. He did his best to yank her clothing to cover her limb not wishing his men to gaze upon her attractive leg. That was reserved for him alone.

"Woman, what are ye about? This way of riding just isn't done."

"Don't concern yourself with my position. I'm safe enough. I tussled with three rough brothers who taught me a thing or two. This arrangement suits me. Now what was I about to tell you? Oh, yes—William." When she placed her hands on his chest, she wore a sympathetic expression.

"Bless that precious boy. He doesn't need to earn my love by showing me what he can do. I fell in love with him the moment he spoke to me at that ill-fated banquet. He can do nothing to change my love for him." She tapped her chin, lashes all aflutter. "You, on the other hand, have much to do to win my affection." Her brow raised.

He roared with laughter. "Oh, wife. I predict a merry chase during our lives together which I intend to enjoy as long as you are the prize." Her impish face flushed at his words.

"You have no idea what I'm capable of doing," she said in jest.

He couldn't resist her inviting lips. With his arm already holding her in the saddle, he drew her flush against his chest. "Ye are most appealing when ye are playful." Surprised at his maneuver, her lips parted, but he captured them before she uttered a response.

When he released her, she flushed. Open affection appeared unfamiliar to her. From all indications, the Fairwick brothers offered rare physical touch to their sister. He planned caresses as a daily ritual with his little wife hoping she grew to enjoy and anticipate these moments of tenderness.

111

William rode close to his father's horse. "Papa, whit ar' ye aboot?"

The magical moment evaporated. He eased his tight hold around her waist. "We were discussing issues." Daniel winked at Brigette.

"Whit ar' issues?"

"'Tis nothing of import. Care to join us?" she asked.

"Nay. Thar is no room, and I have me own pony ta ride." He trotted away shaking his head at her query.

She leaned her head against Daniel's chest. "Oh, me."

With a deep chuckle, he put his chin atop her head. "There will be many a time when we are caught in a tender embrace. Dinna be troubled. 'Tis a normal happening between a man and his wife." Her muffled moan caused a smile to split his lips.

The remainder of the ride home proved pleasurable. Brigette managed to turn herself back around without smacking his already black eye. She viewed the countryside as he described it. Asking her enthusiastic questions, he viewed his homeland with renewed wonder. It didn't take long for her harrowing morning and disturbing afternoon to take a toll on her endurance. He recognized the moment she dozed off. The warmth of his hold and the rocking from the ride must have lulled her to sleep.

"Ah, Brigette. We have much to learn about one another," he whispered. "One day ye will look at me with affectionate eyes and hunger for my touch. Until then, I am satisfied with what ye offer."

The castle came into view as dusk enveloped them. His sleeping wife awoke with a jolt as the horses clomped on the wooden bridge. "Oh, dear. I fell asleep." She rubbed her eyes.

"Ye've had an eventful day. I do hope 'twas a soothing respite. Perhaps it affords ye stamina for our night together." Did she stiffen when he cuddled her close?

"Did ye see her?"

"Aye. He's keepin' her close.

"How will we git near enough to nab her?"

"We're not to nab her, ye dolt. We're to watch her ever'day habits and report back."

"I dinna know how much more I can take muckin' horse dung." He rubbed his knee. "Hey, whatcha hit me far?"

"Cease talkin' so loud. Ye might be heard. We need to stay in service at the McKinnon castle so we can be close at hand. Now quit complainin' and git to work."

Mumbling to himself, he went back to his duty. It wasn't long before horse manure tore through the air and smacked his friend in the back.

"Ye idiot." He charged his partner and threw him on the ground. The men tussled about in the hay with fists swinging. Grunts and vulgar words drifted out the door and straight to the blacksmith's ears.

Hamish marched into the barn. "What are ye aboot? Cease this at once." He grabbed the big man's arm and dragged him off the little one underneath. "Stop this I say."

The two stopped scrapping about and scrambled apart. "We were juist having a bit o' fun," the big one said.

"Not from where I'm standing. Ye were in a heated brawl. What say ye?"

Both men stayed silent and hung their heads.

"I say again, what say ye?" Silence. Not many wanted to muck out stalls each day, so instead of tossing them out on their ear, Hamish gave a warning. "Dinna let me hear o' ye fighting again. If I do, ye git the boot. Understand?"

"Aye," they replied in unison.

Hamish's eyes narrowed. "What be yer names?"

They looked wide-eyed at each other. The big one spoke up, "Me name is Scott and this 'ere is Donald."

"Weel, Scott and Donald, git back to work. Ye have much to do before ye're allowed yer dinner."

Hamish stomped from the barn.

"If we want to keep working for the laird, we moost stay

cautious. We face harsh punishment or mayhap death if we git thrown out."

"Aye," the little one muttered. He frowned. "I dinna like the name Donald."

"Weel, ye fool, I had to think quick like. We can't give our proper names." He hissed and popped his companion in the head. "Ye are daft."

As Donald pulled his fist back to punch Scott, Hamish yelled, "Back to work!"

Both men scurried to their stalls.

Chapter Sixteen

After a week of sharing the bed with her husband, Brigette decided it best to ask for her own room. One way to ensure not growing with child was to stay away from her husband since he delighted in bed sport each night. So terrified of enduring the pain or possible death from childbirth, her self-protection won out over her fear of stirring Daniel's anger.

Her husband rose before dawn to go about his duties. As he shaved, she launched into her idea.

"I think it's time for me to move to my own room."

His hand stopped in midair before he pivoted to face her.

"What did you say?"

Taking a fortifying breath, she repeated it. "It's time for me to move to my own room." When his brows came to a point between his eyes, she failed to recognize the danger and continued. "From what I hear, most women of position reside in a separate bedchamber from their husbands."

With blade still in hand, he stalked over to the bed where she lounged. "Do you know the reason most women of high position dwell in a separate room?"

"'Tis the way of the elite," she answered matter-of-factly while twirling a lock of hair.

"Nay. It's because those husbands invite other women, not their wives, to share their bed." He paused. "Is that what you wish? For other women to share my bed, as well as you?"

Brigette straightened up in the bed pulling the blanket with her. "Of course not! You said that to upset me, didn't you? That's not true."

"I speak truth." He glared for a moment before returning to his mirror propped in the windowsill. "If that is the type of life you wish to lead, it can be arranged." After another swipe of the blade, he said, "Who knows, I might enjoy having multiple women share my bed."

Gasp! "You wouldn't dare. That is disgraceful."

"Remember wife, you are the one who suggested it."

"I did no such a thing. I merely requested my own room." She whipped back the blanket and slid out of the bed. After securing her robe, she marched over to where he stood at the window. "Why are you acting in this manner?"

Daniel wiped his face with a towel and slid his knife into the sheath in his boot. His nonchalant turn put him toe to toe with her. "I'm answering your question." He strode to the door where he buckled his scabbard to his waist.

"Are you leaving? We are having a discussion," she said in a high-pitched voice.

"Yes, wife." His hand sliced the air. "Our *discussion* is concluded."

"You misunderstood my request. You can't leave without resolving our disagreement."

"Brigette, you need to decide if you want to remain a childish lass or be a wife. Most women your age have two babes suckling at their breast. Yet here you are … a … a foolish child."

With the stamp of her foot, her hands knotted into fists at her side. "I don't want to birth babies!"

Daniel stilled. Nothing but their heavy breathing broke the quiet. Her chest rose and fell in quick succession. His gaze lingered on the movement but for a moment.

"That is preposterous. It is a woman's lot in life. Why do you think I married you?"

Her eyes grew round with surprise as pain knifed through her heart. With a rigid back, she replied through a shaky voice. "Well, you should have consulted me before signing the marriage contract with my brother. I refuse to produce children from you or anyone."

His face blazed red. He opened the door and then turned back to her. "Choose any room that is vacant. I care not." Without waiting for an answer, he walked out closing the door with a crash.

Brigette stared at the portal her husband vacated as her eyes filled. "You're a horrid man, Daniel McKinnon." When she blinked, tears slipped down her cheeks. Not sure what to do, she glared at the portrait hanging over the fireplace. "It's all your fault, Anna McKinnon. He still wants you for his wife, not me. I'm just here to warm his bed and produce babes while he dreams about you. That's why you remain in this room even though he's married to me."

After those words escaped into the room, she fell into a heap on the floor. She covered her face with her hands and cried in earnest. "No one wants me for me! I'm required to perform or be cast aside." *My brothers don't want me, and now my own husband has discarded me like rotted food.*

Rocking back and forth while crying didn't bring her the comfort she sought. The weight of her unhappiness held her pinned to the floor. How was she to survive this latest battle with nowhere to go for refuge?

Trying to stifle the sniffles, she wiped her nose on her robe sleeve, and scrubbed her tear-stained face with trembling hands. Sitting silent, Isabelle's words kept pricking her mind. *Pray about everything.* After a sobbing hiccup, she looked heavenward and whispered, "Can you help me, God? What should I do?"

She waited several minutes as her eyes roamed the chamber but received no relief. Certain that praying was a waste of time, her gaze drifted back to the McKinnon family portrait. Anna, with her coal black hair, sat straight and regal while her loving eyes focused on William. Daniel's regard seemed one of adoration with his eyes fastened on Anna's profile. Would he ever look at her in that manner? Doubtful.

With a deep breath, she pushed to her feet. No need sitting on the cold stone floor weeping over a difficult husband. She undressed as she walked to her wardrobe for a day dress leaving her clothing where it fell. Tempted to kick them into the fireplace, she feared Daniel might not provide her a replacement. In her opinion, men were too unpredictable.

Satisfied with her dress, she put her hair in a single braid. Daniel had expressed his desire to see her hair unbound with a circlet around her forehead. His obstinate attitude left her feeling a bit spiteful. She peered into the mirror and smiled at her appearance.

Not wishing to appear foolish to peasants whom she found difficult to understand, she determined some time spent with William would lift her spirits. Such a delightful little boy who adored her and right now, she needed his affection. He was the one person who would not shun her. On her way to the door, she glanced at the looming portrait. Her husband's warm regard for his dead wife disturbed her.

Furious with his wife, Daniel bypassed the grand hall and headed straight for the lists. No morning meal for him. Fighting with his men under the guise of training was just what he needed. So driven by his rage, he marched on disregarding the stares.

"Iain, ye'll be the first to train."

"Aye, my laird."

Ignoring the apprehension on Iain's face, both men stripped bare to the waist with swords in hand. "Gather around, men. Watch and learn. Each of you need to perfect these offensive moves."

Thus, began a rigorous drill on sword methods and maneuvers. Dust swirled as they parried one another with dirt sticking to their sweaty bodies. Lord McKinnon battled each one with aggressive sword action that left the man heaving when he moved to the next. His strength and stamina, astounding.

Just when the men grew weary, Duncan hollered from the

gatehouse, "Rider approaching."

Niall threw Daniel a towel to dry the sweat and mud, followed by his shirt. Not happy with the interruption, he pulled his shirt over his dirty body. Being presentable was not a priority. He sheathed his sword and stalked to the keep steps to wait. When the messenger entered, he found the laird on the top steps with arms crossed and feet apart.

"Are ye Laird McKinnon?"

"Aye."

"I'm Allister, a messenger of the king."

Inwardly, Daniel groaned. It was never good when the king sent his messenger. "Come inside, mon and receive some refreshment. Kenneth. Take the mon's horse."

"Thank you, sir." The messenger followed him inside the castle doors and into the great hall where a tankard of ale was set before him.

"Drink yer fill, and then we'll talk business." Daniel downed his own tankard without stopping. He plopped his mug on the table and wiped his mouth with the back of his hand. "Are ye hungry, lad?"

Allister smiled. "A meal is always welcomed."

"Clara, bring the mon some food."

The young maid ran to do her laird's bidding. Daniel watched her go wishing he could run from the room, as well. Based on previous missives from the king, it would either cost him vast bags of coins or time away from home neither of which he wished to relinquish. His stomach already blazed after the altercation with his wife. Delaying the inevitable could cause flames to shoot from his throat. "Weel, Allister, what is it the king wishes?"

The king's man rummaged inside his haversack and withdrew a rolled document carrying the king's seal. He handed it to Daniel as his meal arrived.

Breaking the seal, he unrolled the parchment anchoring it with his tankard and hand. After reading the first line, he sensed Allister's eyes upon him and glanced up.

"May I eat, sir?"

"Excuse my manners. Please, eat your fill. Clara will fetch more if you deem it so. She awaits your decree on the matter."

As Allister stabbed his food, Daniel returned to his reading. At first scan, the missive exasperated him. King James invited him to accompany the king to speak with the clans north of the border. He couldn't fault the king for trying to keep peace between Scotland and England, but did he honestly need Daniel's assistance? Without thought, he rubbed his stomach that rumbled from the smell of the fresh baked bread, reminding him of his missed meal.

"Do ye care for some of my meal?"

He looked up to see Allister holding out a piece of bread. "No, thank you." He raised his hand. "Clara, please bring me a platter."

"Aye, my laird."

"I missed the morning meal. Please, eat," he said as he nodded toward the food. He returned his attention to the king's missive. The more he contemplated the request, the more he warmed to the idea of traveling from home. Perhaps his absence would force his young wife to see the value of her husband and increase her desire for his presence. A smile broke his face. The idea had merit.

With the delicious aroma of roasted meat and bread set before him, his mouth watered in anticipation. "After we finish our meal, I'll write a response for you to take to King James. I believe I'll join the king's traveling party."

He cared not how Brigette might react.

Chapter Seventeen

When Brigette stepped outside her bedroom door, Mungo stood guard. Once Daniel gave credence to her attack story, he enlisted Mungo to stay at her side. She wasn't sure if her husband tried to scare her or not when he told her that Mungo's name meant *my wolf.* Either way, she was stuck with the giant. No danger of her sneaking about with him in tow.

"Good morrow, Mungo." When he didn't answer, she said, "Come along. I'm going to visit young William." She jumped back when he stepped in front of her as she turned to the right. "I suppose his room is to the left?" When no answer came forth, her shoulders rose and fell with her sigh. "Alright. Which way is correct?" He pointed down the passageway and then jerked his beefy hand to the right.

She closed her eyes and breathed deep. A tedious day loomed if her guard followed her every step. No need to fear not understanding him, he never spoke. Even though he remained silent, she heard his breathing. She suspected he hated trailing behind her as much as she disliked his presence.

As she rounded the corner, she spotted William's guard outside his door. A smile hid behind her hand thinking about the two guards staring at each other in the passageway while she played with William. What a terrible lot in life for those two brawny men.

She stopped in front of his protector. "Good morrow. My name is Lady Brigette McKinnon, what is your name?"

"I knew ye. Me name is Ross, m' lady."

Thankful that at least someone recognized her, she said, "Well, Ross, 'tis a pleasure to meet you. Is the sweet boy in his room?"

Ross cocked a brow. "Aye, m' lady."

Mungo stood guard across from the doorway while Ross remained next to the open door. Surveying the two men, she grinned. "You men enjoy a pleasant chat." With a giggle, she tapped on the door and walked into her refuge.

It took a moment for her eyes to adjust to the dim room. Without seeing him, a muffled noise arose from another open doorway inside the room. Not wanting to frighten her newly acquired son, she called out as she walked toward the sound. "William, where are you?"

A dark-haired little head popped around the door. "Mither!" He scrambled to his feet and ran to meet her. She knelt on one knee, catching him when he launched into her waiting arms. "Whit ar' ye aboot?"

She snuggled him close breathing in his innocence and the mustiness of his clothes. Plopping on her bottom, she pulled him into her lap. "Well, I came to play with my son. Is that to your liking?"

"Och, aye. Ye ar' juist in time. I need help."

Smoothing back his hair, she gazed into eyes so like his father's. A small pain pricked her heart as the memory of their argument surfaced. Determined not to allow any unhappy thoughts ruin their play time, she pushed it aside. "How can I help?"

"I can't find me soldiers ye gave me."

His pouty lips and round eyes created a flutter in her heart. Adorable, and he was hers. The unconditional love he so freely bestowed wrapped around her scarred heart like a bandage. When no one else wanted her, William did. He had no idea how his absolute trust in her began to heal her soul.

"Then let's get started." Once they both stood, he captured her hand and led her into his small wardrobe. "I dinna mean ta lose them."

"I will help you find them. Now tell me where you last played with them."

After he told of playing with them instead of sleeping, she searched his bed covers and found the prize. She lit more candles and opened his shutters wide allowing light to flood the room. They played with the toy soldiers for a while and then a hiding game. Crouched in a dark closet, her growling stomach gave away her secret place.

Standing over her, he said, "Ar' ye hungry?"

"Yes. I missed the morning meal. I'll ask one of the guards to bring us some food."

He wore a perplexed expression. "Thit's not for a mon ta do."

She grinned and shook her head at his lordly attitude. One task she planned to accomplish—teach her precious son proper English while his papa went about his duties. She prayed he wouldn't expose the lessons to Lord McKinnon. "Then I suppose you can show me to the kitchens, and I'll get my own food. How does that sound?"

"Coom. I'll shew ye the pantry."

Emerging from his room, she bumped into Ross. "Oh, dear, excuse me. I forgot you stood guard." She winked at William and grabbed his hand. "It looks like we'll have a procession to the kitchens. Is there a back stairway?"

"Aye. I'll lead the way."

He darted away, and she scampered to keep up. She didn't dare peek at Ross and Mungo afraid she might burst into laughter as they made chase. From the sound of their clanking swords, they hurried in pursuit. For the first time in over a year, she felt carefree. The burdens of her past vanished with each childish act she did with William.

Chamber maids and servant boys popped out from rooms to see what caused the commotion. If word got back to their laird, she felt certain there would be a price to pay for her unladylike behavior.

The two scavengers pretended to be soldiers scouting out their enemy. They slipped behind barrels and boxes to hide from the kitchen help. Of course, a few women cutting vegetables spotted them, smiled, and kept at their task. It was all in fun. Brigette grabbed two meat pies and a small loaf of warm baked bread before they scurried away laughing.

No enemy attacked as they made a safe return to his room. They fell on his bed and giggled into the bedcovers. She rolled to her back. He raised his head and peered at her "That was exciting."

"Yes, it was," she said as she chewed a bite of pie. "And we escaped with a treasure. Mm, this is quite tasty." She leaned back on her elbows and offered him a bite of her stash.

After sending Allister back to the king with his affirmative answer, Daniel set out to find his wife. With glee, he anticipated her reaction when she received the news. Not finding her in their room stirred his anger. Deep in his gut, he didn't want her to wander the castle and get to know his people. He wanted her to suffer a bit of hardship after her announcement this morning.

He chose not to hunt for her and went to inform his son. At times like this William clung to him, heartbroken over assignments that took him far from home. If he promised to bring back a souvenir from his travels, it satisfied and brightened the lad. As he started down the wing, he noticed Mungo and Ross. He guessed his wife hid in his son's room. Coward.

As he approached the door, laughter pushed under the threshold. He thrust open the door to see a lump on the bed. Brigette's feet dangled over the edge while her hands and arms moved about. William's childish gaiety pleased his ears which would end once his presence became known.

"What goes on here?"

Two heads popped up and turned his way. "Papa!" He clambered over his mother and slid to the floor. "Did ye coom ta play?" he asked as he ran and jumped into his father's arms.

"Nay. I have important news."

He grabbed his father's face with both hands and pulled it downward. "Whit papa?"

By this time, Brigette stood next to the bed with hands clasped together. Her face changed from joyous to anxious. He experienced a twinge of guilt for causing her torment, but she caused him equal agony when she announced she wished to move from their shared room. Did she know how her words wounded him?

"Tell me, papa."

Daniel sat in the closest chair, holding the rascal in his lap. "Come, wife, this concerns you, as well."

With slow deliberate steps, she reached the edge of the rug and stopped. She wore her insecurity like a cloak. Seeing her apprehension stirred his compassion.

"Don't look so frightened, wife. Sit and hear my good news." She perched on the edge of the chair as a bird ready for flight. Her rapid breathing pricked his conscience. He needed to tell it quickly before he regretted his decision to punish his wife in this way.

"The king requested I travel with him to a few of our northern clans in hopes of promoting peace."

She sucked in a quick breath as her hand flew to her throat. "Will we travel with you?"

"Aye, papa. Can I go?"

With his eyes fastened on his wife, he said, "Nay. Ye and yer mither will remain here, but I promise to bring a present back to ye." He hoped William didn't press the issue. He watched Brigette struggle to hold her tears at bay. Rubbing William's back, he said, "Make me a list of gifts that might delight you."

William's eyes grew big with excitement. He hopped down and ran to get his writing tablet he kept for special occasions. Brigette continued to stare wide-eyed at him.

"Yer mither and I have much to discuss. Ye work on yer list." Even though his young son could neither read nor write, the assignment would keep him amused.

"Aye, papa."

Daniel encircled Brigette's hand and pulled her to her feet. "We will talk of this further in our room." She traipsed behind him as he walked back to their corridor while grasping her hand.

Mungo followed at a discrete distance.

A smidgen of remorse engulfed him after seeing his wife's reaction to his declaration. However, the closer he got to their bedchamber, his shame evaporated like a mist. Her insensitive words flooded his memory replacing his guilt. After depositing her in the middle of the room, he closed the door and leaned against it.

"What do you mean you're leaving me here, alone?" she blurted.

"Now, wife. I have to go when the king summons me."

"What exactly did he say? Did he know you took a new wife? Did he give you a choice?"

"Wife, one question at a time." Her questions annoyed him.

"Where is the missive? I wish to read it."

'Twas obvious, during the walk throughout the long hallways, his wife recovered from her initial fearful response. She replaced it with feistiness. He regarded the bed. Oh, that she might bring her boldness to their intimate moments. What a vision—nothing but a mere fantasy in his mind.

Disbelieving, he asked, "You can read?"

Her hands flew to her hips. "Yes, I can read."

"Very well." He walked over and unlocked his trunk. After laying aside a few items, he withdrew the king's request. He held it out and made her walk to fetch it—for him, a small victory.

She didn't back down but marched over to the table under the window and unrolled it. He moved about the room choosing items needed for his journey anticipating her negative reaction when she got to the bottom of the parchment. He knew the moment she discovered the truth.

She whipped around as the message floated to the floor. "The king allowed you an exemption for being newly married. You didn't have to accept his invitation!"

Her red face and fiery eyes were no surprise. If the arrows coming from her eyes were real, he would be a dead man. He

126

remained unmoving and waited, allowing the full ramification of her previous actions to come full circle.

Her face palled, and her fiery eyes dimmed. He watched the fight slip away as her body grew limp. "You chose to accept his offer to get away from me," she whispered. She stood still while her eyes scanned the room as if conducting a search. After agonizing minutes, she raised vacant eyes to his. "Well, I understand all too well the sting of rejection, and now that's where I find myself once again."

He made a step toward her with his hand outstretched. "Now, Brigette …" He choked on his own guilt. The idea of punishing his wife had taken a dreadful turn.

She threw her hands up as if in surrender. "Don't touch me." She backed toward the door. "I'll find another room in which to sleep tonight. No need to concern yourself with me ever again."

Chapter Eighteen

In the wee morning hours with her eyes still closed, Brigette lay unmoving in the bed. Her nose wrinkled at the damp, musty smell. *Is it raining?* She listened for the sounds of the morning activity around the castle. Odd. All was still and quiet. Her hand sneaked across the bedcovers and came up empty. As she peeped, memory flooded back.

Realization dawned. A sharp pain flashed across her chest. The heaviness of her despair pushed her further into the feather mattress. Rejected by her brothers and now her husband. Too hard to endure.

After leaving her unbearable husband last night, she had staggered along—blinded by her tears—until she found a deserted wing with empty rooms. With all her strength, she heaved the door open on its rusty hinges to find the room shrouded in total darkness. Frozen in fear of an unknown enemy, a massive arm carrying a torch stretched before her.

Mungo came to her aid. He laid a fire and lit four torches to ward off scary nocturnal creatures. The staleness of the room almost sent her running, but her husband's rejection kept her rooted to the spot.

With a new day dawning, she realized crying herself to sleep produced gritty eyes and an aching head. Would she ever learn that crying helped nothing? Peeking over the side of the bed, she determined it safe to reach for her shoes. Experience taught her that spiders like to hide in dark places. After banging her walking boots several times, she slid her feet inside and laced them tight.

The chilliness of the room caused her to rub her arms as she moved toward the door. With no other choice, she had slept in her clothes. Trying to smooth out the wrinkles was all for naught. Hair that escaped her braid, tickled her face. Stopping at the closed door, she untwisted the braid and worked her fingers through the tangled mess. Her eyes hurt. No doubt puffy and red, but she didn't possess the strength to care. Just as she pulled on the door, it swung wide with ease.

She sucked in and held her breath. Hoping an apologetic husband stood on the other side, her disappointment doubled. There stood her trusty guard, Mungo. Her shoulders slumped. The awareness that Daniel failed to seek her out during the night nor this morning left her disheartened.

"Good morrow, Mungo." Of course, she didn't expect an answer from him, but at the very least, a grunt. "I suppose I should make my way back among the living." When she started down the passageway, he stepped in front of her and shook his head. With a feeble smile, she said, "You lead, and I will follow until we get to a familiar area."

With eyes downcast, she walked on legs of wood—each step burdensome. At one point she walked straight into the back of her protector knocking her to her knees. She mumbled a shaky apology as she struggled to get up. Mungo never touched her—not even to assist her. Strange.

"Did my husband warn you not to touch me?"

He shook his head no and continued along the corridor. All too soon they reached the wing that contained her and Daniel's shared room. With the door ajar, a dim light spilled into the hallway.

She looked at Mungo. "I think I'll stay out here with you until he comes out."

He shook his head and nodded toward the open doorway. Why couldn't she have a guard who agreed with her? Better to face the demon and be done with it, she supposed. She lifted her nose in the air and marched into the room.

When she entered, Daniel continued packing. Her clacking boot heels made her presence known, yet he didn't acknowledge her. She hovered near the door. "Are you ready to leave?"

His failure to answer annoyed her. Now who was acting like the child? "Well, since you seem preoccupied with packing for your journey, I'll bid you farewell." As she turned toward the door, he snatched her hand.

"I expect a proper sendoff as is fitting the wife of a powerful laird."

Her eyes narrowed as they glared at one another. She ground her teeth. "Oh, am I still your wife?"

He yanked her against his body. "I will not tolerate your disrespectful tone. When we stand together as I prepare to mount up, you will act the humble and dutiful wife sending off her husband with a loving kiss."

She jerked her head to the side when he attempted to steal a kiss. He threw her hand aside and stalked over to his haversack. As he buckled on his sword, he added, "Remain chaste while I am away or your unfaithfulness will reach my ears, of this I am certain."

"My unfaithful … you swine," she spit out. "How dare you accuse me of such? 'Tis you that would be disloyal. You care naught about me and have proven it so." When tears pricked her eyes, she forbid them to form. She would not give him the benefit of seeing how his insult affected her.

"You might wish to change your clothes and comb your hair before we break our fast together. I'll await you below. Orders must be given before I depart." With those parting words, he stalked from the room.

She couldn't believe the words that spewed from her husband—cruel and hateful. All she asked for was her own room. Her assessment? Without a doubt, all men were peculiar. Afraid of how he might embarrass her in front of his people if she appeared untidy, she took time to don a clean dress and fix her hair with a circlet. It grieved her to do his bidding, but her fear of his retort won out. The more she contemplated his absence, the more she warmed to the idea.

Daniel and Brigette ate their morning meal in silence. He scowled as she swirled her spoon in the bowl of gruel without eating. No emotion crossed her face. Their hostility toward each other saturated the grand hall and was borne by all. Servants avoided the high table unless summoned.

Sitting by his stoic wife robbed him of his appetite. Not the reaction he had anticipated. She had displayed such maturity at their first meeting, why childish now? Not wanting to belabor their time together, he hurried through his meal. He slammed the goblet on the table and wiped his mouth before grabbing her hand.

Leaning around her, he said, "Come William. 'Tis time I depart."

William jumped down and ran ahead of his parents. In silence, he walked past the other diners with his docile wife trailing behind … head down.

As was custom, the servants and other workers lined from the keep to the gate to cheer their laird as he left on a special journey with the king. This appointment was an honor for the lord of their realm. His few select men packed their weapons and prepared to mount their horses.

Standing close to his wife, he whispered, "Will I receive your tender kiss?"

A forced smile appeared. "Of course, husband. Where would you like it?"

His nostrils flared. "Woman, you test me." He grabbed her around the waist and snatched her close. His kiss, born of punishment not love. When he pulled back, he ignored her reddened lip and swung William into his arms. "Be a good boy while I'm away, and I'll bring you a present."

"Aye, papa."

He bounded down the steps to his waiting horse. Once in the saddle, he waved to the people but reserved a piercing glare for his wife. "Have a care, wife," he said as his horse danced in agitation.

While he waited at the gate, the other horses thundered over the drawbridge. He turned for one last look. On the top step, his child bride held the hand of his precious son. The scene would have been perfect if they were a joyful family. But alas, they were not.

"Good riddance," Brigette whispered. A tug on her hand came when William broke free from her grasp and ran to play. Ross fast on his heels. She watched as the people dispersed to their duties. Some gave her a sideways glance, but no one engaged her in conversation.

Uncertain of what to do, she stood on the steps until everyone vanished. For the first time in her life, she held the power to do as she wished. No brothers or husband to give her orders. For a moment, she allowed her eyes to scan the courtyard while her body stayed fixed in place. She stifled the desire to scream like a stuck pig—free at last!

With great care she turned and viewed her surroundings. She could go anywhere and do anything. What to do? Giddy with excitement, she ran down the steps and twirled in a fast circle. With a hard foot plant, she came to an abrupt stop while her dress danced around her ankles. From the corner of her eye, a movement. In the shadows of the castle stood her faithful guardian.

With a new-found confidence, she marched over to him. "Where can I find a woman who can serve as my assistant? One who is easy to understand?"

Without moving, he let loose with an ear-splitting whistle. One so loud and surprising that Brigette's hands sped to cover her ears. "What are you about?"

When he puckered again, a woman raced around the side of the castle and came to sliding halt. Dust swirled about. "How can I help ye, Mungo?"

Brigette gave the little lady a once over. She was of slight build with burnt orange hair that kinked all around her face. White aligned teeth shone bright.

Mungo nodded his head toward Brigette. "Hello, my lady. I'm Fiona. How may I help you?"

Brigette shook her head in disbelief. "You speak perfect English. Astonishing!"

Fiona giggled. "I suppose I do. Are ye in need?"

"Yes … yes, I am. If it's not too much trouble, might you assist me in a task?"

"Delighted. I've been telling him how I wanted to meet ye, but he said ye were much too busy for such frivolity."

She looked between the two. "He speaks?"

"Oh, aye." Fiona laughed. "Sometimes I barely get in a word."

"Surely, ye jest?"

"Come, tell me how I can assist ye, and when we're done, I'll tell ye all about my Mungo."

Chapter Nineteen

Once Daniel escaped his situation at home, the tension seeped from his shoulders. When he and his men cut through an open field, the subtle aroma of heather filled his nostrils. Even though late fall, the flower still bloomed and possessed a richer, deeper tone. With each hoof beat, he acquired more self-control.

How had he allowed a young girl to upend his well-ordered life? She had burst into his home acting as if in control. No doubt, Lord Fairwick knew his sister would topple his disciplined existence and had planned it all along. Nicolas would claim the last battle victory over him and laugh all the way into eternity.

A battle … that's what Daniel entered when he repeated his sacred vows. Now he was trapped. Or was he? As the landscape blurred, he contemplated how to solve the dilemma with his wife. If engaged in a true battle with an enemy, he would strategize with his choice men and formulate a plan of attack. That's what he needed now—a tactic to bring his wife under his thumb.

Women had very few rights—mere property. He needed to remind his wife of that fact. When he returned home, he planned to take charge of his castle and reclaim the activity in his bedchamber. No more giving into the demands of a child bride.

Before his plan had substance, Iain interrupted. "The scout has returned. We're approaching the king's entourage within half a days ride."

"Thank you, Iain."

"Sir, if I may be so bold, ye seem a wee distracted."

"'Tis nothing of import. Carry on."

"Aye, my lord."

He watched Iain rein in his horse and move back into formation. Angered that Iain detected his irritation, he vowed to put his wayward wife from his mind. Now was not the time to consider his hasty marriage to a Fairwick.

By the time his group reached the outskirts of the king's camp, twilight descended. Thankful a tent awaited his arrival, he stored his gear and drank some ale sitting on a tray. Iain attended to his horse and assumed control of the other men. Niall, his first-in-command, remained in charge of the castle. Even though Iain was next to Niall in prominence, he was an excellent battle commander. One in whom he had great confidence.

As Daniel emerged from his tent, one of the king's men waited to speak with him. "Lord McKinnon, the king wishes to speak with you at your earliest convenience. When you are refreshed, I will escort you to his quarters."

"I'm ready now."

"This way, my lord."

As he weaved his way past tents, the smell of roasted meat permeated the air. Small cooking fires and clusters of men covered the ground in every direction. The king never traveled lightly. Hundreds of knights, clerks, pages, cooks, and servants journeyed with the king. The total didn't even include Daniel and the other prominent lords there to add support.

King James I of England or King James VI of Scotland, depending on where you lived, was attempting to keep the peace between Scotland and England. With talk of an uprising, he prayed a diplomatic visit to the highlands would go far in making peace a permanent reality.

After meandering through the sea of tents, Daniel hoped he could find his way back from the king's shelter. Not wanting to intrude, he waited off to the side while the king completed his conversation with his clerk. When the king spied him, a broad smile broke his stern countenance.

"Laird Daniel McKinnon, I am pleased you have joined my small company to the highlands."

Daniel chuckled. "I'm honored to be included, but small is a misnomer."

King James slapped him on the back and ducked inside the open tent flap. "Now McKinnon, you wound me with those words. I simply brought a few people I needed to accomplish my task."

"Of course, my king."

As soon as they sat on stools before a small table, a cook brought in numerous platters of food and filled their goblets with ale. "So, have you heard about the Elliot's trying to cause unrest?"

Nothing like getting straight to the point. That was one characteristic he appreciated in his king. He wasted no time.

"Aye. I don't see it as a great concern. Not many would follow Fergus Elliot. He has made countless enemies on both sides of the border."

"My report revealed his son tried stealing cattle in England this time last year even though he understood we were at peace."

"Aye, but Lord Nicolas Fairwick stopped them. Brodie and the foolish men following his leadership wouldn't concede to Lord Fairwick. 'Twas an unfortunate ending for the reivers."

"Yes, that's how it was reported to me. I'm glad you confirmed my information accurate. Keep an ear out for any other trouble they might stir up since you are the closest laird to their land holdings."

"Aye, my lord. My scouts can make his realm a part of their mission."

"And McKinnon … use force if needed."

"As you say, my liege."

"Now, on to more pleasantries. I hear, Nicolas Fairwick's sister is a beauty to behold."

"Yes, she is quite fetching."

"That is your only response? Surely, being wed to such a woman deserves more than a frank retort?"

Daniel chewed his meat contemplating what to say. The king noticed his reluctance to discuss his wife and launched into his "fatherly" mode.

"It seems all is not well between you and your new bride."

"We but need time to adjust to one another."

The king threw back his head and roared with laughter. "Adjust? Marriage is so much more than a simple adjustment. Our Lord's Word is filled with scriptures about a relationship between a man and a woman. I'm sure you are aware that an English translation of God's Holy Word was completed in the year of our Lord, 1611?"

"Yes, my lord. I believe it's called The King James Version of the Bible, is it not?"

"Well, they first called it the Authorized Version."

"It's been told that you furnished instructions to the translators on how to translate The Holy Bible."

"This is true. I wanted to ensure that the new version conformed to the ecclesiology and reflect the episcopal structure of the Church of England and its belief in an ordained clergy. Forty-seven scholars completed the translation, all of whom were members of the Church of England. The New Testament was translated from Greek and the Old Testament from Hebrew and Aramaic. I've supervised this project for over seven years."

"In my opinion, I believe it should be called the King James Version in your honor instead of the Authorized Version. It could well be remembered as one of your greatest achievements during your reign."

"It matters not if I'm remembered for this accomplishment. What matters is that the common man can now read God's Word for himself and understand it."

"Of course, you are right."

"Don't worry, Daniel, you have not deterred me from my main quest—to give you aid."

"Give me aid?"

"Absolutely. 'Tis good fortune I have the New Testament part of the Bible with me. Stay where you are." The king rummaged

138

through his chest until he laid hands on his prized possession. He came back to the small table. With the Bible still in his hands, the king reverently ran his hand across the wooden cover. His intense gaze pinned Daniel. "This is the English version of The New Testament. I want to give it to you."

Dumbfounded, Daniel didn't know what to say. His heart raced and his palms grew moist. "My lord, how can I accept such a precious gift?"

"With graciousness, my son, with graciousness. God wants to work in your life, and He has wisdom to impart to you if you will read His Word. How can you read it if you don't have access to a Bible you can understand?"

The king placed the heavy Bible into Daniel's hands. The outside cover was made of olive wood with the loose pages bound together by leather. Two hinges on the left side and one buckle on the right side fastened it closed.

"As you can see, I was in a hurry to have my own copy to take with me on my journeys. You will need to use caution when turning the pages."

"But 'tis your travel manuscript."

"McKinnon, I'm the king. I can get another one in due time. I insist."

There was no help for it. He had to accept the gift or risk offending his king. "I am your humble servant. It's with a grateful heart that I accept this treasure."

He bowed his head with respect to his king. With great care, he placed the Bible on the table and continued to eat his meal. The king had a few details about their next stop where he would be required to be a role player. However, concentrating on the particulars proved difficult with the Bible so close at hand.

On the way back to camp, Daniel held the Bible close to his chest to prevent it being jostled from his grasp. To drop the special gift caused him angst. The king issued distinct instructions on where to search for scriptures relating to being a good husband. He lacked the courage to tell the king the problems with his recent marriage lay at his wife's door.

Campfires lit his path through the mass of men. As he came to the outskirts of the camp, he made a wide sweep around the outer circle to find his site. He blamed the king for his inability to think straight. After the king gave him a "holy" setting down for his treatment of his wife, his thoughts jumbled. At this point, his hands burned from carrying the sacred gift, and desired relief from it.

Iain called out. "My lord. We are here."

He looked around to see Iain waving the McKinnon banner to attract his attention. Relieved, he hurried over to Iain. "Here, put this in a safe place."

"What is it, my lord?"

"A gift from the king. Quickly, hide it away," he rushed to say. "'Tis part of God's Holy Word."

Iain caught the book as Daniel shoved it into his hands. He turned it over and touched the intricate design on the wooden case surrounding the pages. "'Tis beautiful," he said in awe.

"Stop gazing at it. Wrap it in cloth and put it away at once."

Iain's puzzled face stared back at him. For sure Iain wondered at his reluctance to have the present in his sight. The soldier had no idea of the wicked sins he kept hidden. Sins that deserved a lightning bolt from heaven … one to annihilate him upon impact.

After Iain wrapped and stored the Bible in a secure saddle bag, Daniel's breath hissed through his teeth. His breathing came fast and erratic. Wiping his sweaty palms on his pant leg, he collapsed on a log by the open fire pit. Rubbing his hand over his face, he inhaled a deep breath and released it with slow deliberation.

What vexed him? He acted as if he ran a long distance. Iain and two of his men stared at him. "I need some ale … and … and …" He flipped his hand. "… just get the ale."

His brusque manner sent Iain scurrying to do his bidding. The other men ambled away from their laird allowing him privacy. Ever since the Bible touched his hand, he couldn't entertain a level-headed thought. He despised his rudeness toward Iain and needed to apologize. For now, he struggled to formulate more than two words that made any sense.

A voice drifted from the dark. "Having a difficult time of it, are ye?"

Daniel jerked his head around. "Who's there? Show yourself." He rose to his feet and drew his sword.

"There's no need for that sword, laddie. I'm not here to do ye any harm," the old voice crackled. "I've been sent to give ye relief."

Chapter Twenty

Brigette could not believe her ears—a woman who spoke English. Her future got brighter by the minute. Fiona was a hidden treasure she was happy to claim. And to think she was wed to Mungo. What an oddity.

As the two women walked together, Brigette said, "I wish to set out my painting easel and tools. Your help in doing so would be much appreciated."

"Ooh, you paint? How exciting. I've never been privy to know an artist. Does Laird McKinnon know of this secret talent? I dare say that Mungo doesn't know it. What type of paintings do you do?"

"Fiona, slow down." Brigette grinned. "All of your questions make my head spin."

"Oh, my lady, please forgive me. I'm so delighted to talk with you that I forget myself. Mungo keeps telling me I'm high-strung." She giggled.

"Now, that's a concept I'm having a hard time believing— Mungo talking."

"Aye. A man of many mysteries."

The women started up the winding stairway.

"Whew!" Brigette huffed. "I know the curved stairs are a strategic construction for battles that find their way inside the castle, but it makes it hard to traverse with full hands."

143

"Aye, but it presents difficulty for the enemy to use their sword on circular stairs with a wall on their right side unless they are left-handed."

"Yea. My brothers instructed me how it allows the landowner to continue the assault descending on his attackers from upstairs with free range of sword motion. However, today it's difficult to manage."

Fiona laughed as they topped the stairs.

"How long have you lived at the McKinnon castle?"

"Well, let me think. Ever since Mungo captured me, I suppose."

She stopped in the middle of the hallway and spun around to face Fiona. "Captured you!"

"Oh, aye. 'Tis quite a story to be sure."

With slow movements, Brigette turned to Mungo and then to stare at Fiona. "I can't wait to hear the whole of it. It's bound to be entertaining."

The women continued to the room that Brigette shared with Daniel. She paused outside the entry before pushing open the heavy door. As the first one over the threshold, Brigette's knees weakened. Daniel's punishing words rushed to her mind. For a moment, she became light-headed and queasy. When she failed to walk inside the room, Fiona bumped into her back.

"I'm sorry, my lady. I didn't expect ye to stop."

"'Tis my fault. Come, I'll show you my painting instruments."

Both women acted like young girls seeking their favorite doll, eager to play. After Brigette pulled out her paints, brushes, small canvasses, and easel, Fiona stared.

"Oh," she marveled, "ye have such fine tools." She looked at Brigette. "Can ye paint portraits?"

"Yes, but my skill lacks finesse. Nicolas paid for me to study from an artist. The man didn't stay long in our home. He stated I was a difficult student." Gazing out the window, she said, "I suppose I did try his patience." Turning back to Fiona, "He was old and had black teeth." She snickered. "In spite of our many quarrels, I did learn basic strokes that I have perfected over time."

"Where do you want to place your paints?"

"I know the ideal place. Let's gather these items, and I'll show you or rather Mungo will lead the way." Brigette arranged her paints and small utensils in a wooden box with a handle while Fiona lifted the easel and canvas.

"I stumbled upon a quiet wing of the castle where no one seems to inhabit. It will allow me to remain undisturbed while I paint. As a novice, I must concentrate on my techniques, or it will be a muddled mess."

Bridgette grabbed the broom from behind the door as the two women left the room. She walked over to Mungo who waited in the passageway.

"Kind sir, I need you to lead me to the room where I slept last night." She watched his eyes cut to Fiona before swinging back to her. Without a word, he started down the hallway.

Brigette looked at Fiona trying to understand what had just happened. Her new friend offered an innocent smile and started after her husband. Something strange passed between those two, and one way or another she would know of it.

On this trip, Brigette catalogued each turn they made to arrive at the darkened wing of the castle. Their guide stopped at the entrance of the corridor and stared into the darkness.

"What is it Mungo? Why don't you get a torch and light our way?"

As he stood unresponsive, Fiona answered for her husband. "This is the forbidden area of the castle," she whispered. "Laird McKinnon has deemed it so."

"Why?"

Fiona turned to Brigette. "It is not our story to tell, but we mustn't go down this passageway."

"I slept in one of those rooms last night, and your husband didn't stop me. He even lit the torch for my room. Is there danger?"

Once again, a silent communication swept between Fiona and Mungo. "No. No there is no danger."

Brigette set her toolbox on the floor and walked over to an unlit torch on the wall. She snatched it down and marched back the way they had come to find a source to light it. Mungo caught up to her and retrieved it from her hand. He placed it next to a burning one on the wall, and it caught fire. He glanced at her before leading her back to where Fiona stood.

With a nod he indicated for Brigette to proceed down the dark wing. He stayed close at hand to light her way. She grasped her wooden box and with uncertainty started walking the long hallway. She couldn't remember which room she slept in, but thought it sat at the far end. Last night she had wanted to escape her husband's dreadful anger and had run unaware.

She stopped in front of one closed door and looked at Mungo. His brows raised. She examined the area to get her bearings and then proceeded farther along the hallway before stopping again. This time he awarded her an affirmative answer. He pushed open the door and stepped back allowing her to enter. She hesitated inside the doorway and breathed in the mustiness of the room. At last, the correct chamber.

Fiona brought in Brigette's easel and canvas. "Where would ye like these, my lady?"

"Mungo, please light the other torches so I can better see the room."

As light penetrated the room, it appeared less ominous as when she first entered. She walked over and yanked back the heavy curtains. The sunlight peeked through the dingy windowpanes allowing a beam of light to enter.

With extra light Brigette observed her sanctuary through clearer sight. The sparse room contained elaborate yet worn embellishments. The bedside table had a thick layer of undisturbed dust waiting to be blown away. The once ornate coverlet and curtains on the platform bed hung shabby from neglect. Walking over to the washstand, she fingered a brush and a hand mirror. Those two items were reserved for the most privileged in a household. What had happened in this area to warrant abandonment?

She whirled around. "Who occupied this room?"

"My lady…" Fiona's voice faltered.

When her eyes grew fearful, Brigette raised her hand. "Cease. I no longer wish to know. I plan to paint in this room and don't want any prior knowledge to hamper my mood." She shrugged. "I paint best in a pleasing atmosphere. Come. Let's get this room cleaned up, shall we?"

Mungo, who had joined Fiona near the doorway, nodded to his wife and left the room. He stood guard outside the door. Threats from any source would be held at bay as long as he stood watch.

"Fiona?"

"Yea, my lady. How may I be of service?"

Finding another broom by the cold fireplace, she gave Fiona the task of knocking down cobwebs and killing spiders that might live in said webs while she swept the floor of dirt and debris. Even though Brigette concluded the room was indeed where she wanted to be, she couldn't quite shake the feeling that something troubling had transpired here. Readying the room for her use as a studio overpowered her misgivings.

It was obvious the space had been ignored for years, but it was the why of it that kept her mind occupied. Not wishing gloomy notions to cloud her mind, she said, "Fiona, tell me how Mungo captured you. It sounds fascinating."

Fiona paused in her spider squashing and leaned on the broom handle with dreamy eyes. "'Tis such a romantic yet tragic tale to be sure." With a deep sigh she went back to her chore.

"I'm of Irish decent but raised in England. My father was Irish but fell in love with my English mother during his travels. Since my father adored my mother, he agreed to find work in England if she agreed to become his bride. Their time together was difficult because of my father's Irish heritage. Work was hard to find. Yet my mother remained loyal. Once he had a way to support his wife, he…"

Brigette stopped her sweeping to watch Fiona's expressions as she talked about her parents wishing she had such a memory of her own. Fiona's face glowed when she reminisced about her family.

147

Brigette's memory of her father was scant, and she had no recollection of her mother. Would she be as content as Fiona if she had had a mother and father who loved her?

"…and my father allowed me to travel with him to deliver the wool across the border. Of course, my mother didn't know about our journey until hours after our departure. Father worried I was too sheltered by my mother and wanted me to see the world—even if only Scotland. Sadly, we met with an unsavory lot. The men intended ill against our traveling group."

"Oh, dear. What happened?" Entrapped by the tale, she grabbed Fiona's broom and pulled her arm until they reached the bed. "Let's sit here while you tell the rest of your tale."

Both women crawled into the middle of the dusty bed and sat cross legged facing one another.

Fiona leaned in and with a hushed voice resumed her story. "There was much clashing of swords and loud cries of fighting that surrounded me as I sat in the wagon full of wool. I was so frightened that I knew not what to do. All of a sudden, a huge man on horseback galloped out of the middle of the battle, snatched me around the waist and lifted me onto his horse. Of course, I pounded his chest, face, and arms to try and escape. I'm not sure where I would have gone had I gotten loose from his grasp, but I tried."

Brigette's heart beat wild from fear. "What about your father? What happened to him?"

Fiona's eyes filled with tears. "After my unsuccessful attempt to flee my captor, I peered around his big arms to see that my father and his traveling companions had fallen to their deaths. Such a horror. Now evil men pursued us." With the edge of her apron, she wiped her running nose.

"Oh, Fiona. I'm so sorry. You don't have to finish your story if it's too difficult."

"No. I want to tell of Mungo's heroic feat. My Mungo is an intelligent man. He knew those men would expect us to stay on the road, so he darted into the forest. He held me tight as he rode his mighty horse, weaving through underbrush and trees. I kept trying to see behind us, but his focus never wavered from where he was headed. Little did I know that he was well acquainted with the forest because he lived there."

"Mungo lived in the forest?"

"Aye. I cried for my father and feared for my life all at the same time. For all I knew I could have been headed to my death with a man I didn't know in a country far from home. Once we reached a small stream, Mungo ran his horse right into the water and headed upstream. His mighty horse never slowed. They were headed home, and the dark fazed them not."

"It was night?" she asked with alarm. The scene unfolded right before Brigette's eyes.

"Aye. Night had swallowed us during our time in the water. A blessing to be sure. The wicked men couldn't see us nor find us. At one point we stopped under a rock overhang, and Mungo put his hand over my mouth and shook his head. Our faces touched. I gathered my silence was essential."

"Dear me, I can't imagine your fright!"

"When Mungo determined the danger had passed, he found us a small cave in which to stay the night. Since a fire would have drawn notice, we huddled together for warmth." Fiona grinned. "My gentle giant radiates much heat." She took a deep breath. "The sadness of my heart weighed heavy on me. I fell into a restless sleep where frightening dreams chased me through the night. Mungo kept vigilant watch through the long hours. Before first light, we mounted again and galloped all the way to the McKinnon castle."

"I thought Mungo lived in the forest?"

"Yes, but he did work for Laird McKinnon, too. The McKinnon welcomed us and provided a haven. He also offered his assistance in finding the culprits who had murdered my father and his men."

"Oh, my. Your poor mother."

"Yea. She was quite distraught. Since Mungo and I had spent the night together without a chaperone, he insisted that we wed post haste. I'm not sure which was worse for my mother, losing my father or watching me leave for Scotland never to return."

Brigette's eyes widened. "You've not seen your mother since that day?"

"Oh, nay." Fiona smiled. "Mungo made sure my mother was cared for until we convinced her to move to Scotland when our first child arrived."

Brigette's jaw fell open as she leaned forward. "You and Mungo have children?"

"Aye. We have a swarm of youngins."

Brigette couldn't believe her ears. Fiona rejoiced in her marriage. Mungo, who never uttered a word in her presence, was married with children. What an odd twist to Fiona's tale of grief. "Did you love Mungo when you wed?"

"Oh, aye. His gentleness and kind ways won my heart. He wanted nothing but the best for me. How could I not love him?"

"Are you happy here?"

"Aye. The McKinnon is such a fair man, and his castle provides us a safe place to live and raise our family."

"You live in the castle?"

"In truth, The McKinnon allotted Mungo a small, dilapidated hut not far outside the castle walls. We could have it for our very own, but it was our task to make it habitable. Without a doubt, we were verra pleased with Laird McKinnon's generous offer and received it with a grateful heart. My Mungo has such a tender heart for others." Her eyes misted with emotion. "We are truly blessed beyond our hopes."

Brigette sat contemplating all that Fiona had shared. Incredible. The miserable reality was that Daniel could be beyond lavish with how he treated others in his realm, but for his own wife, he had nothing but contempt. Her chest constricted at the memory. With a heavy heart, she said, "Thank you for telling your remarkable journey."

With a soft touch Fiona squeezed Brigette's hand. "My prayer is that one day you and Laird McKinnon will have a castle full of babes."

Brigette's eyes grew round with fear. *Never!*

150

Chapter Twenty-One

Daniel crouched ready to pounce. "I said, show yourself."

Out of the darkness hobbled an old man in full knight dress: sword, shield, chainmail, and helmet. He emerged as if he had walked off the battlefield of the Christian crusades complete with a red cross on his breastplate.

"Put away your sword. I'm here to offer ye relief from yer concerns. Might I have a seat next to your fire?" he asked in a raspy voice.

The young laird relaxed his stance and sheathed his sword. The crusty old man looked as if he might topple over from the weight of his heavy armor. "As you wish."

Daniel extended his hand toward a vacant spot near the fire. He watched as the man removed his helmet and sword belt and laid them down with care. At one point Daniel had to offer his hand to steady the man before he fell.

"Might I offer you some food and drink?" Daniel asked.

"Nay."

The old warrior heaved a sigh while staring at Daniel. When he was not forthcoming with his intentions, Daniel said, "Again, I ask you, what is your purpose?"

The man held up his hand as if to stop Daniel. "All in due time. I need a moment to gather myself. I'll accept yer offer of some ale."

Daniel huffed out his frustration. He was in no mood to deal with an old man who didn't know his own mind and seemed determined to impede Daniel's intentions.

"Iain. See the man gets some ale."

Guilt pricked him at his gruff tone but not enough to act upon it. He wanted to hurry the man with the telling for he needed time alone to reason through his reaction to the king's gift. It was unsettling.

"Ye appear to be out of sorts."

"Old man, instead of judging me, why don't you identify yourself?" Daniel's frustration escaped through his words.

"Always impatient. It will be a detriment to ye." He slurped a long drag on his tankard. "Ah. I was thirstier than I realized."

Daniel recognized the man would be forthcoming with information in his own time. 'Twas obvious he was not to be hurried. Mayhap he was daft. No doubt, that was the problem.

"My name is Tancred. I've been sent to offer ye relief from yer difficulties—those concerning yer wife."

It was all Daniel could do to remain seated and not attack the old man seated across from him. His heart pounded in his chest. Who was this man who knew about his wife? Had the king told him?

"You talk gibberish, old man," he snapped.

Tancred sat his empty mug on the log and focused on Daniel. "Ye wed a woman ye didn't love to gain a mother for yer young son. When she didn't perform to yer expectations, yer displeasure grew, and ye made it known."

Tancred's penetrating stare pinned Daniel to his seat as if skewered by an arrow. "How do you know this?" Daniel ground his teeth. "Did the king send you?"

"Nay. I'm not privy to know the king."

Daniel staggered backward until he connected with the log and plunked down. Blood drained from his face. "Are ye an angel?"

Tancred's hearty laughter rang loud. "Examine me, son. Do I fit yer view of an angel? I move like a slug in my armor, and some say I'm near the grave. An angel indeed." He grinned.

"You are a prophet then?" He vetoed that suggestion with a shake of his head. Afraid of his own next question, Daniel hesitated. With a quick turn, he glanced right and left. "Were you sent by God?" he asked in a low voice.

"Does it matter who sent me. I'm here to clarify the scriptures and give ye direction about yer wife. Believe me when I say, it's all for yer good."

Dumbfounded, Daniel stared. He might choke from his rapid heartbeat. Again, he rubbed sweaty palms over his trousers. What was happening here? Had he been snatched up and dropped into another world? For sure, he faced an adversary he didn't know how to battle.

"Instead of pondering where I gained my knowledge, why don't ye allow me to offer some advice? My advice is free and ye don't have to adhere to my suggestions. Ye have nothing to lose but yer time. Are ye willing to give me a few moments?"

The old man's short speech calmed Daniel. His breathing returned to normal, and his attitude shifted from provoked to receptive—puzzled, yet open to hear from Tancred.

"I will listen to you for a brief time, and then I must retire. I have much to do for the king on the morrow."

"Ye don't live as long as I have lived and not learn important lessons. But before I talk about them, can I get some more ale? Talking makes me parched."

Out of the dark, Iain materialized with two full cups of ale and handed one to each of the men. Afterwards, he vanished like smoke in the wind.

"Do ye walk in the light?" Tancred asked.

"What mean you, walk in the light?"

"Do ye live righteously and avoid evil ways?"

Daniel squirmed. Tancred was prying into his private affairs. Should he answer or refuse the old man his request? For now, Daniel's curiosity was peaked, and he chose to indulge the old fella.

"I try to shun wicked ways. I treat my fellow man with respect unless they are my enemies… so, yes, I suppose I live righteously."

"Do ye walk in God's wisdom?"

Daniel drained his mug of ale and let it drop to the ground. "I consider myself a wise man. Now, do I have God's wisdom… ?"

While Daniel considered his answer, Tancred went on with his questioning. "Do ye agree that God created man?"

At last, one he could answer with conviction. "Without a doubt."

"Do ye believe that God's Son, Jesus Christ, died on a cross for yer sins and mine?"

"Aye." Daniel was pleased at this line of questioning. There was no harm in responding. He knew all about these facts since he received instruction as a young child. "I go to confession on occasion and pay alms to the church." He was relieved that he had paid his taxes to the church before leaving on this expedition.

"Do ye believe that God sanctioned marriage between a man and a woman like Adam and Eve of old?"

"Oh, Aye."

"Did ye know that God's Holy Word says the wife is to be submissive to her husband?"

Daniel sat tall. This was good news to his ears. "Is that found in The New Testament?"

"Aye. It's found in Paul's letter to the Ephesians in chapter five. This submission by the wife is to be given willingly and lovingly."

Daniel massaged his hands together. Now the questions were more to his liking. He looked around before asking in a hushed voice, "How is a husband to get his wife to submit in such a way?"

Tancred rubbed his neck and then his face. "Ah, Daniel. Ye have much to learn."

He was confused. Why did his question about Brigette's submission draw that type of reaction from the old man? "Is there not a method to use that would ensure her submission?"

"The book of Ephesians has the answer to yer question."

"Shall I go and retrieve my portion of the Bible for you?"

154

"I don't need the Bible to answer yer question. God created man to give leadership to the wife…"

Daniel interrupted. "I am trained in leadership. This I do well."

"That's not the leadership of which I speak. The husband is to protect, preserve and love his wife. When ye love yer wife with the unreserved, selfless, and sacrificial love that Christ has for His church, then and only then, can ye garner the submission of yer wife, and it will be given with a free will."

Daniel's brows came together. He stared at Tancred as if he were a troll. Bewildered. "You mean, I have to love her before she will submit? We are barely acquainted."

"Nay. Ye misunderstand. Ye need to care for yer wife with the same devotion that ye care for yerself. But more than that, ye must exhibit a self-sacrificing love that puts her first in yer marriage… where ye are more concerned for her than for yerself. This love should come because of yer deep devotion to Christ. It should show in yer actions and yer spoken word to her. Ye want to see her grow in Christ while giving her comfort and security. Is that true in yer marriage?"

Now he was meddling. Daniel stood and began pacing. He stopped at one point with his hands on his hips staring at the ground. His mind whirled with ideas and strategies. Spinning on one foot, he faced Tancred.

"I can do this. I have this entire journey to form my plan before returning home."

"Form yer plan?"

"Aye. A strategy to get my wife to submit."

Tancred shook his head as if defeated.

The king traveled up the east coast with a stop in Edinburgh. He and some of his chosen men were the guests at the Hamilton's castle. A great feast and celebration were planned in honor of the king's appearance.

Upon arrival, King James and his men occupied one wing of the castle devoted to their comfort while Daniel was allowed three men to stay with him. His other men were to camp outside the castle surroundings.

"Iain, I need you to remain with our men in the tents for the first night. You will oversee their conduct and see that our clan's behavior is above reproach. Much depends on this meeting with the local lairds in this territory. I will check with you tonight after the festivities."

"Aye, my lord."

"A word with ye, my lord?" Tancred asked.

Daniel turned to see the old man waiting for an audience with him. He took a deep breath and let it out with a huff. "Tancred, to what do I owe this pleasure?"

The old warrior was once again dressed in full armor. Sweat dripped from under his helmet, but today he used his sword as a staff to steady himself. "Will ye be residing inside the castle tonight?"

"I'm not sure why you need to know this information, but, yes, I will."

"I sense a great evil will pass yer way tonight." His withered hand grasped Daniel's arm. "Ye must run from it," he said with conviction.

When Tancred touched his wrist, a charge ran up his arm. The words were disturbing enough, but to have a flux vibrate up his arm was most troubling. He tried to shake free, but Tancred held fast with the grip of a young warrior.

"Promise me, ye will run," he said with urgency.

Daniel was beginning to believe Tancred was daft. What harm could come if he did promise? "Aye, Tancred. I plan to avoid being lured into any resemblance of wickedness."

"Nay. Ye must promise to run far from it. It's of great import."

Realizing that he would be late for the celebration if he didn't leave soon, he said, "I promise to dash away from any evil. Now will ye release your hold?"

Tancred exhaled his breath. "Ye have promised. All will be

156

well. Thank ye, my lord." His hand dropped from Daniel's wrist, and he backed away with his head bowed in respect.

He watched Tancred hobble out of sight wondering why he had appeared in Daniel's life. He didn't pose any threat, but what was the true purpose? And who had sent him?

Thankful he would sleep in comfort, Daniel dreaded the pageantry of the evening. Women and men would be dressed in all their finery requiring him to wear his ceremonial dress complete with kilt and accessories. Proud to wear his clan's plaid, he didn't relish the false flattery that was required at these social events.

Upon entering the grand hall resplendent with beautiful ornamentations, Daniel stopped near the archway awaiting his introduction. Flanked by his three guards to watch his back would allow him to move about the room with ease. Even in peaceful times there remained the possibility of conflict.

He studied the crowded room. The Hamilton coat of arms along with embellished tapestries hung high on the walls. Long tables covered with white linen cloths were laden with platters of food and drink. Numerous candelabras garnished every table with a large, iron candelabra suspended from the wooden support beams.

As he walked toward the dais, a sweet aroma arose from the rushes scattered over the stone floor. Lord and Lady Hamilton and King James I were seated high on the dais in canopied chairs. The wealth of the Hamilton's was easy to see all the way to having wax candles instead of tallow. Impressive.

Daniel bowed before the head table. "Your Majesty, King James, Lord and Lady Hamilton." As he backed away to allow others to greet the king, a hand touched his arm. He turned to see Lady Millicent Scott.

"Lord Daniel McKinnon, what a delight." She dipped into a deep curtsey.

Daniel enfolded her outstretched hand and bowed low over it.

157

"Lady Scott, what a surprise."

"I hope it's a pleasant surprise."

He stood and released her hand. "Of course, my lady. You brighten anyone's day with your dazzling smile." He offered his arm to escort her away from the dais.

"Oh," she twittered and fluttered her eyes behind her silk fan. "I'm relieved to see you." She scrutinized the room before continuing. "I've been quite bored for days," she whispered. "But now that you are here, I know my time will be more satisfying."

Daniel held his head higher as he walked toward a table. On his arm was a woman who complimented a man of prominence. They had met when he was married to Anna five years hence. At that time, she was betrothed to Lord Alfred Scott, a man twenty years her senior.

"How is Lord Scott?" Daniel inquired.

"Ugh. You can see him at the table over there." She pointed with her fan. "I imagine he is in his cups and half asleep."

Daniel twisted around to see her husband talking with Laird Gavin Buchanan. Lord Scott's head neared touching the table as he cradled his tankard while Laird Buchanan rested against the stone wall. In his view, they had been celebrating for quite some time. "Yes, I see him engaging Laird Buchanan."

After seating her at the table, Daniel walked around to the other side to sit across from her. He didn't want to sit too close with her husband nearby. That could cause a stir especially since her husband was drunk. When he sat, Daniel noticed her pouting lips.

"What troubles you, my lady?"

"I wanted you to sit next to me," she murmured.

Daniel grinned. "I can better view your beauty from this vantage point." His words brightened her countenance as he expected.

The servants poured drink into their goblets, as well as, placing a cloth napkin in their laps. Most days the action made Daniel uncomfortable when he wore his kilt, but not tonight. His mind dwelt elsewhere. Making idle chatter, he asked, "Do you find Scotland to your liking?"

Her chest lifted on a deep sigh. "I do miss my England. All of the splendor of court is lacking here."

"Now that you are off the market, so to speak, doesn't that change the way you see your role?"

She leaned over giving Daniel an easy view of her near exposed bosom. He jerked his eyes upward but not before she observed his line of sight. Her sly smile was all he needed to know she had accomplished what she wanted.

"I'm married to an old man who is more interested in his horses than his wife. 'Tis my good fortune, he already has two heirs from his first unlucky wife, and I didn't have to produce. Childbearing is disgusting."

Daniel bristled. "Lady Scott, this is not appropriate conversation between us. Cease this line of discussion."

Inspecting his platter heaped with roasted duck, wild boar, carrots, peas, cabbage, fresh bread, and an assortment of fresh berries, he ignored Lady Scott. He needed to focus on eating his fill before meeting with the king and the other local lairds.

"Oh, pish, posh. We are adults at this table. Nothing has transpired except words." She then turned to the man sitting to her right and batted her long lashes at him leaving Daniel alone for the duration of the meal.

He wondered at her boldness and what trouble she might stir.

Chapter Twenty-Two

Determined to have a new portrait to hang over the mantle in Daniel's bedchamber when he returned, Brigette painted for over two weeks. Instead of Anna, it would contain his new wife to catch his notice before laying his head down for slumber. The painting pleased her, until it came to capturing her own face.

At her request, Mungo had removed the mirror from the dresser in her secret workroom and placed it next to the window. Having bright light was imperative to seeing her reflection more clearly. She had but one chance to get the new portrait correct and didn't wish a disaster.

She resolved it was easier to leave Daniel in the same posture as the original painting since he was absent. Yet she left his face blank hoping to capture a more pleasing expression from him when he returned. One clothing change was needed. Instead of trousers, she portrayed him in his kilt with cowhide knee boots as he wore on their wedding day.

With William, she wanted to bring out his bright eyes and five-year-old countenance. Therefore, she insisted he be her model which had proven a challenge.

She bribed him with a new puppy if he would sit still while she completed his part of the painting. Poor Kenneth had the task of finding a mother dog with pups. She hoped Daniel's anger would be short-lived when he found out about the new puppy that he

161

didn't get to choose.

"When can I hae ma new pup?" William asked one morning while sitting for the portrait.

Brigette glanced around the easel and smiled. "We have to wait until the mother has her pups. Then you can choose the one you want."

"Whaur is the mither? Did Kenneth find one?"

"William, be still." She made a few strokes with her brush. "Kenneth hasn't found a mother yet, but I'm sure he will soon."

"Will I hae one afore father gits home?"

Brigette laid aside her brush and came to kneel before William. He put his arms around her neck, and they touched noses. "I have a secret plan," she whispered.

He leaned back. "Whit is it?"

"You and I will make a visit to Fairwick castle. They always have new puppies running free. You may choose one there. It will be an enjoyable time to visit with Isabelle and see her new baby. What say you?"

William pulled away and jumped around the room with arms whirling. "Thon will be splendid. When will we leave? Will we be gone long? Will ma puppy be black? Will it be a lad like me?"

She rose to her feet. "William, too many questions. I have much to do to prepare for our journey. For today we are finished here, so you may frolic outside." He was almost to the door when she called out. "Have a care."

Shaking her head, she realized that William had burrowed deep inside her heart. She had grown to love his sweet innocence and exuberance for life. Oh, to be young and carefree again. Her shoulders rose and fell as she remembered how her innocence had been stolen on her wedding day.

Walking back to the canvas, she analyzed the portrait, satisfied with her efforts. There was still work to be completed on William, but it could wait. Once the fresh paint dried, she would cover it with her linen cloth to protect it from dust and the dreadful spiders that continued to haunt her nights.

Holding her brushes, she cleaned them with great care before putting them away. Her teacher had tutored her on the proper care of her tools which she followed without wavering. Otherwise, Nicolas would have ceased her art instruction and locked away the one area where she excelled. She blew out the candles and removed the torch from the wall to carry with her. Stopping at the door, she viewed the room. Her eyes scanned every corner. One day she would know what had transpired in the room that she seized as her studio. She pulled the door until it latched.

Kenneth waited for her to exit the room. Whenever he relieved Mungo of his watch-care duty, he seemed frightened to be in this part of the castle. Curious.

"Come, Kenneth. I've completed today's work."

"Aye, m' lady. 'Tis near the midday meal." He took the torch from her hand and followed close beside her.

Just the mention of food turned Brigette's stomach. She must have breathed too much of her dyes and henna.

"I will retire to my room. You may eat your meal in the grand hall. My door will remain locked. I will be safe without your watch."

"Oh, I think not. Mungo told me I had to endure until he returns on the morrow. He widnae like it if I left me post."

Brigette halted outside the door to Daniel's room and turned to face Kenneth. "Am I not the lady of the castle?"

A frown formed between his eyes. "Aye."

"Then what I say supersedes what Mungo says. Is that not so?"

As he went from foot to foot, he said, "Whit mean you?"

Brigette closed her eyes for a brief moment and then smiled. "It means that what I say is to be heeded above what Mungo says. Go take your meal while I rest. All will be well." Without waiting for him to reply, she went in the room and latched the door. She stood still until Kenneth's weighty tread faded away.

She breathed a sigh of relief. There were so few times to be alone. As she entered the room, she viewed the empty spot above the fireplace and grinned. Soon another woman would grace the blank location. One with blond hair and blue eyes instead of black hair and dark eyes. Her stomach rolled, and she automatically rubbed it hoping to curb the queasiness. Ever since she had begun to paint, her stomach had been unsettled. She didn't remember the smell affecting her with such intensity.

She pulled a bowl next to the bed in case she heaved up her morning meal. Sitting on the edge of the bed, she unlaced her boots and snuggled under the comforter. Her weariness began the day her husband left her on the keep steps. Could she be missing him? Unlikely. Whatever the reason, she found their huge bed calming and reassuring. Her heavy lids soon closed in slumber.

Two days hence, Brigette, William and their protectors left for Fairwick castle. Niall and Mungo disapproved of the journey without her husband's approval. Of course, she had argued that he assigned her no boundaries when he left. It was rewarding to be in charge for a change. No man in Daniel's service would dare oppose her wishes.

She and William rode in a wagon filled with hay and blankets should either need to rest during their travel. She was relieved when Niall suggested it since she had yet to learn the proper way to ride a horse. Her husband had left before she picked her horse and received riding lessons.

"Read it to me again," William said as he fidgeted next to her.

Brigette reached inside her pouch and pulled out a note from Isabelle. It had taken less than two days for her to receive word from Isabelle when she had requested an audience to meet her new nephew.

Dear Brigette. It was such a wonderful surprise to hear from you and to know that all is well with you and yours. I would be delighted for you and William to make a visit to Fairwick castle. Safe travels as you hurry to me. Your loving sister, Isabelle.

Before she had even finished reading the missive, William's interest had turned to the countryside. He had seldom traveled to

England and could barely contain his excitement.

After rereading the letter from Isabelle, her joy diminished. Brigette's heartache caused her stomach to swirl. There was no mention of anyone else being happy about her visit, just Isabelle. Had she made a mistake? Was it still too soon to face her brothers? There was no turning back now. She would never disappoint her son just because her brothers were scoundrels. They would find a puppy and then be on their way home.

Most often, the men rode to Fairwick castle in about two hours, but the wagon slowed the progress.

"'Tis time to stop for a repast," Niall said.

Niall had insisted on making the journey to provide additional protection. It was obvious to Brigette that her husband had spread the word about her near abduction by two unknown men. Now she had Niall and Mungo at her every turn. She should be grateful for extra guards but instead felt suffocated.

When the wagon stopped, William jumped out and ran into the woods. Brigette raised a hand to call him back when Ross sprinted after him. There were certain advantages to their guards. She eased off the end of the wagon. How was she to relieve herself without notice while twenty men milled about?

Mungo must have anticipated her needs. He returned from the forest and pointed to an area on the opposite side of the road from the others. She had wanted Fiona to travel with her, but she remained home with the children. Instead, the servant girl, Clara, had agreed to come with her.

"Come, Clara. It seems Mungo has cleared a safe area for us to use."

"Aye, m' lady."

One stood at the entrance of the wooded area while the other became swallowed up in the bushes. After both women took care of their needs, they rejoined the men to eat a small meal. Brigette nibbled on some cheese and crusty bread but wasn't too hungry.

"William, come and eat," Brigette shouted. He was running around the men and horses, and she feared he would get hurt.

William fell upon the blanket on which Brigette and Clara sat. He huffed to catch his breath. "I'm nay hungry. I want to chase afta the wind."

Brigette ruffled his hair. "Oh, William, you are such a delight. You may romp but stay away from the horses."

"Aye, mither. Thank ye." He gave her a quick kiss on the cheek and away he ran.

Brigette laughed. "Poor, Ross. He will be weary at the end of this journey. Watching out for William is like herding a wild horse."

"Aye. 'e keeps Ross hopping," Clara added. "Dost ye not like the fare?"

Brigette dusted off her hands. On a loud exhale she said, "I've had an unsettled constitution since I started painting. Mayhap the fresh air will improve my condition."

"I daresay 'tis true."

Brigette stood and walked around a bit, stretching her legs and trying to calm her quivering stomach. It felt as if ants crawled on her insides. Why did she ever imagine visiting Fairwick castle was a good idea? All too soon the caravan resumed its quest headed toward the unknown.

William had worn himself out with play and lay asleep in Brigette's lap while Clara sat next to Ross on the wagon seat. As familiar terrain came into view, her heart banged against her chest. What type of reception would she receive? Would her brothers even speak to her? What if they made tasteless remarks about her in front of William? Would Niall and Mungo defend her? She would wring her hands if they weren't occupied stroking William's hair.

Her breath caught in her throat when the castle came into view. It was just as she had left it. Nothing out of place, yet she felt an intruder. The rapid beat of her heart made it hard to breathe. *There is no need to fear. Nicolas does not control me any longer.*

"William, 'tis time to awaken. We have arrived."

His childish groan provided a sweet distraction. He rubbed his eyes and sat up. "Mither, we're haur. Luek at the banners." He pointed to the colorful pennants waving in the breeze. His head jerked from side to side so as not to miss a thing.

Niall halted the wagon in the middle of the courtyard and walked his horse to the keep steps. Brigette twisted around in the wagon to see Nicolas and Thomas standing with arms crossed glaring at Niall. She was too far away to decipher their exchange, but they must have allowed them entry for Niall rode back and issued orders.

"What did he say?" she asked Niall.

"We are to dismount and escort our immediate party into the great hall on the first floor to the left of the entryway. Here, permit me to assist you."

Once on the ground, she grabbed William's hand and leaned down to give him instructions.

"William, you must obey me inside this castle. There will be time to explore and have fun after our introductions, but for now, you must come with me."

"Aye, mither."

It was refreshing to have this small child obey her and offer his love without conditions. He had no idea how his presence uplifted her spirits and encouraged her to continue. Unsure of her reception, she gripped his hand as if to release it meant sure death.

Brigette floated weightless through the doors and into the grand hall as if in a dream. She froze inside the archway to the hall. There stood Phillip and Abigail with Philippa, all wearing smiles of greeting. After a moment, William tugged her hand. "Is the babe William?"

Coming out of her stupor, she turned to William who watched her. "No. That is Abigail's babe."

When she made no move, William broke the hold and marched up to Phillip and Abigail. Abigail stooped for him to better see the baby.

"Is the bairn a lad?"

Abigail smiled. "No, this is a little girl. Her name is Philippa."

William brushed the hair off her forehead and leaned to give her

167

a kiss. "She is bonnie."

Seeing him respond with such love and kindness, shattered Brigette's petrified stance. She moved into the room and stopped a few feet away from the loving scene. Uncertain, she remained speechless.

"Brigette, 'tis good to see you again. You look well," Abigail said.

Transported back to her childhood, she didn't know what to do or how to respond. It relieved her when Phillip came forward to embrace her. Once in his arms, she melted into the familiar.

"We have missed you, sister."

Not wishing to become nostalgic, she pulled out of the embrace. "Let me introduce my son. This handsome boy is William."

"He is a charmer much like his father if you ask me," Phillip said grinning. Phillip shook William's hand as if he were an adult. "Pleasure to meet such a fine young man."

"I've been here afore." He glanced at Brigette. "Remember, mither. I played in yer room."

"Yes, you did."

Brigette eased up to Abigail to peep at Philippa. "She is beautiful, Abigail." She looked to see Abigail staring at her instead of the babe. "Is something amiss?"

Abigail shook her head. "No. It's just that … well, you seem different than before."

With a sad smile, Brigette said, "I suppose I am different. I'm no longer an innocent young woman. My view of life has altered. What I once cared about is no longer my concern."

Phillip interrupted. "I'm sure you're anxious to see Isabelle and her new baby boy. First, let's get you settled in your rooms and then partake of our noon meal."

When Brigette reached the bottom of the stairs, she saw Nicolas waiting above. Their eyes locked. She refused to cower under his scowl. Without hesitation, she lifted her dress and marched toward her fate.

Chapter Twenty-Three

As Brigette reached the top of the winding stairs, Nicolas stood with his nose in the air.

"Brigette."

It required great effort for Brigette not to roll her eyes. His posture of intimidation did not disturb her.

"Nicolas."

With head held high, she stood waiting for his warning sure to come.

"You may see Isabelle after the midday meal if you agree not to cause her undue distress by your theatrics."

His gruff voice cut. Brigette clamped her teeth tight. She wanted to lash out at his hateful remark but suspected it would expedite her removal from the castle. Her love of Isabelle burned hotter than her loathing of her brother. She nodded her head in affirmation.

Nicolas spun on his heel. "Follow me."

It wasn't like she didn't remember where her former room was located. His formalities were grating on her resolve. Bless William. He never uttered a word in the wake of Nicolas's impolite manner but stayed close to Brigette's side. She looked down to see his face scrunched in displeasure—her little protector.

Instead of being shown to her usual room, she and William were taken to another wing in the back of the castle. The area had

169

been closed off for repairs that were never completed as long as she lived at Fairwick Castle. 'Twas evident Nicolas wanted her far from the family. So be it.

The passageway was dark and foreboding, but she had Mungo at her back. Without a word, Nicolas let her know her status was a visitor, no longer family to him. Glaring at his back, she refused to allow his actions to wound her.

At the end of the long hallway, Nicolas opened a door. "You will reside here for the duration of your stay. There is a doorway that adjoins two small rooms. It should be sufficient to accommodate you and your son." He stepped aside for her to enter.

"It is adequate." She glared at Nicolas. "You may leave. Your presence is not needed." She didn't think it possible, but his frown grew deeper—his piercing eyes aflame with anger.

"As you wish," he snapped and left in a huff with a final scowl at Mungo.

Brigette blew out her angry breath. How dare he be so inhospitable toward her and her guards? He made it clear that she was not welcome and was here because Isabelle wished it. She determined at that moment her time at Fairwick castle would be short. A puppy for William, a visit with Phillip's family, and time with Isabelle was all she required. Nicolas was no longer her family. A slight ache passed across her chest at the thought but was not worth dwelling on. She was thankful that Mungo had remained silent during the whole exchange even though his countenance expressed murderous intent.

"Mither, why was that mon so angry?"

Not wanting to taint William's view of others, she said, "Pay him no mind. Let's get our things stowed away and go take our meal. Shall we?"

She showed William his small room that appeared to be a closet with a bed in one corner. "Look at your cozy room. I am glad to have you close at hand in case I am fearful in the night." She watched him strut into his private area and drop his bag of clothes on the floor.

"I'm ready to eat."

"Of course, you are." Brigette pointed to an empty space for Mungo to place her baggage. "I'll hang my dresses later. Come."

After eating, William ran to play with Henry, Patrick, and Pierce while Brigette was escorted to Isabelle's bedchamber. It comforted her knowing Ross would watch over William in her absence. Nicolas's guard left her and Mungo standing outside the door that was slightly ajar. As she raised her hand to knock, she heard Nicolas's deep voice.

"Don't let her stay overlong. I don't want you and our babe worn out by her visit."

Brigette lowered her hand. Did she have to endure his presence? She wanted Isabelle all to herself without his interference.

"Nicolas, all will be well. Please, be gone."

Brigette stepped back from the door. Her brother's footsteps grew louder. He jerked back when he came upon her near the open door. Her raised brows let him know she intercepted his words.

"I see your habit of eavesdropping is alive and well."

Brigette couldn't let that pass. "Don't invite me to see your wife, and then leave the door ajar and speak with a loud voice. Whatever I heard, the fault is yours."

Without giving him time to reply, she pushed passed him and clicked the door closed. He muttered something to Mungo, but she was unable to distinguish the words. Certain that Mungo could hold his own, she focused on the scene in front of her.

What a delightful sight before her as she leaned against the door. Isabelle propped up on fluffy pillows with a swaddled babe in her arms. Isabelle's eyes remained shut until Brigette walked farther into the room. At the sound of her boot heels they popped open, and a brilliant smile graced her lips.

"Brigette. You are here at last." She reached out her left hand. "I have missed you sorely. Come to me."

All thoughts of Nicolas vanished at the soothing words from

Isabelle. Just being in her presence transformed Brigette's fuming attitude.

"'Tis so good to see you again. You look radiant." She took Isabelle's hand and kissed her on the forehead. "Now let me see this new babe." She leaned in close.

"'Tis a boy," Isabelle announced. "His name is William after my grandfather."

Brigette grinned. "Well, I'm relieved he is named after your grandfather and not my husband's son."

"Nicolas was not happy that your son was already named William, and I wanted our son named William," she giggled. "He feared Daniel would believe I held feelings for him."

"Men. Their pride can cause difficulties, can it not?"

Both women burst out in laughter waking the baby. "Oh, dear. I'm afraid our merriment has disturbed William," Brigette said.

Isabelle calmed him and then offered for Brigette to hold him. Once he was placed in her arms, she was smitten. His tiny fingers and nose were so sweet.

"He's perfect," she whispered while stroking his face.

"Holding him fits you."

Brigette flinched. Still gazing at the babe, she said, "I think not." She turned her eyes on Isabelle. "I've told you, I don't want to have a babe."

"Look at me. I had no trouble birthing William and Abigail had no misfortune with Philippa. Women were created for this."

"I'm not sure why I was created," Brigette muttered.

Isabelle released a gasp. "Will you place William in his cradle? I want us to talk without any distractions."

Brigette complied with Isabelle's wish and then returned to sit in a chair at her bedside.

"Tell me how you have adjusted to your new home and being wed."

Brigette's dilemma … lie or tell the truth? She saw Isabelle giving her the look. The one she reserved for her serious talks.

"I'm adjusting."

"Now, Brigette. It is I with whom you speak. Truth please?"

"Oh, Isabelle," she moaned. "I'm not happy."

Isabelle waited when Brigette laid her head on the soft mattress and sobbed. Isabelle stroked her hair.

"Oh, my sweet Brigette. Tell me what is happening, and I will fix it."

After a few moments of self-pity, Brigette wiped her tearstained face. Her story came spilling out like water from a broken pitcher. She was distraught when Isabelle found her horrific wedding night amusing. That account was followed by the delightful ride in her husband's arms and the rope bridge catastrophe and how her day ended with a disagreement with her husband.

"Brigette, the tales you are telling are not unusual when one first gets married. All men and women go through numerous adjustments before settling into a routine together. Do not let these small skirmishes cause you discontent."

"Oh, that's not the worst of it. After several weeks of sharing a bed with Daniel, I asked for my own room."

"You what?" Isabelle exclaimed.

Brigette grimaced and ducked her head. "I asked for my own room."

"I'm sure Daniel was not pleased with that request."

"Indeed, he was not."

"Why did you want your own room?"

She leaned back in her chair and crossed her arms. "You know of my fears. I do not wish to get with child. The anger he displayed surprised me. He spoke cruel things to me from which I might not recover."

"Oh, my Brigette. Asking for your own room harmed Daniel's pride as a man. It was as if you were rejecting him as a husband and a protector ... and a lover."

She flung her arms out to her side. "We know each other not. There is no love."

"What does God's Word tell us about creation?"

Brigette pulled her hands into her lap, confused. "Pardon?"

"Tell me about God creating man and woman. What do you

173

know about it?"

"I don't see how this ..."

"Brigette."

Brigette rolled her eyes. "God created all of the earth, animals, and man and woman."

"Who was created first, man or woman?"

"Man."

"Yes. Then He removed a rib from Adam's side and created woman. A rib, Brigette. Not a bone from his head so he could rule over her or one from his foot so she would be beneath him but a rib bone so she could be his helpmate. The married pair are to complete each other, to live in harmony, and produce children."

"But I don't want that." She whimpered. "I'm afraid."

Isabelle patted the bed. "Come sit close beside me."

Brigette crawled onto the bed.

Isabelle held her hand. "Take care to listen to me. I don't want you to interrupt until you've heard the whole of it. Agreed?"

Brigette searched Isabelle's face. There was no denying the request. It was best to let her have her say and be done with it. "Very well."

"When God created man and woman, His plan for them was perfect. We also know that the serpent brought sin into God's perfect world. Adam and Eve fell for the serpent's temptation for wickedness, and their lives changed forever. Man had to labor to provide for his family and woman had to go through childbirth."

"So, it's a curse on women?"

"Both Adam and Eve paid a high price for their disobedience, and that punishment has been passed to all of us. The main problem? Sin separated them from God. However, God knew this would happen, and He had a plan that would allow them to have fellowship with Him. Do you know what that plan was?"

Brigette blinked several times and scanned the ceiling. "Christ the Son?"

"Correct. He planned from the beginning to send His only son to pay for our sins by dying a terrible death on the cross. His blood covered all our sins if we would but accept God's free gift of salvation. Have you accepted His free gift?"

Brigette hung her head. "Yes. The local priest spent many hours teaching me and mentoring me so I would stay out of trouble. I prayed for God to forgive me of my sins and to save me from my own wretchedness when I was a young girl." Her eyes watered. "But I haven't lived like I believed it."

Isabelle pulled Brigette into her arms. "My sweet girl, none of us are perfect. We all sin each day. That's why we go to chapel services every day, so we can confess our sins and keep a clear conscience. We don't want unconfessed sin to block our path to God."

She clung to Isabelle and sniffled. "But what does all of this have to do with me and Daniel?"

"I'm getting to that. Do you remember the story of how King Nebuchadnezzar of Babylon captured Israel?"

"Some of it."

"The children of God had disobeyed Him over and over again. God had given them hundreds of chances to confess their sins and turn back to Him—to follow Him alone, but they refused. So, God raised up a pagan king, who didn't even serve the Living God, to punish His wayward children. They were taken captive for seventy years as punishment. You see, God will bring about His will for His children in whatever way He deems best—even to use an unbelieving king. During those seventy years His people realized that Jehovah God was the one true God. They repented and were allowed to return home to Jerusalem."

Brigette rolled out of Isabelle's arms onto the bed. Staring at the ceiling, she rubbed her stomach. "I still don't see how this pertains to me."

At the moment when Isabelle turned on her side to continue talking to Brigette, William began to cry.

"Stay here while I get William." Isabelle walked over to the cradle and changed William's nappy. "Come, my sweet. 'Tis time for your meal." She got back into bed to breastfeed her son.

When Brigette comprehended what Isabelle was doing, she

175

twisted to her side away from her sister-in-law. She didn't want to see Isabelle feeding William, but she could still hear it. *Oh, me.*

"Now, where was I?"

"I hope you are about to explain how I fit into this lengthy discussion about creation."

Touching Brigette's shoulder, Isabelle said, "You do make me smile. I have missed you so much."

Brigette deemed it safe to lie on her back as long as she didn't watch Isabelle and William. With their hips touching one another, somehow it comforted her.

"Just as God used King Nebuchadnezzar to restore His people back to Himself, I believe that God used Nicolas to push you out of the nest. God knew you wouldn't leave here unless forced much like a mother bird shoving her babies out. Otherwise, they would never learn to fly."

"You mean you believe God planned for me to marry and since I wouldn't do it, He used Nicolas to make me?"

"Yes, I do."

Brigette lay there considering all that Isabelle had expressed. She didn't want it to be true, but it made sense when Isabelle told it. If God truly wanted her wed, then what else did He want for her?

"Why do you believe God wants me married to Daniel?"

"I can't possibly know what God has in store for you, but I know that it is for your good. It tells me that in the Bible. There is a verse in Jeremiah when he spoke to the Israelites while they were still captives in Babylon. It says, '*For I know the thoughts that I think toward you, saith the Lord, thoughts of peace and not of evil, to give you an expected end.*' Or in other words, to give a hope. God wants nothing but good for you, little sister."

"It doesn't feel like it's for my good. It's more like a hardship filled with woe."

"There are times when we are put through trials. God uses those times to position us for greater blessings than we can imagine. He will use those trials and suffering for our benefit. I compare it to the silversmith who uses fire to refine his silver and make it usable.

God refines His children to make us more like Him."

"I don't want to go through a fire." Brigette pouted. Her eyes met Isabelle's and she grinned. "But I wouldn't mind if God ran Nicolas through hot flames."

Chapter Twenty-Four

Daniel's head pounded as he came out of the royal meeting. At one point, he believed Clans Stewart and Kennedy were going to draw swords against Lord Hamilton and Lord Montgomery. If it had been left to him, he would have knocked them all in the head with the hilt of his sword. Thankfully, King James used his diplomacy and brought all into a tentative agreement about reivers and uprisings against one another.

After checking with his three men, Daniel concluded a walk in the moonlight might sooth his throbbing head. He walked past the grand hall filled with snoring men on pallets and went straight for the doorway to the outdoor court. After stepping outside, he took a deep breath of the crisp air and filled his lungs full. As he slowly released it, the tension ebbed from his shoulders.

He gazed at the bright stars winking at him. What was Brigette doing? Did she watch the twinkling stars and miss him? Did she regret her recent actions toward him? The tension began to return the longer he reflected on his wife. A stroll through the gardens would clear his mind. Whistling a tuneless song, he sauntered down the steps and turned left for the gardens. Torches on poles lit his way as he walked through the maze of hedges and flowers.

Always aware that danger could be lurking about, his hand never left the handle of his sword. The farther he went from the castle, the more peaceful the night became. Rustling of animals and insects buzzing were his companions. At one point, an unusual sound caught his ear. He stopped whistling and stood unmoving, listening. It sounded more like a struggle.

Running back through the hedges would take too long, and he might lose the location of where the sound originated. Instead, he drew his sword and cut his way through the thick hedge just enough to see in both directions. Nothing. He pushed his way through the shrubbery into the next lane of the maze. Turning his head one way and then the other, it sounded again. Someone was in distress.

Running down the grassy row, he paused at the end to listen again. Certain of the location, he sprinted off with his sword held at ready.

A woman's voice protested. "Stop this at once, I tell you." A moan with crunching followed.

Daniel called out, "What are you about?"

When his voice floated through the night, a scream erupted, and someone crashed through the bushes. Pounding feet ensued. His heart raced as he tracked the sound.

"Help me!"

"Keep speaking so I can find you in this maze of brush," Daniel yelled. He was met with whimpering, but it was enough. There sprawled on the lawn was Lady Scott. He ran to her side to find her lip bleeding and a cut above her eye.

"Lady Scott, what has happened here? Are you greatly harmed?" He sheathed his sword and pulled out a cloth to dab her cuts.

"Oh, Daniel, I'm so glad you were here to scare off my attacker." Her horrified eyes assured him she was not acting.

"What are you doing out here alone?"

"First, help me up, and I'll explain all."

"Let's get you back inside where you will be safe, and then I'll hear your story." He lifted her under the arms to a standing position. "You tremble. Can you walk?"

"Yes, I believe so."

With his arm around her waist and one holding her arm, she

limped back toward the castle. "You mustn't tell anyone," she said with urgency. "My husband would blame me for being careless."

"I'm sure when he sees your distress, he would come to your aid."

She stopped walking and grabbed his arm. "No, I tell you. He would not understand."

The fear in her eyes concerned him. "As you wish."

Daniel remembered an entrance near the kitchens that had a back stairway to the second floor. Used by servants, they should enter undetected. While in the gardens, he kept them in the shadows, so no one watching out the windows from above could see their movements. Before entering, Daniel peeked inside the door to find the kitchens empty.

"Come. The way is clear," he whispered. Once inside, Daniel perched Millicent on a stool and got a wet cloth for her face. "Here, let me wipe away the blood."

She flinched each time he touched her. "Ouch. You are hurting me."

"Please excuse my rough handling. I'm not used to tending delicate women."

She snatched the cloth from his hand. "I'll do it myself. Are you this rough with your wife?"

Daniel let that question die away. He didn't need yet another person telling him how to treat his wife.

"You will have a bruise above your eye and a swollen lip in the morning. Now tell me why you were in the gardens alone this late in the evening."

"I wasn't alone. You were there," she drawled as her finger slid along his arm.

Daniel snatched his arm away. "Tell me of your attack."

She rolled her eyes and blew her breath out through her pouty lips. "I waited in the shadows outside the war room until your meeting concluded. When I was about to make myself known to my husband, he walked into the grand hall and plopped onto a pallet by some filthy knights." She blinked several times. "I had

181

been rejected, yet again." She shrugged one shoulder. "So, I followed you into the hedges."

He frowned. "I didn't see you."

"That was obvious when I tried to get your attention and you kept walking … rather briskly, I might add. I slowed my pace and started back the way I had come. When I came around a corner, a man grabbed me from behind. He put his grimy hand over my mouth and dragged me down another Labyrinth. He had ill intentions in mind, of that I am certain."

"Let's get you back to your room before we are discovered. This would not go well for either of us. In the future, stay in your room when night falls. Not all men are noble."

Daniel found a candle on the chopping block and used the smoldering wood in the fire pit to light it. He assisted Millicent off her stool and led her up the back stairs. The dark passageway appeared deserted. Once arriving at her room, he searched it before allowing her to enter for the night.

"You should be safe. Latch the door for the remainder of the night if you are certain Lord Scott will not be returning."

"He will not." She touched his arm when he turned to leave. "Thank you, kind sir, for coming to my aid. I'm forever in your debt."

He nodded and left with haste after hearing her bolt the door. Making his way to the kitchens, Daniel went back to the maze to see if he could find anyone prowling about. Of course, the perpetrator was long gone.

Women baffled him. Do they not see the danger that lurks in the dark of night? Shaking his head in disbelief, surely, Lady Scott had more sense? He trusted that Brigette would not be so foolish. After spending time in Millicent's presence, he was grateful that Brigette had become his wife. She might be young, but she had intelligence.

After his rescue of Millicent, not only did his heart throb in his head, but his insides coiled tight. Since his stroll outside had turned out less than desirable, he elected to check in with Iain before turning in for the night. The guard at the rear of the castle allowed him to depart through the postern gate if he returned within the hour.

Once he reached the area of tents, he strolled through the middle of the camp instead of walking the perimeter. He didn't want to be mistaken for an enemy. He picked his way over snoring men. The few men left to guard the camps permitted his passage.

Upon reaching his camp, he found Iain waiting up. "Iain, why are ye the one guarding the camp?"

"I'm awaiting yer word."

Daniel chastised himself. He had specifically told Iain he would check with him before retiring for the night. Securing Lady Scott's safety addled him.

"Please forgive the lateness of the hour. I was detained." Both men sat on logs around the smoldering campfire. "How goes the day?"

"Naught mooch to tell. Two men from Clan Spaulding tried to birth a fight, but when Dand stood up, they took their sairy selves away." He grinned. "Ye know Dand. He looks like a Balloch."

Daniel smiled at the picture. Dand was not his best warrior, but his size caused most men to run in fright. "Our assembly went well. With any luck, we'll be on our way home in another day or two."

"Canna be too soon," Iain said.

"I deem it best ye stay with the men, Iain. Ye are my best mon at keeping the peace. What say ye?"

"Thank ye for yer faith in me. I'm pleased to stay. Better than what ye are about."

"Iain, ye have no idea the true words ye speak." Daniel smacked Iain's shoulder as he stood to his feet. "I must return."

"Aye, my lord. Until the morrow."

As Daniel made his way back toward the castle, he remembered how fortunate he was to have loyal men in his service. Niall and Iain were two of his best but not to forget Kenneth, Ross, Mungo and countless others. Anyone of his men would come to his clan's aid even if it meant forfeiting their lives. Dwelling on those gratifying reminders was enough to alleviate his sore head. If only the difficulties with Brigette were as easy to solve.

When Daniel squeezed through the rusty postern gate, the original guard met him and allowed him safe entry. "Be on yer guard, m' lord. I've 'eard mischief is afoot this verra night."

"Thank you for the warning. It's never a good thing when you have this many pompous men in one place, aye?" Daniel replied with a grin.

"Aye, m' lord. 'Tis not." Shaking his head, the guard walked away chuckling.

Daniel blew out a snort relieved his rescue of Lady Scott had not circulated. That bit of information could cause an uproar between the Scotts and the McKinnons.

Daniel trudged up the back stairs so as not to attract undo attention of his late-night prowling. He rubbed the back of his neck—so weary. As he approached his room, he found one of his men propped next to his door, asleep. His tread was light as he eased past Alain and closed his door. Odd that Alain didn't stir. He must have been exhausted or too much drink.

When he walked into the center of the room, he detected a presence. He whipped out his dagger and hunkered low as he scanned the darkened room. With all his senses on alert, he identified breathing.

"Make yourself known for I hear your loud breathing." Waiting, his eyes continued to roam. Whoever had crept into his room was no warrior worth his salt—too noisy.

"'Tis me."

"Millicent?"

She peered from behind the bed curtains. "Yes."

"What the devil?"

When her feet touched the floor, Daniel's eyes grew round. The light from the low-burning fire cut through her sheer bed clothes! He whipped his face to the side.

"What are you doing in here," he hissed. With his eyes averted, her rose petal scent alerted him to her approach.

"I hoped you wouldn't mind keeping a lonesome friend company for the night," she said in a sultry voice.

Daniel spun around giving his back to her. "You cannot be here. Your husband ..."

She pressed her body against his back and wrapped her arms around him. He sucked in a quick breath from the warmth and caress of her body. His eyes drifted shut.

I sense that great evil will pass yer way tonight. Ye must run from it. Run from it.

Her hands slid up his chest and were headed back down when he stilled them with his own. Tancred's words rang loud. He had to remove himself at once. He pulled her arms from around him and stepped away. Grabbing a blanket from the bed, he threw it around her shoulders.

"This will not happen. We both repeated sacred vows that must not be cast aside."

"Our marriage vows have nothing to do with having a bit of pleasure with another." She moved toward him holding the blanket with a loose grip.

Run.

"Stop this attack. I will not be unfaithful to my wife. You must leave before you are discovered."

She dipped her head and peeked upward through her lashes. "You don't sound too convincing." Her pout broke into a sly smile.

He needed to turn aside from her seductive advance. "What did you do to Alain?"

"Oh, he was an easy mark. With a few sweet smiles and perfectly placed touches, he was eager to drink from the cup I offered. It might have had a wee bit of sleeping potion in it."

This caused his anger to flare. His grip was tight when he grabbed her arms. "You had better pray no harm comes to Alain."

"No need for concern. He should wake in a few hours with no ill effects."

Nose to nose, neither was ready to relent.

"Your hold is too tight. Free me at once," she snapped.

Daniel gave a slight shove when he released her. He snatched his belongings folded on the chest and stuffed them in his saddle bags.

"You may have this room."

"Surely, you jest? You would dismiss my proposal as if I were rubbish?" She dropped the blanket to the floor to give him full view of all she had to offer.

Daniel pointed at her, "Dinna come near … not now nor in the future." He threw his bags over his shoulder and stalked out the door.

Chapter Twenty-Five

"Mither, Henry kens of some pups," William exclaimed. "Can I hae one?"

"First, it's 'knows' instead of 'kens.' Can I have one? Try saying it again."

"Henry kn-o-ws of some puppies," William repeated. "Can I hae one?"

"That's a great start. I'll have you talking like me in no time. And yes, let's take a gander at those puppies. Lead the way."

William grabbed her hand and tried to run while pulling her along. His infectious enthusiasm made her laugh as she ran to keep step with him.

She giggled. "Slow down, before I trip on my dress."

They passed Phillip in the hallway. "What is all the excitement about?"

"William has found a puppy he would like to take home. I am going to view them and see if we can agree on the one he should choose. Join us?"

William came to a quick stop. "Can Feelapa come too?"

Phillip laughed. "Let me check with Abigail first."

Brigette and William waited outside of Phillip and Abigail's bedchamber. "Her name is Philippa," Brigette corrected.

"That's 'ard to say." She watched as his little face scrunched in thought. "I will call her, Pippa."

187

"Pippa?" Brigette asked.

"Aye, Pippa. That is better." He gave her a sweet smile. "And she's quite bonnie."

"Yes, she is a beautiful baby girl."

Phillip emerged from the room cuddling his daughter. "Speaking of a beautiful baby girl, we will join you as you choose your first puppy. Mayhap you can give her suggestions for her first puppy."

As they proceeded down the passageway, Brigette said, "William concluded Philippa is too hard for him to say. He has chosen to call her Pippa. What think you of that, my brother?"

Phillip smiled at William. "I think Pippa is a wonderful name for my little daughter."

It pleased Brigette when her brother accepted William's new name for the baby. She was especially thankful that Phillip had been kind toward her son. At least William would have some pleasant experiences while at Fairwick castle and see that not all of her kin were rude.

When they got outside, William met Henry. They both ran toward the back stables allowing Phillip and Brigette some time alone. Their pace slowed, and Phillip glanced sideways at her.

"How are you, sister?"

She inhaled a deep breath of the fresh air that smelled like home and gazed at all that had once been so familiar. A small smile crossed her lips. "I'm learning to adapt."

With Philippa in one arm, he put his other arm around Brigette's shoulders as they walked on in silence.

Once entering the barn, it was not hard to locate the boys. Their voices echoed with each passionate expression. "Choose that one," Henry suggested. "It's a boy."

"I'm not sure I want a boy. Look at that one," William said.

Brigette and Phillip leaned an arm on the top of the stable door of an empty stall where the mother dog lay with her puppies. "Look, but don't touch them," she murmured not wanting to upset the mother. "Which one do you like, William?"

"I canna decide. Can I hae more than one?" he asked hopeful.

"No." She gentled her voice. "We want your father to be surprised not shocked when he comes home."

"Aye, mither."

While the boys discussed which pup was perfect, Phillip said, "William seems to have accepted you as his mother easily enough."

A smile spread across her face. "Yes. He is the one pleasing gift I received in this marriage arrangement. And he is so easy to love." She removed her arm and turned toward Phillip. "He loves me with no conditions. How could I want anything more?"

Phillip blanched at her remark. "Brigette, I know we made some mistakes with your upbringing. And we might not have handled your betrothal in the best way, but we do love you," he said with beseeching eyes.

Brigette stared into her brother's imploring eyes. It seemed he wanted her to absolve him of all guilt that he and the other two brothers possessed because of their neglect of her. Could she forgive the three after all she had endured? Phillip was the sensitive brother that had tried to care for her. Nicolas and Thomas had shoved her off on servants.

She stared unblinking. "Are you asking for my forgiveness?"

Phillip shifted Philippa to the other arm, his red-rimmed eyes held unshed tears. "Yes, Brigette, I am asking that you forgive me for not raising you like a parent should." Shaking his head, "I didn't know what to do with you. I'm sorry for my inattentiveness. Will you forgive me?"

As she regarded her oldest brother's face, he was not to blame for her terrible childhood. Her middle brother, Nicolas, had been the one in charge of her after Phillip suffered a near death incident. Phillip had struggled to overcome his injuries and had no time to raise a little sister. Yet, he had been quick to give her a smile or a hug when needed.

With sadness, she said, "Yes, Phillip. I can forgive you because you showed me love even when I didn't deserve it."

He placed his hand on her arm. "Thank you," he whispered.

189

"As I attempt to care and cherish Philippa, it's obvious to me how we failed you. I know I cannot replace those years for you, but I hope, in time, your life with Daniel and William will be rich with love and acceptance."

"Mither, can Pippa see ma new puppy?"

Brigette was thankful she didn't have to respond to Phillip's last statement. How could she explain that her husband didn't want her either? That only William accepted her.

"Aye, my love."

Phillip stepped into the stall and squatted so Philippa could see the boys and pups. She cooed and giggled as her body squirmed trying to get down.

William's gaze shifted from the pups to Philippa. While kneeling in the straw, he crawled over to her. "Pippa, do ye see the pups?" He kissed her pudgy hand. He looked at Brigette. "Mither can we take Pippa home, too?"

Phillip frowned, but Brigette found his question endearing. "No, my sweet. Pippa must stay here with her mother and father. Perhaps one day she will visit us in Scotland. Would you like that?"

He wore a huge grin. "Aye."

As the puppies yelped and jumped around in the straw, Brigette asked, "Which pup will be yours to take home?"

"I want the orange and white one."

"Oh, what made you choose that one out of all these pups?" Phillip asked.

"The white is like mither's hair and the orange is like Pippa's hair."

"It's a girl," Phillip announced after turning the pup over.

"How sweet," Brigette said to William. "But you must leave her in the barn until we are ready to depart. She will want to spend time with her mother before leaving."

"Aye, mither. Can I play with Henry?"

"Yes, but stay inside the castle walls."

"Aye." The boys left the stall and dashed out of the barn laughing and pushing as they ran.

"He seems quite smitten with Philippa," Brigette remarked.

"I have much to worry about. She's not even one year old and boys are giving her the once over." Phillip came out and closed the stall door.

They walked toward the barn door, "Now that William has chosen a puppy, we will be headed home on the morrow."

"Why are you leaving so soon? Two days is not long enough."

"Nicolas and Thomas do not want me here. Their hostility is unmistakable making it hard for me to breathe." She peeked over at Phillip. "I need to be home when my husband returns from his travels with the king. He would not be pleased to find us gone when he will be expecting a festive homecoming. I have accomplished what I set out to do. I visited with Isabelle, got to hold baby William, spent time with Philippa and picked a puppy. My tasks are complete."

Phillip observed her. "In such a short time, I see before me a lady. No longer the insecure young girl that left here on her wedding day, but a mature wife and mother. I'm proud of you, my sister."

"Thank you, Phillip." She chuckled. "It's good to know that I can still fool you when I put my mind to it."

Taking her hand, Phillip squeezed it. "Come and see Abigail tonight. She desires to talk with you but fears you might reject her invitation. She, too, is keenly aware of her ill treatment of you and wishes to gain your forgiveness."

"Of course. I'll come after the evening meal." Brigette walked beside Phillip as if she fit in the family for the first time in her life. No longer was she the little sister that manipulated her siblings with her childish theatrics, but one who was of equal standing. Her sunnier heart warmed her thoughts about the future.

191

Chapter Twenty-Six

"William, you may play outside with Henry, Patrick and Pierson while I say my farewells to Isabelle." He ran to hug her leg and dashed out the door without a word. Knowing that Ross would keep him safe allowed her the freedom to do as she pleased.

"Mungo, please take our baggage to the wagon. I will make a final visit with Isabelle, and then I will join you in the courtyard. Please make sure we have ample food for our journey. I have already spoken with their cook and the provisions should be waiting for you in the kitchens."

She watched her gentle giant lift their heavy gear without any strain and depart to do her bidding. What a treasure Fiona had in her husband ... so strong and mild tempered. Was Daniel those things too? Had she failed to see his chivalrous temperament because of her tainted view of men?

Now was not the time for such questions. She sipped some water hoping to settle her upset constitution and headed toward Isabelle's room. Ever since she had resumed painting, her appetite had waned. Perhaps Isabelle would have a solution to her dilemma since she was versed in herb concoctions. She remembered how Isabelle had mixed her a drink to alleviate her belly pain when she thought she had been dying. Brigette chuckled at the memory.

She slowed her pace to a stop as she came to the main corridor leading to the master bedchamber. The passageway was empty of anyone except her. She let her eyes scan the décor along the long hallway. Urns, lampstands, ancestry armor, and a few tapestries lent themselves to a homey feel, one she hadn't known she would miss until it was too late.

Even though her tread was heavy, she plodded on. Each doorway she happened upon, she viewed the room to capture a last image of her family home. In a short time, she reached her destination and knocked before she became too melancholy.

"Enter," Isabelle said.

Brigette peeked around the doorway. "'Tis me."

"Oh, Brigette, I'm so delighted you have come to see us this fine morning."

After a quick inspection of the room, Brigette assessed that Nicolas was not present. Such a relief. With a smile affixed to her face, she went to the bed and kissed William and Isabelle.

"You two look splendid."

"Sit, sit. Nicolas reported you are leaving us this morning. Tell me it isn't so."

"Yes. We must arrive home before Daniel returns to find us missing." She sat in the chair closest to the bed.

"We've not been able to spend ample time together."

"You have much to do with caring for my sweet nephew and recovering from his birth. Rest is what you require not conversing with me. There will be another time, I'm sure." She balanced on the edge of the chair with hands clasped in her lap and doubted her own words.

Isabelle studied her. "You appear pale this morning. Are you ill?"

Brigette looked away wondering if she should bother Isabelle with her malady. Nicolas would be furious if she caused Isabelle any distress. When she decided to pretend to be in fine health, her stomach lurched. She swallowed hard to keep her meal in place.

"Well ... since you have broached the subject, I did want to ask if you had some herbs that might settle my stomach. It has been circling about when I first rise in the morning. It started when I commenced painting again. The smell of the dyes and henna were quite strong and made my belly ill, but I have endured."

Isabelle sat straight up and laid William in the middle of the mattress. She swung her legs over the side of the bed and clasped Brigette's hands in her own. "When did you start painting?"

Brigette tilted her head upward. Her nose scrunched as she remembered back. "It's been about six weeks or more I suppose. Why?"

"Are you ill all day or just in the morning?"

"It's always in the morning because I don't paint after the midday meal. I spend that time playing with William. My stomach settles once I'm breathing fresh air."

"Do you remember when you came to me and expressed you were dying?"

Brigette rolled her eyes and felt her face flush. "Yes. That was a terrible awaking. I had no idea a woman would go through that every month."

"I mixed herbs to help with the cramping. Remember?"

"Of course. It was a wonderful remedy. I recorded on parchment so I could take it with me."

"Have you had to mix my potion since you married?"

Brigette grew quiet. "No ... no I haven't. Isn't that odd?"

"No, Brigette, it's not odd. You aren't ill from the paint smell. You are going to have a babe."

Brigette's eyes grew large with fright. She jerked her hands free and stood to her feet. "No, I'm not. Why are you trying to frighten me right before my departure?"

Isabelle pushed off the bed and stood before her. "Oh, my sweet Brigette. Yes, you will have a baby in about seven months based on your calculations."

The trembling started in her head and traveled to her legs. She reached back with one hand to grab the chair as she sank into it. "This can't be," she whispered. "No, no, no! I've slept in another room for weeks. It can't be true."

Isabelle eased back to sit on the edge of the bed. William remained right where she had laid him. He slept without a care of what was happening around him.

"It's possible I'm mistaken. Missing your monthly courses could be from the misery you have undergone the last few months. Or … I could be correct."

Brigette slumped against her chair. "Of course, that's it. I've been in great distress these last several months with the forced marriage and living in Scotland with a husband I didn't want. That has caused my body to be out of sorts." She perked up and smiled. "In addition, you aren't yourself since having a baby. I'm sure you've misjudged the signs."

"Let me tell you a few things just in case I'm correct. Humor me?"

Reasoning that Isabelle had misread her symptoms, she remained open-minded to mollify Isabelle. "Carry on."

"I will send some of my special herbs that will alleviate your sour stomach with directions on how they should be dispensed. You must eat less greasy food. It's best to eat fresh fruits, roasted meat, and fresh vegetables with little added to flavor them. It might not satisfy your palate, but trust me, your unhappy belly will thank you."

"That won't be hard to do. I'm not too fond of Scottish fare."

"If this continues for many more weeks, you must tell Daniel."

Brigette frowned. She was not pleased with this line of discussion. "I will tell him if the need arises. Thank you for helping with my queasiness." She silently prayed that Isabelle was wrong about a babe.

Isabelle placed her hand on Brigette's knee. "Remember, Brigette, if you are indeed with child, it's part of God's plan for you. I have four words I like to repeat to myself when troubles come my way: *Thy Will Be Done*. God is in control even in our sufferings. He has a purpose for the pain and will work out something good for you in the process. You mustn't give into despair. Promise me?"

Brigette had to smile. Isabelle wanted to mother her even though she was a woman full grown with a husband and son of her own. It was Isabelle's way, and she was content with it.

"I promise not to give in to despair," she repeated hoping if the need arose, she would be true to the promise.

Isabelle went to her cabinet of healing herbs and portioned out some in small bottles for easy travel. While she was busy, Brigette picked up William and snuggled him close. He smelled so uniquely baby, and it was nice. She sang a soft lullaby and ended it with a kiss to his cheek. She whispered, "I hope you are nothing like your father."

"Here they are. Be careful with them." She removed William from Brigette's arms and gave her a sideways hug. "I will long for you until we meet again. Have a care."

"Until then. I love you, Isabelle."

"As I love you, my Brigette."

Brigette made a hasty exit before she gushed as a waterfall. She didn't want her son alarmed by her red eyes and running nose. She dashed down the hallway and the curved stairway but skidded to a halt at the bottom. There stood Nicolas and Thomas. Glory be her suffering knew no bounds. She tried to brush past them, but it was not to be.

"Safe travels," Nicolas said.

Thomas stood off to the side and nodded his head as if in agreement.

Brigette couldn't contain herself. She squinted her eyes, and then presented a smug face. Without a word, she walked outside and left them wondering what she was about. Once her back was to her brothers, a wide grin graced her face.

"Mither, I hae been waiting overlong."

"Let's be away, shall we?"

Mungo assisted Brigette onto the wagon seat while William and Clara sat in the back with his new puppy. They had fresh hay piled high for a comfortable ride home. There was a loose cord tied to the pup's neck to keep her better contained. Brigette held a regal posture with her face averted from the keep steps. There would be no last waves or nods to her dreadful brothers. She had made peace with Phillip and Abigail, and that's all that was required.

197

Half of her men rode before the wagon, and the other half guarded her back as they journeyed home. The sunrise graced the sky burning a brilliant pink and yellow. A beautiful sight.

Brigette had been glad to hurry out of the gates. Her stomach spun, and she didn't know how long her morning meal might stay put. What if Isabelle was correct, and there was a babe growing inside? The thought alone made her cringe. It wasn't long before they had to stop.

After her heaving subsided, she emerged from behind the bushes. Clara met her with a wet cloth and a cup of cool water. "Haur, m' lady."

"Thank you, Clara. Do you mind riding on the seat with Kenneth and letting me lie in the wagon bed?"

"Oh no, miss. Ye need some rest, ye do."

Brigette wasn't sure rest would cure what ailed her but was grateful to stretch out on the soft hay. From her previous experience, the queasiness would soon pass. Clara held the wiggling pup in her lap while William was happy to ride pillion with Ross.

Before pulling out, Niall came alongside the wagon. "Lady McKinnon, can ye stand a quicker pace?"

"Yes, Niall. I'll signal if we need to slow down." She moaned. Oh, how her stomach rolled. To be home snug in her bed would be blissful. She shielded her eyes with her arm and drifted into a fitful sleep.

After traveling an hour, Niall rode from the front of the sentry to where Mungo rode beside the wagon. "Is Lady McKinnon asleep?"

Mungo gave a slight nod.

"We will soon be approaching the shaded pathway. I dinna wish to tarry there. 'Tis a good place to harbor ruffians. So, when we enter, we will make haste."

Brigette awoke at the lurch of the wagon. She roused enough to see the canopy of trees speeding by. Mercifully, her stomach was settled because she was being jostled each time the wagon wheels found a hole. She struggled to sit up but wobbled about as the wagon pitched to and fro.

"Clara, what is amiss?"

"'Tis naught to be concerned. Niall is in a hurry."

Brigette grabbed the sides of the wagon to keep from hurling out to the road. "Dear, me, tell him to slow down."

No sooner had the words taken flight, a battle cry arose that caused the hair on her neck to stand. She had never experienced such a noise until coming to Scotland. The Scottish men were heathens to be sure.

"Clara, what is happening?" She tried to twist around but could not hold her position. "William? Where is William?" she screamed.

Clara shrieked as the wagon ran off the road, tipped on two wheels and bounced to a stop. Brigette's fear rose in her throat with a cry for help. Mungo was nowhere to be seen, nor could she spot Ross and William. When she pulled herself to a sitting position, a man grabbed her from behind and hauled her out of the wagon.

His dreadful odor was nothing she had smelled before. She tried to see him, but to no avail. The constriction of her chest grew tighter as she recognized he was not one of her men. She saw objects falling from the trees and trapping her guardians in a mangle of netting.

"Mungo!" she screamed right before a hood covered her head. Her struggles to be free were met with wicked laughter.

"Ye will nay escape."

With her arms pinned to her sides by the man's tight hold around her body and no sight, it put her at a terrible disadvantage. She squirmed and thrashed with her legs.

"Release me at once," she demanded. "Where is my son? Please don't hurt him. He's but a lad," she cried.

She found the raised part of the saddle and clung to it for fear of falling from the galloping horse. "Who are you? Why have you done this despicable thing?"

Each of her questions met silence as they continued to ride. Trees and brush smacked against her head as the rider weaved through the forest. Her fear gave way to soundless tears. From what she saw, her men had been rendered powerless with those nets. They would not be rescuing her.

Lord God, Almighty, help me!

Chapter Twenty-Seven

By the time Daniel returned to the campsite, a few hours remained before sunrise. Deciding to rest outside the tent, he built up the cooking fire and pulled a seat close by. His emotions jumped from annoyance to relief to fury. Why had he been surprised at the depth of depravity to which Millicent had stooped? She had been conniving when he and Anna had first met her. Without a doubt, she had gotten worse after she married old man Scott.

He scrubbed his face with his hand before pinching the bridge of his nose. What scared him most was his own reaction to her seduction. Would he have succumbed if Tancred hadn't warned him about evil lurking about? Staring into the fire, with a quick jerk, he straightened. Had Tancred put Millicent up to the invitation? Since Tancred was privy to the coming wickedness, it made sense. Daniel continued to stew over the puzzle until his men stirred.

Iain lifted open the tent flap to find Daniel sitting by the fire. "M' Lord, what brings ye oot this early morn?"

"I dinna sleep at the castle last night. 'Twas some mischief afoot of which I wanted no part."

Iain smiled. "Sairy to hear it. A meal is what every mon needs to put 'im to rights." He roused the other men to forage for food. They carried their bows and arrows in hopes of bringing back squirrel or rabbit. In the meantime, Iain laid out a platter of cheese and bread for his lord. "Do ye fancy some oats? I can make ye some pottage."

Daniel looked up as if coming out of a daze. "I'm sairy?"

"Would ye like some pottage?"

"Oh. Nay. This cheese is enough for now."

"Did ye hae a bad night?" a voice asked from behind him.

Daniel jerked around to find Tancred standing at his back. How had he approached without him being aware?

"Tancred." Furious, Daniel rose and grabbed him by his breastplate causing him to stumble. "You knew about my midnight encounter. Are you responsible for putting her up to it?"

Tancred fell to one knee when Daniel released him.

"No, my lord. I sense things before they happen." He struggled to right himself, but the heavy armor kept him rooted.

There was no help for it, Daniel had to assist Tancred or watch the old man thrash about. Needless to say, he didn't want his men to take notice of him shoving an old warrior to his knees. He caught hold of Tancred's arm and pulled him to the vacant log.

"Sit here, old man." Daniel had some remorse for his actions toward the ancient warrior. He would have run a man through if they had treated his grandfather with such disrespect.

"Please forgive my rough handling. I'm quite vexed by the whole ordeal."

Tancred didn't answer. He laid aside his helmet and his sword belt as was his usual sequence. He removed a cloth from his pocket and wiped his sweaty face. "'Tis of no consequence. I hae more to say."

Daniel dreaded what Tancred might reveal this time. He had never disclosed anything good.

"I ran as you suggested," Daniel said trying to lighten his own mood. "What words of wisdom will you impart this morn?"

"'Tis nay good."

Daniel hovered over Tancred. "Oot with it."

"I sense a great disturbance. I dinna know what." Regret filtered through his words.

Daniel sank to the edge of the log. "What am I to do?"

"Go home now. Do not delay."

At that moment some of his men returned with meat to cook for their morning meal. Daniel helped Tancred to his feet and tugged him away from their hearing.

"Did one of my clan meet with tragedy? Is someone dead?" he demanded with urgency.

"I dinna know. I'm sairy. God dinna reveal all to me."

"So, you are a prophet?"

"I'm juist one of God's messengers."

Daniel didn't know what to believe about Tancred. However, he did know that Tancred had been right about the evil he encountered last night. Could he be telling the truth now? Could one of his family be in great danger? His stomach roiled. He needed to see if the man had other insights before letting him escape.

"Share our meal with us?"

"Thank ye, m' lord. I am grateful for the offer."

As Daniel's men prepared the meat, Tancred settled on the log furthest from the fire and rested. Daniel could see the sag in the old warrior's shoulders as if a great weight pushed them down. Was he a mad man, or truly a messenger from God? He carried the cheese over and offered some to Tancred.

"Thank ye, m' lord." He lifted a small piece, but before placing it to his lips, he turned to Daniel who was squatted near him. His boney fingers gripped Daniel's arm. "Ye need to forgive."

A jolt shot up Daniel's arm causing him to drop the platter of food. His teeth clinched. "What are ye referring to?"

"I no naught, but ye know. Of this, I am sure. God hath good for ye if ye but obey Him."

Once again Tancred's words mesmerized Daniel even though the old man talked in riddles. "Who are you? And why have you chosen me to harass?"

His old eyes focused over Daniel's shoulder. "Someone is coming far ye. Beware, all is not as it appears." His hand slid from

Daniel's arm and hit the log with a thud.

Who had Tancred seen? Daniel whipped his head around to see his men cleaning and cooking their meat. No one of surprise. Before he turned back to Tancred, a shout came from the road near their site. Daniel stood to see a rider approaching their encampment. The rider did not slow until he came to an abrupt halt at the edge of the tent that flew his clan's colors. The man jumped from his horse and removed his helmet. Daniel's legs nearly buckled.

"My Lord," Kenneth exclaimed. "Ye are needed at home. Post haste."

"Is William safe?" His son had always been his main concern ever since his first wife had died.

"Aye, my lord."

Relief soothed his soul. "Then what is amiss?" Daniel demanded.

"Lady Brigette has been captured," he blurted out.

Daniel hadn't given his wife a thought. He sank to his knees with his chin to his chest as horrific scenes played out in his mind with lightning speed. She was so young. She wouldn't know how to defend herself. He had left her vulnerable with his absence.

His men stood motionless as they watched their leader struggle with the dreadful news. Iain came to his aid. "M' lord, let me help ye up."

As Iain clutched his arm, Daniel stumbled to his feet. His men waited for him to give a command while his petrified state fed their fears. He turned to speak to Tancred. The man, his sword belt, and his helmet had all vanished in a matter of moments. Daniel glared at the empty log while his fury gained momentum over the injustice of life. He had wasted too much time with his indecisiveness. He needed to act.

"Iain, break camp and be ready to mount up within the hour. Kenneth, how long ago did this transpire?"

"Taday is day three. 'Twas hard to track ye."

"I must speak with the king. Be ready when I return."

Daniel's discussion with the king went as he had expected but with a twist. The king extended his consent to depart straightway and with God's speed. He even offered to send some men to aid in the search if needed, but it was his parting words that rang loud in Daniel's ears.

The king had told him he would pray for Brigette's safe return, and that God would work all things out for their good. Those had been similar words of Tancred, yet the king denied knowing anyone by that name.

Daniel hurried back to his men dismissing the peculiar happenings that had taken place while he had been in northeastern Scotland. He had no time to delve into the bizarre occurrences. His wife's life was in peril, and the fault was his to bear.

No words were spoken as he and his company of men rode hard until the noon hour. They had cut across pastureland to quicken their travels. When they happened upon a tree-lined stream, Daniel raised his hand. "We will stop here long enough to rest our horses and eat a quick repast."

The men dismounted and tended to their horses first. Iain took care of Daniel's horse while Daniel sought out Kenneth. "Kenneth, come with me. I will hear the whole of the tale." They found a grassy spot in the shade in which to converse.

"Whaur do ye wish me to start?"

"At the beginning."

"Lady McKinnon wished to visit Lady Fairwick to see the new babe. Niall advised agin it, but she insisted. Niall took twenty men to protect yer lady and wee William."

He gasped. "She had William with her?"

"Aye."

Daniel gritted his teeth. "Continue."

"All was weel until our return. M' lady was ill."

Daniel's brows met between his eyes. "What kind of illness?"

"We made many a stoop for her to retch, my lord. She had to lay in the wagon bed. William rode with Ross. Clara and the new pup sat beside me on the wagon bench."

"What new pup?" Daniel asked with exasperation. "Oh, never

ye mind, tell the tale." He noticed the rest of his men came close to listen to the depressing account

"Niall made us pick oop speed when we came to the shaded pathway. He was afeared of ruffians and rightly so. That's where they attacked. We dinna see them in the treetops. They draped nets on us. All except Lady McKinnon. While me and Clara fought to be free, a mon grabbed yer lady and left with swiftness."

"What was their clan colors?"

"They wore nay colors."

Daniel bounded to his feet. "Do you have any information as to which direction they went or who they might be?"

"Nay, my lord." Kenneth rose to stand before his lord. He produced a lopsided grin. "But we captured one."

Daniel grabbed Kenneth by the arms. "Well, why didn't ye say so from the beginning? Let's be away." As Daniel mounted his war horse, he had renewed hope that Brigette would be found ... her condition at rescue is what haunted him.

Brigette's body trembled. She endured a lengthy horseback ride in the arms of a foul-smelling Scotsman who wouldn't tell her anything. Her mind whirled with possibilities, but none that made any sense. Once they arrived at their destination, her captor dragged her off the horse and led her up crumbling stone stairs. Without sight, she tripped hearing broken stones fall with each step. After stopping at the top of the stairway, he shoved her into a room and shut the door with a bang.

For several moments she stood still waiting for instructions, but none came. She removed the hood from her face and was met with near darkness. Light cut through the gloom from four small slits in the outside wall. It took a moment for her eyes to adjust to the dimness of the room but was then able to distinguish the furnishings.

To the left, an old collapsed fireplace empty of wood graced the wall. One broken wooden chair leaned in the corner near the window slit. Her eyes swept right and fixed on a rope bed with a straw mattress. Upon further inspection, she found the straw molded from age. Thick dust and dirt covered the stone floor. She picked her way to the arrow loop to peer outside. Her limited view revealed an unharvested field. From what she could discern, she was in a castle tower. That explained the small slits used for archers.

Torment plagued her all during the day. No one came to her room to offer food or drink. As the day turned to night, her fears multiplied. Not only did she fear her captors and what they might do to her, but she remained terrified of spiders that might crawl about unseen. She stood in the slash of moonlight until her legs became too weary to hold her. At that time her body inched down the wall until her backside plopped onto the floor.

With her dress wrapped tightly around her up-drawn knees, Brigette dozed. She awakened several times to mice scurrying across the floor. Her heart doubled in time from the fright of a creature running across her boots or crawling on her person. Dreading the day to come, she cried herself to sleep

.

Chapter Twenty-Eight

Daniel's party of men went without sleep in order to quicken their return home. Travel at night required torches to light their way, but they persisted onward. Their diligence was rewarded when the McKinnon castle came into view on the eve of the second day of their journey.

The illuminated sky from lighted torches across the parapet served as beacons to the weary travelers. At the sound of the trumpets heralding the homecoming of their laird and his men, Daniel's heart leapt in his chest. The pounding of his heart increased when they rode through the raised portcullis. Shouts and cheers arose from men lining the walls and encircling the courtyard. On the top keep step stood his son.

Daniel jumped to his feet when he pulled his horse to a hasty stop. Overcome with joy, he ran up the steps and snatched William in his arms. "William," he whispered as he breathed in the aroma of his son. He rubbed his face in his son's neck and held him tight.

"Papa! Mither has been taken!"

He shifted his son to one arm and stalked through the doors and into the great hall. "I will find yer mother. Of this, I promise."

"She screamed for help." He dipped his head and cried. "She needed ye, Papa." With arms wrapped around his father's neck, he buried his nose into his father's shoulder.

He rubbed his son's back. "I will make it right. You'll see. But I must set you aside so I can make my battle plans to save your mother. Alright?"

William lifted his troubled face and gave his father a quick kiss on his cheek. "Thank ye, Father."

Daniel was humbled by the faith his son placed in him—no doubt blind faith. He prayed he could fulfill his promise and that Brigette still lived.

He handed William over to Ross. "Men, let's eat our meal and talk of our strategy. Has Fairwick castle been alerted?"

Niall stepped forward. "Aye, my lord. Lord Nicolas said he and his men would be ready at yer command."

Daniel rubbed his hands together. "Good. Good. Now, tell me about the man you captured."

Several of the clan moved the tables and benches to form a square. The men sat around the outside of the tables so each could be seen and heard.

Niall began the tale. "As Kenneth doubtless told ye, we were ambushed. Nets were dropped from above. It was weel thought out. Nygell obtained freedom first. He was able to discharge an arrow that found a home in a mon's leg. When the mon tried to run, Mungo wrestled him to the ground. My lord, he worked here."

Daniel's gut wrenched. "He was one of our own?"

"He helped in the stables, m' lord," Niall continued, "but for a brief time. He goes by the name of Donald."

"Where is he now?"

"He's been in the oubliette for three days now," Nygell said. "We've kept him alive with some water and a bit of food."

Daniel shuddered at the mention of confinement in the oubliette. A deep, narrow hole with a trap door high above the prisoner's head. There was not enough room to turn around or sit. They had to stand the duration in total darkness. The one way out was a rope tied to their waist to haul them to the surface.

"Open the trap door enough to give him food and drink. I will speak to him within the half hour."

"Aye, my lord," Niall said. He left the room to prepare the prisoner.

210

"Once we know who we are dealing with and where we are headed, we will gather with Lord Fairwick's men. Iain, speak with Hamish. We need all available weapons not necessary to protect the castle. The rest of you, eat and get some rest. You will require sharp wits for this encounter."

Little talk transpired as the hungry men devoured their food. As Daniel allowed his mind to drift to Brigette and what she might have endured, his stomach churned. His food refused to be swallowed.

"Come, Iain." Wiping his hands, Daniel left the meal and headed toward the oubliette, a dreadful place for dreadful business.

Niall met Daniel and Iain in the passageway toward the oubliette. "He's crying like a babe to be released. Ye should be able to find out the truth."

"Thank you, Niall. Go and finish yer meal. Iain will accompany me. Oh, and send Kenneth with two pails of water with which to douse our foul-smelling prisoner."

"Aye, m' lord."

The only sound in the hallway was the echo of Daniel and Iain's boots as they clicked on the stone floor. The farther they got from the central hub of the castle, the dampness increased. They descended some back stairs and walked across a covered corridor to another small building. Daniel pulled open the heavy door and stepped into darkness.

"Bring the torch from the outside wall," he instructed Iain.

As the light cut through the blackness, Daniel knelt to open the trapdoor. He strained to lift the stone seal over the oubliette. The odious smell that wafted upward caused him to fall backward.

"Ech, the smell is repulsive."

"Aye," Iain said as he hid his nose in the crook of his arm.

"Bring the torch closer."

As the light traveled into the tunnel of darkness, a weak voice rose up. "Git me oot."

"Weel, now, Donald. I believe ye have some explaining to do," Daniel said as if he were in no hurry.

"I told yer mon, I canna reveal me master or I forfeit me life."

"And ye think I'll allow ye to live if ye refuse?" Daniel asked with deceptive calm.

"Ye're a mon of honor. Of this I ken. The master is nay of yer ilk. I beg ye."

"I lost my honor when ye took my wife. A name, mon or I'll leave ye here to rot." His voice ricocheted around the walls.

Donald whined. "Please?"

"Iain, replace the cover."

"Nay. Nay. I'll tell all if ye'll juist git me oot. Of this I swear!"

Kenneth slipped in with the two buckets of water. He set them near the open door to the building and stepped away with haste to wait in the corridor.

"Iain, light the other two torches on the wall, and then hand me the rope. Now, Donald, if I pull ye out and ye refuse to be forthright, I'll put ye back in the hole, but it'll be headfirst. Understand?"

"Aye! Git me oot!"

Iain dropped the looped rope over the edge. He inched the cord downward to avoid the bottom floor covered with human waste.

"Reach yer hands upward until ye touch the rope."

When Donald had placed the twine around his waist, he gave a slight tug to signal the men. The remainder of the rope was attached around an iron pulley system anchored in the wall. Daniel and Iain positioned themselves on either side of the two-handed crank and began the slow process of reeling him upward. The closer he came to the opening, the stronger the stench.

"Kenneth, get back in here and be ready to douse our nasty hostage," Daniel grunted.

Kenneth eased inside and pinched his nose while gagging. Donald's bloody hands grabbed the stone lip around the edge of the opening before his head came into view. With one last full crank turn, the upper half of Donald's body sprawled across the floor.

"Slither on up, ye snake and stand ready for yer bath," Daniel snapped. Gone was his diplomacy. He needed quick answers.

Every minute spent prying out the full account of his wife's abduction was another moment she had to endure her treacherous ordeal.

The three men watched as Donald struggled to stand. No doubt, weak from lack of proper nourishment and from standing with a punctured thigh for two days. Kenneth poured one full pail over his head, but it didn't touch his filth. After the second bucket splashed over him, Daniel said, "Remove yer disgusting clothes and yer shoes." He turned to Kenneth. "Hurry and gather men's clothes from the discarded pile in the rear of the kitchens. The ones I keep on hand for orphans and the deprived."

"Aye, m' lord."

"And be quick about it!"

Donald shivered.

"Get yer clothes off, now!"

Donald jerked into action at the sound of Daniel's angry voice. His hands shook as he tried to discard his ragged clothing. At one point he wobbled. He cried out in pain when his leg buckled under him, and he crashed to his knees.

"Stop yer howling." Daniel gritted his teeth. "Yer pain is nothing compared to what ye will suffer if ye don't divulge all ye know with haste."

By the time Donald stood quivering from his nakedness, Kenneth dashed in with a pair of trousers and a torn shirt. "Here." He threw the clothes to Donald.

"You two cover the oubliette while I stand watch," Daniel said.

Donald's shaky hand caught both items from Kenneth and dressed with promptness. His encounter with the floor had reopened his leg wound left from the arrow. Blood oozed. The holey shirt swallowed his frail body but accomplished what Daniel needed. Anything other than his original garments.

"Bring him," Daniel commanded.

Neither Iain nor Kenneth touched Donald. Kenneth led the threesome out and Iain brought up the rear with Donald in between the two. They needn't fear that Donald could escape. He hobbled

213

onward at a slow pace much to Daniel's annoyance.

Daniel led them to a secluded room at the entrance of the long corridor that connected the main castle with the room containing the oubliette. Daniel, Kenneth, and Iain placed their torches on the wall inside the room. There was no seating in the chamber used as a sentinel in times of invasion.

"Ye may sit upon the floor," Daniel said.

Without a word, Donald eased to his knees and then fell onto his backside. The three warriors surrounded him four feet away from his smell.

"Without delay, tell me the name of the mon leading the abduction."

"The mon is mad."

"Name!" Daniel roared.

"Brodie."

"Brodie? Brodie Elliot?" he asked in disbelief. "Fergus Elliot's son?"

"Aye. He's the mon," he croaked.

Daniel could tell that Donald was weak from his harrowing experience from which he deserved no mercy, but he needed him strong to help track the beast who stole his wife. "Kenneth, fetch more bread, meat, and ale for the mon."

Kenneth stared at Daniel with wide eyes. "M' lord?"

"Now!"

"Aye." He scurried off with his running footfalls growing weaker with each step.

"Continue with your account. I want every detail. Nothing is to be disregarded as unimportant. Do ye comprehend?"

"Let me tell how I came to work far the mon. We was starving … me and Scott. Our real names be Gawain and Osborn. Osborn said not to use em. Anyway, we wandered up to the Elliot stronghold. Old mon Elliot turned us away, but his son, needed us far a task. He promised to feed us if we but do one duty." He looked at Daniel. "We had to eat," as if in a way of an apology.

"Hurry yer tale. My wife's life is in his hands." Daniel's spittle flew.

Donald's eyes grew large. "Aye. He had us come here and work far ye to git close to yer wife."

"Why does Brodie want my wife?"

"To be 'is wife."

Iain gasped.

Daniel's rage chocked him. "That's preposterous! She is already wed."

"I think Brodie is a mad mon." Donald shrugged one shoulder.

Daniel paced around the small room. "Did they take her to the Elliot castle?"

Kenneth rushed in holding a platter of bread, slices of roasted quail and a mug of ale. Daniel signaled to place the food on the floor near Donald.

"That was the plan."

Daniel stopped in front of Donald. "Where is she being held at the castle?"

"Brodie had shown us an old tower in the back of the castle that wasn't used. He said she would be taken there. He dinna want his fither to ken." Donald tore off a bite of the fresh bread.

"Is there a secret entrance to that tower?" Daniel asked.

"Aye," he mumbled. He gulped some ale before continuing. "Me and Osborn searched aboot to see if there was a way to escape juist in case Brodie changed his views on us. He appears to be daft." He shoved meat and bread in his mouth before anyone could take it away.

"Ye better slow down," Kenneth muttered under his breath.

"Iain, see that this man is properly bathed and clothed. Get his leg stitched up for he will come with us to the Elliot castle."

215

Chapter Twenty-Nine

With lids still closed, Brigette shivered. Why did her shoulders ache? She peeped her scratchy eyes open to see dust dancing in a stream of light that cut through the darkness. Confused, she turned her head to the right and glimpsed a bare fireplace. Her eyes slid shut on the memory of her previous day. Daybreak had brought queasiness as Isabelle had predicted. God help her! She was with child and a prisoner.

As she tried to lick her parched lips, her tongue stuck to the top of her mouth. At the moment, a sip of water to wet her dry lips would be worth a piece of gold. Unwrapping her stiff legs, she stretched them out and wiggled her arms. Making the stone floor her bed might not have been her finest decision. She unfolded and stood. Once up, she extended her arms above her while reassessing her situation.

In a standing position, Brigette comprehended water or not, she needed to relieve herself. But where? From the bit of light coming through the small openings, she determined there was no chamber pot under the bed or in a corner. Now, what to do?

She assessed her limited options. There was no hope for it. She would need to use the corner of the room furthest from the bed and the window slits. What a disgusting proposition. If someone didn't soon bring food and drink, she would need to add vomit to the corner.

217

After her deed was done, she walked back to the windows trying to see if there was any activity outside. The gray and pink sky told her it was near daybreak, and there was not one person in sight. Should she bang on the door and see if anyone came? If they came, would she be in worse danger?

Thirsty. Hungry. Cold.

Leaning her shoulder against the cool stone, she whispered, "Almighty God, do you hear me? Why am I here? Am I being punished for my past?" She sniffled. "Isabelle said when I prayed for forgiveness, You forgot my transgressions at that very moment. Is that true?" With the sleeve of her dress, she dabbed her nose. "She also said that You will work all things for the good of Your children. I know I've done some terrible things, but am I still one of Your children?"

The longer she contemplated her fate, despair washed over her and robbed her of breath. Sucking in through her nose, she blew it out on a huff. "This doesn't seem good to me ... this whole matter of being captured and all." She massaged her hands together for warmth as she walked to a different opening in the wall and looked out.

"I'm alone, far from home, and in probable danger." With a feeling of hopelessness, she slipped to her knees and bowed her head. Misery had taken up residence in her heart, and she didn't know what else to do.

"Almighty God, please help me." Placing her face in her hands, she allowed her tears to fall at will. "Please help me." She inhaled a shuttering breath. "I need Your power. Give me Your sustaining strength for without it, I'm sure to crumble." She reached to stop the tears that dripped from the end of her nose.

While she knelt, a clang came from outside her door. Her eyes popped open, and her head jerked up at the sound. Pushing off the floor, she stood as the door creaked open. A tiny woman carrying a tray of food and drink came in before the heavy door banged shut. She watched as the woman looked for a place to set the tray. Seeing none, she headed toward the moldy straw bed.

"Where am I?" Brigette whispered. When the woman ignored

her, she went on. "Who are you? Can you help me?" With each question she edged closer to the woman. After moving a few steps, the woman threw out her hand and shook her head no. Her tight lips and frightened eyes held an untold story. The woman trembled as her eyes cut toward the closed door.

A hunk of molded bread and a cup of murky water sat on the tray. The way the woman eyed the meager meal, mayhap, she would be glad to eat it. "Won't you stay and share my meal?" Brigette asked with kindness.

Once again, the woman's frightened eyes darted toward the door. She shook her head no and scooted backwards toward the entry as if she feared Brigette might attack her. "Oh, please, don't go yet. I need to know who holds me and why. Please, help me," she said as she reached toward the woman.

On a quick turn, the tiny woman rapped on the door. It cracked open wide enough for her to squeeze through and nothing more. Before Brigette could grab the door, it was bolted shut. With fisted hands, she stomped her foot and grunted. Her one contact since being snatched disappeared like leaves in a windstorm.

With no other options, Brigette walked over to the bed and stared at the food. She picked up the bread and broke it open hoping to find less mold inside. Pinching off a small part that held no mold, she smelled it. Ugh. Perhaps eating the small nourishment might calm the queasiness.

After a few bites, a scurrying sound and blinking eyes from the dark corner stopped her. Mice! She backed away from the bed. Afraid they might attack her, she threw the molded part of the bread at their beady eyes and stuffed the remainder of the unspoiled part in her mouth. With such a dry tongue, she had to take a sip of the water in order to swallow the clump of food. She pinched her nose and drank the cloudy water forcing herself not to spew it out.

Gulping air, Brigette struggled to hold down the ghastly mess. She used her sleeve as a napkin, and realized she needed to remember which sleeve was used for what. A small moan escaped her at the injustice of her situation. Oh, how she longed to be anywhere but in this despicable room.

A squeak brought her attention back to her immediate dilemma. Mice. If those mice came exploring for crumbs, she wanted them far from her. She moved the tray and deposited it by the door. After completing that job, sitting under the window slits with her back against the wall, she stretched out her legs. What to do?

With her dress snug around her crossed legs, she laid her clasped hands in her lap. She closed her eyes and allowed her mind to wander home. In her daydream, the McKinnon castle was warm and clean. There was a blazing fire in the room she shared with her husband. The food was tasty and plentiful. There were people who cared for her … or at least she hoped they did. A picture of Daniel came to her mind. He stood smiling at something William had said … then he turned to her. His expression unreadable.

She opened her eyes to her reality. Looking inward, she recognized there was much she admired about her husband. He was strong and provided well for his clan … even her. She remembered the fun they shared when they rode on his war horse. Their time together had been agreeable, and both were growing fond of the other. What had gone wrong?

"I went wrong," she said in the stillness. "Isabelle was right. I made a poor decision. My choice insulted my husband in some way." She pondered a moment. Not understanding the way a man thinks, she decided she didn't have to know every aspect of Daniel's character to live in harmony with him. If Isabelle was correct in her assessment that God had orchestrated the marriage between her and Daniel, she could help it succeed by putting his desires above her own.

That one choice lightened her hopelessness. She had something on which to focus besides her own predicament. If her conduct toward Daniel was unselfish, maybe … just maybe she could repair the damage she had done to their union. As she visualized a cheerful home, warmth enveloped her heart shoving aside the bleakness trying to overtake her spirit.

Suddenly, the door burst open wide, and a man's shoulders

filled the entryway. "Weel now, yer still here," he drawled.

Brigette scrambled to her feet. She put her hands on the wall behind her to steady herself. Her eyes grew round with fright as light slashed across his face when he sauntered into the room. She tried to mask her response fearing he would use it against her.

"Do ye ken me?" A sly grin spread on his face.

"Brodie." His name came out with a croak.

He approached with slow deliberate steps until he stood within a handbreadth of her. "Ye ken I would find ye. Ye canna escape me agin."

"What are you talking about?" She pushed her boot heel against the wall and raised on her toes. Flight was her strategy. One tactic she learned by watching her brothers was to stay on your toes so you can move at a moment's notice to escape your enemy.

When he wrapped a long curl around his grimy finger, she turned her head to the side. Even though her brothers told her to look your enemy in the eye, she couldn't bring herself to carry it out.

"Ye are me bride, and I've been searching far ye."

His statement startled her. She frowned. "That's preposterous. I'm Laird McKinnon's wife."

A quick slap knocked her head against the stone wall. Her eyes closed at will from the pain.

"Ye are mine now," he growled. "Ye willnae play the harlot with me."

Afraid to speak, she stared at him. Spittle dripped into his nasty beard as he ogled her from head to toe. His smell resurrected her nausea. What would he do if she retched on him? Likely kill her.

"This eventide, I'll share yer bed." He flipped his head toward the mice infested bed across the room.

When she tried to jump aside, he grabbed her arm and dragged her from the wall. She struggled against his hold but to no avail. Her feet skidded through the dust and dirt until she was within a foot of the bed. At first his words stunned her, but the image of her fate brought her boldness. She wrestled free from his grasp and backed up a few feet. The speed of her thoughts made her dizzy until one idea roared to the front.

"You don't want to do this shameful act. I'm already with child," she said in hopes he would reconsider. Instead, he snarled like an animal.

"No!" he bellowed and raised his foot.

The kick to her stomach came so fast and hard, it lifted her off the floor and propelled her backwards into the wall. The force of the impact slammed her head against the stone. Dazed, her body slumped into a heap on the floor.

Brodie continued to kick her. On instinct, she curled into a ball as his onslaught was unrelenting. When she thought her death was imminent, another man burst into the room.

"Brodie, stoop this at once." His thundering voice hurt her head. A scuffle between the men erupted as she slipped in and out of consciousness.

"Nay, fither. I'm to be 'er hoosband, nay Daniel!" Brodie yelled. "She is a harlot! Nay worthy to live."

"Guard," Fergus hollered while restraining his son. "Take Brodie oot and send in a servant."

Brodie's angry voice grew faint as the guard hauled him out the door. She couldn't move her throbbing body. One side of her face lay on the floor with her lid swollen shut. Fergus Elliot's feet came into her blurred view. She expected him to finish what his son had started. Instead, he grabbed her hands and jerked her across the floor toward the bed. Her teeth clinched as pain radiated through her body.

"Mara, take 'er feet and I'll take 'er hands."

Brigette couldn't see, but another person clutched her feet while Laird Elliot snatched under her arms to lift her onto the bed. Each tug like a sword slice, separating her limbs. Her face scrunched in agony with every yank. At long last, they dropped her onto the hard, straw mattress.

"Leave 'er til the morrow."

The woman shuffled out the door leaving old man Fergus alone with her. She tried to open her one eye, but the pain was too great.

What more suffering would she endure at his hand? She sensed his presence next to the bed, thankful he didn't touch her.

"Oh, son. Ye have brought our doom." He uttered his parting words before shutting her prison door.

That was the last she heard before slipping into oblivion.

Brigette woke to a stabbing pain in her belly. Her stomach cramped, followed by brief moments of relief. However, the dull ache in her back never yielded. Her eyes traveled around the room hoping to see Mara watching over her. But no. There was no one concerned about her welfare. The darkness that filled every corner made her believe it was still nighttime. Turning her head toward the window slits, the dim light that touched her legs came from the moon as it snuck through the tiny openings.

Her nausea had returned with a vengeance which was uncommon since it most often attacked in the mornings. When the cramping struck, she curled tight to relieve her pain. Even that motion brought more agony. Brodie's beating was to blame.

She wrestled in the bed, but no relief was forthcoming. Not wanting to cry out, she tore off a piece of her dress and made a gag to bite on. Her thrashing about did nothing to stop the hurting. The piercing cramps increased in intensity.

Yanking the gag from her mouth, she panted like an animal. "God, help me," she cried. When she thought to die from the pain, a gush of fluid left her body. With so little light with which to see, she squinted. Her dress had a dark spot forming as the cloth absorbed the fluid. What was it? Had Brodie's kicks damaged her? Would she now bleed to death in this horrible room and all alone? "God, please," she begged. "I don't want to die. Please, save me."

Since the bed offered no reprieve, she scooted off the edge and walked around the room. There were times when she doubled over in pain. After the brutal cramp eased, she persisted on until running into a spider's web. The web wrapped around her face and stuck like tar. Stumbling around the room, she clawed at the webbing as she bounced off the walls. Was there no end to her torment?

Bile rose in her throat as another sharp pain slashed through her upper body. The acute agony drove her to her hands and knees as another deluge of blood pushed from her body. Her woozy head nearly caused her to black out. She slipped to the floor and rolled to her side. Tears dripped over the bridge of her nose and fell to the dusty floor.

"God ... forgive me of my transgressions. Please, please, release me from this cruelty. I can't bear it any longer. I entrust my spirit into Your hands. Take me home."

Chapter Thirty

The crashing door rocked on its hinges. Brodie's torch cut the darkness. He attached the light to the wall near the doorway and rushed to where Brigette lay on the floor.

"Lass, whit ar' ye doin' on the ground?" His rough handling caused her to moan as he rolled her onto her back.

"Git up. Ye need to git ready."

Brigette's head lolled to the side. Her weakened state prevented a response to his request. She cracked open one eyelid to see him on his knees bending over her. Her strength had vanished in the night and left her helpless to defend herself.

"I'll git ye a chair." He brought the broken three-legged chair to the center of the room and placed it beside her. Putting his hands under her arms, he pushed her to a sitting position. "Help me, wummin. I canna git ye oop alone."

She tried to stand but couldn't gather enough might to make a difference. Unprepared when Brodie let go, her shoulders hit hard as her head bounced against the floor. A bleeding gash followed.

"Guard. Assist me," Brodie yelled.

The soldier's sword clanked as he walked toward Brigette.

"Put 'er in the chair."

As the guard lifted her off the floor, excruciating pain plagued every part of her body. He plopped her into the chair which promptly tipped over with her weight. She tried catching herself with her hand, but her arm buckled.

"She needs a bath. I'll return soon. Stay here," Brodie said before skipping from the room.

When Brigette fell, she landed facing the door and saw Brodie's strange actions. His behavior didn't fit a man of his age and rank. The son of a Scottish laird brought with it a position of significance. Yet, one moment he acted as a wild animal in a rage, and the next, a docile child. Verily, he was daft.

She heard the guard pacing behind her as if he didn't know what to do. "Can you help me?" she whispered. "Please?"

"Ask me not," he growled. "Ye wilt git me killed."

Brigette's eye closed realizing there was no help for her. God had not seen fit to remove her from the situation, so He must plan for her to die here. Her priest had often lectured how sin had dire consequences, but she didn't think it applied to her. As she lay on the cold floor in her own filth, unconfessed sin from her past popped into her head. Sure that death was imminent, she started confessing and asking God's forgiveness for all that came to mind. She wanted a clean conscious when she met God face to face.

While she remained where she fell, Brodie stalked into the room carrying two pitchers of water.

"Git up," he demanded.

Oh, dear. 'Twas the animal Brodie that returned. With agonizing effort, she pushed herself into a sitting position. That was the limit of her strength and will.

"I'm too weak to stand," she murmured.

"I see ye have blood in yer hair. It moost be cleaned." Without warning, he dumped one pitcher of cold water on her head that drained down her face and back, soaking her clothes. "There. That should suffice."

Brigette shivered as she used one hand to wipe dripping hair from her face. Afraid of what he might do next, she remained silent. No need to poke an angry beast. It would go poorly for her. Of course, she almost snorted at the absurdity of her thought ... go poorly, indeed. Maybe she should ask him to use the guard's sword and run her through now. That would speed events along.

"Stand 'er oop."

Without hesitation, the guard lifted her off the floor and held her limp body against his chest in a standing position. The second dousing splashed her straight in the face and spattered the guard, as well. She had opened her mouth in hopes to receive enough to wet her parched mouth but didn't expect such force. A small amount made it inside while the biggest quantity stung her face and fell to the floor.

"Now, ye'll satisfy me lusty appetite. Take 'er to the bed."

As the guard yanked her toward the bed, a shout came from a second guard outside the room. "Stoop. Yer fither is cooming."

Without hesitation, the guard dropped her before reaching the bed and headed toward the open doorway dragging Brodie along.

"Have no fear, I'll return to ye," Brodie warned. The door thumped shut and was bolted from the other side.

If she wasn't in such misery, she would have grinned. Just when she thought she had suffered her worst, another threat rolled in like a fire in the wind. No longer would she wonder if her affairs could worsen—they most definitely could.

"Well, Brigette, you can sit here like a dumb sheep awaiting your slaughter, or you can figure out a way to fight," she muttered.

Crawling on her hands and knees, she inched her way to the chair. She didn't have enough strength in her arms and legs to fracture a chair leg to use as a weapon, but she knew who did. "In the name of Jesus, I ask for Your power to infuse my weak body."

She sat back on her haunches and scooted the chair legs around to face her. After a few yanks, she figured out it was sturdier than she first perceived. She hooked her foot through the rung and drug it across the floor as she crawled toward the wall. If she could brace the chair against the wall with one foot and bash the chair leg with her other foot, then maybe it would loosen enough to gain a fragment for a club.

With fortitude born from her God-given strength and her fear of Brodie, she attacked the chair. She rested in between kicks until at last one chair leg splintered. Grabbing the leg, she wiggled it until

227

it broke away. She held a sharp-pointed club.

Hysterical laughter spewed out. "I have a spear. I have a spear!" She clung tight to her weapon and crawled to the wall furthest from the door and hid beside the bed. Propping her back in the corner, she pulled her legs up to her chest and tucked her dress around them. She heaved a deep sigh. With a feeble smile affixed to her battered face, she praised God for her renewed hope. Brodie would not have her without a fight.

She gingerly touched her head and flinched where a knot had formed. Another injury to add to her swollen face and bruised body. When she brought her arm down, fresh blood stained her fingers. A shiver raced down her back and angry determination fueled her resolve. With her hand fisted around her spike, she stared into the darkness.

"Come near me again, Brodie Elliot, and I will stab you."

Thunderous hoof beats shook the earth as Daniel and his men rode to rendezvous with Lord Fairwick at the border of Clan Elliot's land. Daniel was all too aware of the notorious border reiver family. They had come down from the central highlands at the invitation of Robert the Bruce to hold lands confiscated from William de Soulis, a reputed devil worshipper and traitor to the Scottish crown. The land now belonged to the Douglass Clan and Fergus Elliot's Clan were nothing more than military vassals of the Douglass's. Even though the king demanded they cease the border raids, skirmishes persisted.

What caused Daniel's fear to escalate was the Elliot's reputation of showing no mercy. Their violence to avenge their grievances was notorious. If Brigette still lived, the thoughts of what she might have endured burned in his gut—all the reason needed to press on without a reprieve.

"M' lord?" Niall spoke from his side.

"Aye?"

"The horses have run hard and need to rest. 'Twill nay end weel if we keep on. Juist for a moment?"

Daniel signaled a halt to his group of men. His reluctance to rest was born from his guilt. His wife's capture was because he had failed her in many ways.

"A short reprieve is all we can afford."

His own horse heaved with each breath. It would not profit him to run the war horses into the ground and leave them without strength to fight. They were an integral part in every battle. He walked next to Niall.

"Thank ye for bringing me to task."

"Yer focus is elsewhaur. That's why ye have me."

Daniel gave him a hearty thump to his back. "Aye, 'tis true. Go. Take ye a rest with the men."

Daniel had left Iain, Ross, and Mungo in charge to secure his castle. They were well versed in managing the garrison of men. At his word, the gates were to remain closed until he returned home with his bride. He needed to know that his son and those left behind were well protected, for he wanted no distractions on this dangerous mission of rescue. It always troubled him to know some of his men might be injured or possibly killed when they headed into battle, but there was no help for it this day.

He watched Niall join the others before he walked a ways down the road. With hands on his hips and eyes open, he prayed. "Lord God of the Heavens cover my Brigette with Your protective Hand. Be her refuge in her time of trouble." He raised his eyes heavenward. "Ye have revealed my errors, and I vow to make amends if Ye will but give me the chance. Please ... please, Almighty Father, provide what she needs to stay alive. And Father, shield my men from harm."

Even though bolstered after his prayer, the weight of his shame pierced his heart like a sword. Not wanting to wallow in despair, he walked back to where his men awaited his directions. He saw Kenneth had a tight hold on Donald and Donald's horse. He nodded at Kenneth.

"Let's mount up."

In less than an hour, the assembly of Nicolas's men came into view. Daniel was taken aback by the sheer mass present but was equally comforted. According to Donald, a surplus of men guaranteed a victory. Nicolas stood holding his horse when Daniel approached.

"Daniel," Nicolas said.

Daniel hopped off his horse and threw the reins to Gavin. "Bring your commanders, and I will draw out our battle strategy in the dirt." He picked a sturdy stick and walked over to a large dirt patch in the road. Outlining the Elliot castle, he pointed out the secret passageway to the abandoned tower.

"This passageway is a tunnel underground. According to Donald, no one guards the forgotten entrance nor the door once inside. We will split our men into five groups. Four will surround the castle and remain hidden until Niall gives the signal to attack. The fifth group of our best men will accompany me through the tunnel."

"I wish to accompany you through the tunnel," Nicolas said.

"I, as well," Thomas interjected.

Daniel contemplated their request. When he looked into their eyes, he saw remorse. It appeared their poor treatment of Brigette was wreaking havoc on their senses. The guilt etched on their faces told of regret and shame. His first inclination was to let them wallow in their dishonor but having them watch his back was a sound decision. They were great warriors.

"You may journey with me through the tunnel, but you will obey my commands. She is my wife and my responsibility to liberate."

Nicolas and Thomas eyed one another and then nodded their approval.

He proceeded to sketch the buildings around the castle grounds and the whereabouts for each group of men. Once the men traversed the tunnel and reached the door inside the castle, Niall would signal with a lighted torch for the men surrounding the castle to attack in a specific order.

"Donald will lead us to the tower where Brigette is being held."

230

Nicolas squinted and frowned at Donald. "Can he be trusted?"

"We have reached an understanding. If at any time I sense he has played us foul, I will run him through his gut with my sword and leave him to die a slow death. Given those stipulations, he agreed to be of assistance. With my dagger against his back, he will be the first through the tunnel door into the castle."

He was relieved when his explanation appeased Nicolas since Daniel had a few qualms about the whole idea. Yet, he had no other choice since time was of the essence.

"I've appointed a commander for each group to carry out my attack orders. After the signal from Niall, men will ride to the front and remain out of reach of arrows while a hidden group attacks the castle with flaming arrows. With luck, the surprise assault will throw the Elliot clan into a frenzy of retaliation. During their initial state of chaos, those of us in the tunnel will make our way inside the castle while the rear squadron filters through the postern gate that Donald revealed." Daniel prayed that Donald had given accurate facts, or there could be a disastrous ending to their encounter.

"With men attacking from inside the walls and inside the castle itself, it will provide an opportunity for warriors to get the front gates opened. At that time, the front battalion of men will rush the open gates and proceed to bring the Elliot clan to heel. Are there any questions to this plan of attack?" Daniel asked the men surrounding him.

Nicolas spoke for them all. "It is as you say. We will carry out your course of action."

"Let us be away." Daniel scanned the group of hardened warriors knowing that some might not return. "Go with God."

Chapter Thirty-One

Shivering, Brigette faded in and out of awareness. Following her baptism with the icy water, she had been unable to dry out. The dampness of the room had kept her dress cold and moist causing her to quake with chills. The dark shadows made it hard to distinguish if it were night or day.

At times, the quivering of her body became so violent, she almost dropped her spear. Fearful of losing it in the dark, she laid her hand in her lap to cradle the weapon. If she happened to be conscious when Brodie entered her room, she planned to have her spike hidden in the folds of her dress until needed. Fairwicks never gave up without a fight, and she intended to initiate a surprise attack on his person.

When Brigette possessed a clear mind, she reflected back on her life. Remaining angry at her brothers had been a waste of her precious time. Here she sat at death's door, either by the hand of Brodie or from her own illness that racked her body, and all she dreamed about was Daniel's embrace.

Why had she squandered his affection? If he knew about her capture, would he search for her? Those questions brought sickness to her heart. As her eyes drifted shut, she pushed aside her gloomy queries and dwelt on the faces of Daniel and William … 'twas pleasing to her heart.

The clamber from the other side of the closed door roused her.

233

"Open the door. I have to see her," Brodie said.

With little effort, Brigette stayed motionless and quiet when the door creaked open. She could see a stream of light cast across the floor and hitting the opposite corner. Brodie's shadow remained stationary as he swung his torch back and forth. "Whaur is me wyff?" he asked the guard. "Did ye let 'er oot?" His angry question bounced off the walls.

"Nay, my lord. She remains."

Brodie's footsteps were slow-moving as he came around the edge of the bed almost as if he were afraid. A mouse scurried next to his foot. He whipped around to his left brandishing his torch. "Whit goes there?"

"'Twas a mouse," the guard replied from the threshold before pulling the door closed.

After a moment, Brodie turned slowly to his right. His torch cast a shaft of light across Brigette's face where she hid in the corner.

"Lass, why are ye hiding? Coom to me."

Brigette cracked open her one eye. From where Brodie stood, he couldn't possibly tell she was awake. Because of the dark shadows, her mere slit allowed her to watch his approach without his knowledge. Her grip tightened on the spear. He crept closer as he squinted to see if she lived.

"Are ye dead?"

Brigette wanted to roll her eyes at the stupidity of his question but didn't dare reveal her alertness. He placed the torch in a holder on the wall and loomed over her. She held her breath and waited. He stooped and came within inches of her body. When he grabbed her arms to pull her to him, she thrust her hand-held spear into his gut with all her might.

Warm blood spurted onto her hand as he screamed in pain. He fell backwards with the wooden spike protruding from his middle. She came to her hands and knees. They both reached for the weapon at the same time, but Brigette's speed won out. She seized the handle and drove it deeper into his body.

"Help," he hollered.

Before he had time to say more, Brigette climbed over him and pulled his cloak up to his face. As he writhed in pain while trying to snatch her, she stretched the cloak over his face and pulled downward gagging off further cries. Presumably, her life would be forfeit when the guard came to check on Brodie, but she would not have to endure any more torture.

As her arms grew weak from the strain, Brodie reached over his head and yanked her hair that hung over his face. She cried out yet was unrelenting with her hold on his gag. Just when she feared all would be lost, the door whacked open.

"Brodie, we're under attack. Coom." The guard marched around the bed to find Brigette and Brodie wrestling on the floor. With one arm he lifted and threw Brigette against the wall. The guard eased out the spike, pulled Brodie into a shoulder hold and ran toward the door leaving her alone. She prayed the door would stay open, instead it banged shut and locked.

At least the torch remained on the wall. It provided enough light to see the wooden chair leg on the floor. With the little strength left in her battered body, she scooted toward the weapon. She cringed when she passed through his fresh blood to reach it. The smell of it nearly choked her as she swallowed several times to keep from retching. There was no need to add vomit to her area of refuge.

Once settled against the wall, holding tight to her one defense, the reality of what she had done collided with her feelings of victory. She repeatedly wiped her hands on her dress. Yet, they remained stained. The repulsiveness of her action was more than her delicate emotions could handle. Tears leaked from her eyes as her head fell to her chest, and her arms lay limp beside her. *God, forgive me. Please, forgive me.*

Daniel left a small contingent of men to guard their horses deep in the forest. Once the castle was breeched and under the control of The McKinnon, they would bring the war horses closer to the castle gates in case they were needed to pursue those fleeing capture.

The crunching of the leaves under foot sounded loud to his ears. If a patrol was within hearing, the fight could end before even reaching the castle. He prayed not. As they snaked their way among the trees, he held tight to the back of Donald's tunic. Each warrior kept his sword at ready while scanning the area as they moved closer to the castle.

At one point, Donald stopped, causing Daniel to bump him. "What are ye about?" Daniel hissed.

"The tunnel is nearby," Donald whispered. He marked off ten paces from a gnarled tree. He fell to his knees and raked his hands across the ground. Daniel stood close by and watched with eagerness. Soon he would be inside the castle and have his wife in his arms.

Hold on, Brigette, I'm here. Lord God, Almighty Warrior, please preserve her.

After a few moments of searching, Donald's hand wrapped around an iron ring attached to metal trap door. He looked up at Daniel.

"I found it." He tugged upward, but his strength failed him.

Daniel pushed Donald aside, grabbed the ring, and yanked it open. The squeaky, rusted hinges echoed through the stillness of the moment. Each man ready for possible assailants. The dark pit looked ominous. A thunder cloud formed on Daniel's face as he grabbed Donald around his scrawny neck.

"How are we to see?"

"There ar' two unlit torches once ye lower yerself into the tunnel," Donald said with haste. "It's aboot a six-foot droop."

"You will drop in first, and then hand me the torches," Daniel said to Donald. "Just remember you have nowhere to hide if you play me false."

"Aye," he said as he rubbed his throat.

"I don't like this arrangement," Nicolas said.

Aggravated at Nicolas's superior tone, Daniel clinched his jaw. "Ye agreed to it. Do ye have a better plan at this stage of our

236

attack?"

Nicolas released a loud breath. "No."

"Then dinna stop our progress again," Daniel said. He turned to Donald and shoved him. "Down ye go."

"Thomas, start a small fire in yonder dirt spot," Nicolas instructed. Thomas rushed to do his brother's bidding while Nicolas joined Daniel. They both leaned over the opening to the tunnel and heard Donald sliding down the dirt embankment. He shuffled about before handing up two unlit torches. Nicolas snatched them from his hand and ran to where Thomas's fire began to take hold.

"Keep your face in my sight," Daniel said to Donald in a low tone. The waiting on the fire for the torches seemed to take overlong. Daniel marched around the trap door while keeping Donald in his sights. Whenever his mind had an idle moment, thoughts of Brigette snuck in. He scrubbed his forehead in hopes of banishing the distraction. Sharp wits were needed.

"We're ready," Nicolas said.

Daniel looked to see two glowing torches. He needed to get them in the tunnel before they blazed bright. "I'm entering. Move out of the way," Daniel said. He dropped into the hole and reached for a light. Nicolas handed him one, and then he followed Daniel into the passageway. Thomas handed the other light to Nicolas before trailing behind them.

Daniel shoved Donald to the front of the raiding party. They trudged ahead as other warriors plunged into the unknown. With only two torches, the men in the center had little light to direct their steps since Niall carried the last torch at the rear. Daniel left five warriors to guard the trap door. He wanted no surprises coming from his back.

The earth beneath their feet consisted of dirt, rocks, and a few tree roots. The underground dampness caused the dirt to pack down as they tramped through the dark passageway. They walked single file with a couple of feet on either side of their shoulders. When Daniel's hand touched the wall, he jerked it away as a shiver ran down his back. The wall crawled.

Donald hurried toward the castle as if the hounds were chasing him. He panted for breath and stumbled several times before Daniel insisted he slow his pace. Sounds ricocheted through the tunnel—clinking swords against rock and heavy exhales. Halfway through the passageway, Daniel spotted another unlit torch lying in the dirt. He lit it and passed it back.

They hiked another hundred paces when Donald held up his hand. Daniel removed the dagger he held against Donald's back and waited for an explanation.

"The door is up ahead," he said in a quiet voice and pointed to a tiny beam.

Daniel spread the word down the line of men. "Nicolas, I will take Thomas, Donald, and Kenneth to the tower. You command the others and secure the inside of the castle," he said in a hushed voice. After Nicolas's gesture of agreement, he edged closer to the door.

When word reached Niall, he waved the torch to signal Gavin waiting at the other end of the channel. Gavin in turn told Robert, Nicolas's man, to ride and give word for the archers to begin their assault.

When the flaming arrows sailed through the air, the front contingent of men rode close to the gates and told Fergus Elliot to surrender or prepare to meet death.

With his ear to the closed tunnel door, shouts came from within. Feet pounded past their hideaway as the enemy ran to prepare for battle. Donald stood between Daniel and Nicolas so Daniel could listen. After the yelling and running feet subsided, he eased the door open. After shoving Donald through the door, Daniel followed which put them in a deserted hallway.

Daniel scruffed Donald's shirt like a cat. "Make haste and lead me to the tower."

Donald steered them left and walked at a brisk clip. Daniel, Kenneth, and Thomas followed close by while six men spread out along the hallway to protect their back. There was one more left turn before meeting a set of curved steps. Donald pointed upward and held up two fingers.

Daniel indicated for Kenneth to grab Donald's tunic. Then he gave a hand signal to stay put. He motioned to Thomas and to himself and pointed up. With swords in hand, Daniel and Thomas crept up the stairs one at a time while listening. As they rounded the first turn, a small light filtered down to the step above their feet. They stopped and waited. Once they made themselves known, anything could happen. Daniel spotted two of Nicolas's men who had mounted five steps and stopped—ready to attack.

They ascended one step at a time until the top of the stairs came into view. There, poised and ready, were two huge warriors. Climbing the stairs, Daniel and Thomas were at a disadvantage. However, they had rage fed by the injustice done to Brigette that fired their intensity to win the encounter. Daniel prayed it would be enough to carry them through.

As they stormed up the remaining steps, Daniel yelled, "Attack from the back."

His declaration caused one of the men to glance behind, and that's all the distraction needed for Daniel and Thomas to gain the advantage. Thomas engaged the first guard while Daniel occupied the second. By the time the second guard turned around, Daniel was on the landing.

Thomas struck fast and hard with his sword. He and the guard were of equal stature, but Thomas held a dagger in his left hand. They shoved and clanged swords until Thomas jabbed him in the ribs with his short dagger. The sudden thrust caught the guard by surprise, allowing Thomas to give him a mighty shove. He tumbled down several steps with Thomas hot on his trail to finish the deed.

Daniel deflected each strike from the other guard's sword. They grunted with every solid blow to the other. Each understood their life depended on winning the match. From the corner of his eye, Daniel noticed Thomas and two other men ready to assist. With his free hand, Daniel pushed the man against the wall, and then kicked hard against his knee. The strike caused the guard to stumble which afforded Daniel the advantage needed to thrust his sword through the heart. The guard sank to the stone floor as Daniel's raised boot pushed him off his sword.

"You two secure the bottom of the stairs. Thomas, guard this door. I'm going in alone." He tried several keys before finding the one that opened the heavy door. Taking the torch off the wall, he stepped into the dark room.

Chapter Thirty-Two

Daniel waited a moment to let his eyes adjust to the dimness of the room. The smell of blood and human waste assaulted his nose. He moved the torch to his left and spied an empty fireplace and a broken chair near the arrow slits. Swinging it to his right, an empty bed. Blood stained the straw, but no Brigette.

When he looked behind the door, he found an empty corner containing human waste and more blood. Bile rose in his throat as his eyes closed on his morbid thoughts. A mouse scurried by which brought him to acute awareness. He made two steps inside the doorway and found a pool of blood.

"Brigette?"

No sound was forthcoming. He eased farther into the room and stopped to listen. Where was she? He stooped to examine under the bed and spotted a dark form huddled on the other side. He ventured close to the foot of the bed.

"Brigette, are ye here, lass?"

A whimper reached his ears.

He came around the edge of the bed where his torch illuminated a huddled mass in the corner. Still clutching his sword, he placed the torch on a wall mount and knelt on one knee.

"Brigette?"

As her head raised, his insides twisted at what he discovered. One side of her face colored black and purple with one lid swollen

241

shut. Dried blood matted her hair and stuck to her face. What concerned him more was the fresh blood covering her clothing. Not wanting to frighten her, he made no sudden moves.

"Brigette, may I come close so I might be of assistance?" He noticed her dull eye followed his sword that still dripped with the guard's blood. Placing his sword on the floor, he reached out his hand to her. Her gaze homed in on his outstretched hand. When she didn't respond, he started scooting toward her. Her stare shifted to his face.

He stopped within a foot of her person. The stench of blood and sickness permeated the area. She had a continuous shiver radiating from her body. Her parched, cracked lips bled.

"My sweet, I have a pouch of water I'm going to take from my belt. Don't be afraid." To prevent frightening her, each move was slow and deliberate. He was grateful when she permitted him to dribble water in her mouth.

"Daniel, did you find Brigette?" Thomas called from the door.

"Aye, she is here," he said with a soft voice.

Thomas's footsteps echoed inside the stark room. He gasped. "What have they done to her?"

Fear shadowed her countenance when Thomas's harsh question rang through the room. Without moving or taking his eyes off his wife, Daniel responded in a quiet yet firm voice.

"Thomas, I need you to retrieve my medicine bag and Brigette's cape from the tunnel. Post another guard at this door. See to it."

Daniel was thankful at the retreating footsteps. Her brother's presence might compound her distress, and he didn't plan to let it happen. Most important, did she have a life-threatening wound?

He used water to wash the blood from her hands. Some dried and some fresh. As he methodically washed the blood away, he asked, "Do you have a wound I need to see to?"

"No."

He cringed at her raspy voice. He frowned. "Is this your blood?"

"No."

When she offered no other explanation, his mind whirled with possibilities. Proceeding with caution, he said, "I'm going to remove my plaid and wrap it around your shoulders if that pleases you."

"Aye."

His head jerked at her response. She had never used any Scottish brogue since becoming his wife. He offered her a brief smile and then draped the plaid around her for warmth.

"I need to get you off this cold floor. Strengthen your resolve for this might cause you pain."

As he scooped her into his arms, she moaned. The pitiful sound stabbed his heart and twisted his gut. It alarmed him that her fragile form weighed that of a child. Daniel clinched his teeth. Brodie's punishment and torment would have no bounds.

Brigette panted, no doubt from the excruciating pain, while Daniel eased her onto the edge of the mattress. He kept his arm around her waist to add support and security as she laid her head against his shoulder. Questions about her abduction and torture stormed through his mind like a whirlwind. Yet he withheld.

She momentarily tilted her head toward him. "William?"

"He is safe and asking for his mother." He watched relief flood her countenance.

With a more direct stare she whispered, "The babe is lost." Silent sobs racked her body. "The fault is mine." She hiccupped.

Daniel looked behind her to see the blood stain on the straw. "The blame is not yours to bear," he said as he snuggled her closer. She buried her face in his neck and continued to cry. It took all his restraint not to leave her to go find Brodie and run him through with his sword.

He stroked her hair. "Shh, now. Quiet your cries. You must preserve your strength to make the journey home. God will provide." As her body relaxed into his, he caressed her arm to help soothe away her unfounded guilt. He, too, deserved retribution for his ill treatment of his wife, but that would have to wait until Brodie had received his judgment for the violence against her.

He presumed she had dozed until she mumbled, "I pierced him

243

with my spear."

Daniel placed his ear closer to her chin. "What say you?"

She tilted her face upward. "I stabbed Brodie … with my spike."

He frowned. "A spike?"

"Aye. He tried to … force me … but God … delivered me."

Her labored breathing caused him concern. "Ah, my wife. You are such a brave and courageous woman. I desire to hear all about your heroic deeds when you are stronger. Especially, how you vanquished that depraved man. But for now, it's best for you to conserve your energy. You have a long ride ahead." As she leaned into him, he seethed with pent up anger.

When he feared his fury might burst forth, Thomas returned with his bag of soothing ointments and the cloak. He approached where the two sat on the bed. His lips pinched tight.

"Here." He held out the cloak and bag.

Without releasing his fragile wife, Daniel took them and laid them on the bed. "How goes the battle?"

"We have prevailed. Nicolas is standing guard over Fergus Elliot who is near death, but Brodie has not been found."

Daniel's anger blazed. "Is the path safe for us to exit the castle through the keep?"

"Yes, my lord. Your guards line the passageway to guide you."

Daniel's hand cupped Brigette's cheek. Her tears had plowed a path down her dirty face. Using his thumb, he wiped her streaked cheeks.

"I'm going to fasten your cloak, and then I will carry you from this wicked pit. Since you have no open wounds, I will apply the healing ointment once we are away from here."

He stood to his feet and used one hand to steady her as Thomas put the cloak around her shoulders. When Daniel reached to pull her hood up, she grimaced as he grazed her head.

"Please forgive my roughness."

Thomas, who had waited in silence, blurted out, "Brigette, please forgive me."

Infuriated, Daniel said, "We are here to retrieve my wife and carry her to safety. Your absolution will have to wait." In his arms, he cradled her close. With her shielded by the hooded cloak, he stalked out of the room with Thomas at his back.

"Keep your face turned into my neck." He was thankful she obeyed as he stepped around dead and dying soldiers from the Elliot household. However, he couldn't block her from the cries of those with fatal injuries. The carnage was great.

When they walked past the grand hall, Daniel noticed Robert and Kenneth attending to the wounded. With Thomas at his side, Daniel asked, "What about my men?"

"No one was killed this day, but some have wounds that needed tending."

Upon hearing the report, a bit of Daniel's tension eased. When he stepped out of the Elliot keep and into the sunshine, he gulped a deep breath. On their knees before him were the surviving captives. Nicolas had his sword pointed at the neck of Fergus Elliot who lay on his back in the dirt.

"Thomas, commandeer two men and see if there is a decent cart to carry your sister. Make sure there is an abundance of fresh hay for a pallet in the back."

"Yes, my lord." He ran to carry out the request.

While standing on the top step of the keep, Niall appeared at his side. "Our wounded have been bandaged and are ready for departure from this filthy place."

"Thank you, Niall. Please draw fresh well water for our journey. Lady McKinnon will need an ample amount to replenish what she has been denied."

"Aye, m' lord."

Daniel could see from Nicolas's frown that he wanted to assess Brigette's condition, but he had no plans of stirring from his spot until her cart became ready. He endeavored to protect her from seeing the slaughter that was before his eyes. Slain men still lay where they fell. Their sightless eyes would cause her distress.

He was thankful when, within a short time, Thomas emerged with a horse-drawn wagon filled with hay. With a jerk of his head, he signaled for Thomas to locate it near the front gate.

"Brigette, I'm going to place you on some soft hay in the back of the wagon." He winced at her frightened face. "Do not be afraid. I will ride by your side until we reach our home." He started walking toward the wagon. "But first, I must give some instructions before we depart. I will leave Niall and Thomas by your side till I return. Does this plan meet with your approval?"

"Aye," she whispered.

With great care, he positioned her in the wagon and wrapped his plaid tight around her for warmth. Thomas and Niall stood on either side to provide security and shield her from bystanders. Though reluctant to leave her even for a moment, it was necessary. He didn't want her to hear his orders.

He strode back to where Nicolas held Fergus Elliot at sword point. Blood oozed from Fergus's mouth and from his gut wound. "Where is Brodie?" Daniel demanded.

"I know not," Fergus gasped.

Daniel put his boot on the old laird's chest. "Did you know about my wife's abduction?"

"Oonly afta the fact."

Daniel's boot slid to Fergus's neck. "Why didn't you release her?" When Fergus refused to answer, Daniel jerked his foot away and spun on his heel. "Burn the place to the ground!"

Daniel's fierce glare panned the crowd of peasant women and children huddled together. "You served a wicked man. He permitted his son to kidnap and beat my wife. Now you will see what happens when evil men meet their fate."

One young boy scowled at Daniel. His face twisted into a snarl when he shouted, "Ye are the evil mon."

"Hush, son," the boy's mother pleaded. She pulled him into her embrace.

Daniel stalked over to the frightened group. "Woman, what is your name?"

"Mara."

"Weel, Mara, yer son has much to learn." When Daniel grabbed the boy's tattered shirt, the young one lost his bravado as his eyes grew fearful. "Ye know nothing of which ye speak. If ye were a mon, I would have killed ye for that remark. Instead, ye can watch the place burn."

He dragged the boy out of his mother's grasp and closer to the castle steps. Men ran into the castle with flaming torches. "It won't be long now." Daniel growled deep in his throat.

With the boy in tow, he tramped over to Fergus. "Look, boy. Here is what happens to cruel men."

The boy started to cry as he gazed upon Fergus. However, he regained his boldness at the same time. He jerked and twisted out of Daniel's hold and faced him with fisted hands at his side.

"One day I weel slay ye."

Daniel released a harsh laugh at the boy's audacity—misplaced bravery at best. "Weel, it willnae be taday. I have won the day."

Mara edged closer and grabbed her son when Daniel lost interest in their dispute. She hurried him back to the cluster of women, and the crowd swallowed the two in their midst.

He watched the flames lash out of the open windows from every side. Nicolas joined him.

"A castle made of wood is risky in times of war," Nicolas said.

"Aye."

"Will Brigette live?"

The questions jolted him. "I know not her true condition."

Nicolas placed his hand on Daniel's shoulder. "Be away with you. My men and I will stay the duration to witness the full annihilation of all involved with this horrendous act. We will search out Brodie and leave him for you to finish. Take my sister home."

His head lowered—ashamed. For a brief moment, he had forgotten Brigette's precarious condition. The aftermath of the rescue had ensnared his attention. More guilt heaped on his head. "Thank you." His burning eyes bore into Nicolas. "Don't allow that depraved man to escape. Promise me."

"We will search and interrogate the whole lot of them until his hiding place is revealed. Of this you have my word."

Daniel rolled his tight neck and shoulders. "I am grateful for your help. When you complete this gruesome task, bring Isabelle to see Brigette, post haste. Her life hangs in the balance."

Nicolas's face dropped. "With all speed."

Chapter Thirty-Three

The trip proved long and arduous. Daniel gave Brigette a mixture to drink, and she slept most of the way. The brief times she awoke, she recounted another part of her tale. Each new disclosure more horrendous than the first. At times he had to fight to keep his stomach from rebelling at the descriptions of what she had endured.

The caravan made several stops to allow him to put ointment on her cuts, bruises, and swollen eye. At one point, he dipped a cloth in a cool stream to apply to her face. Otherwise, he avoided touching her for fear of causing her more discomfort. From what he noticed, not a place on her body remained untouched by trauma. Seeing the results of what she described was punishment to his soul.

He motioned for Niall to come alongside the wagon. "Niall, send three men ahead to the castle. Have them fetch Alice and give word to Fiona to prepare for her lady's return with a warm bath and clean bandages," he said in a soft voice.

"Aye, my lord."

"Am I dying?" Brigette muttered.

He glanced to see his battered wife awake and staring at him. "Nay. I want you treated by our village healer. She is distinguished in the art of mending the broken."

"Ah, that is not of what I speak. You told Nicolas to bring

249

Isabelle post haste."

Daniel gaped at her.

"My body is in need of mending, but my hearing is exceptional." A violent shiver shook her body.

"It would appear so." With a feather touch, he brushed a wisp of hair from her face and did some quick thinking. "I knew you would wish to see Isabelle. She can calm your spirit while offering aid as well. Is that not so?" he asked with hope.

"Aye, it is as you say." Her eye blinked slowly as she held his gaze.

"I've noticed you speak with a bit of Scottish brogue, my wife."

The corner of her lips crooked up. "I thought it might please you."

He took her hand in his. "However you wish to speak is a joy to my ears." After a moment, he placed her hand under the plaid. They rode in silence until he could withhold no longer. He had to reveal the depth of his heart for fear he might not get another chance. "Brigette, might I speak from my heart?"

She opened her one good eye. "Indeed, but I may wish to close my eye while I listen."

"Surely. Do what is best for you." He watched as she closed her lid but tilted her head as if ready to listen. "As you are aware, I was with the king in the highlands when I first got word of your capture. I recognized how I had failed you with my absence when you needed me the most."

Her battered hand reached over and patted his arm. "'Tis not your fault."

He covered her hand with his own. "Be that as it may, let me bare all while I possess the fortitude to do so."

"Yea, my husband."

Those three words brought a drop of water to his parched soul. In her condition, he didn't deserve her acquiescence but was deeply humbled by her agreement to hear him out.

"There was a man named Tancred. He traveled with the king but had not met the king in person." He paused. How much to tell? "He told about events before they happened. I witnessed one of his predictions come true."

She stirred and peeped at him. "Was he a prophet? Isabelle said prophets tell of things to come."

Daniel rubbed his eyes and pinched the bridge of his nose. "I'm not sure, but he told me there was trouble afoot and I needed to return home immediately. That was before I received word from Kenneth." *Give forgiveness ... give forgiveness.* He hung his head in shame. "But first, he told me I needed to offer forgiveness."

A frown formed between her brows. "Offer it to whom?"

Tortured of spirit, he watched her. "I'm to offer forgiveness to you and ask for your forgiveness as well."

"What mean you?"

He presumed her mind was hazy from the sleeping potion since she didn't quite grasp what he meant.

Tell all ... tell all ... she might die. His guilty conscious refused to give him any peace. "I was outraged that you requested to sleep in a separate room. My way of punishing you was to leave you alone and travel with the king. You were correct, I didn't have to go. Can you ever forgive my prideful actions?" While he awaited her answer, no matter how she responded, there was relief in the telling.

Brigette heaved a sigh and wore a sad smile. "We were both at fault. Of course, I forgive you. During this harrowing ordeal God revealed to me my own selfishness and pride."

"Pride?"

"I thought myself wiser than God when I announced I didn't want to have children. Isabelle explained God is sovereign, and He knows what's best for me. I need to trust Him." Tears ran into her hair. "Now our babe is dead."

Daniel couldn't contain his own sorrow for the catastrophe that had invaded their lives. With gentleness, he gathered Brigette into his arms. They both wept for their babe and their poor decisions. He recognized how words spoken in haste could change the course of their lives. Now, his delicate wife hovered near death making their future together uncertain. He kissed her forehead but found

251

small comfort in the embrace understanding that their prospects of growing old together were not assured.

"My lord, the castle is in view," Niall said.

"Thank you, Niall." With his wife cradled against his chest, he gazed upon the castle with renewed hope. Having no control over her survival, he, too, would have to trust God for their future.

Relief flooded Brigette when they rode through the curtain wall into the courtyard. Even from her limited view, those stone walls brought solace to her battered body. She was weary. Shivers continued to torment her since losing the babe which made her grateful to be home in case she succumbed to green fever. At least she wouldn't die alone in a nasty tower prison.

"I will carry you to our room if you have no objection."

"No. No complaint."

She kept her face turned away from the people lining their way in hopes they wouldn't see her abused face. The cheers for her return were subdued but appreciated none the less. She prayed to rally enough to say her farewells to those closest to her: William, Fiona, Mungo, Kenneth, Niall, Iain, Clara, and others. Considering her own demise was depressing—nothing like she had envisioned.

She peeped at her warrior husband. He was indeed a handsome man. Strong bone structure with his features placed in perfect symmetry. He had a bit of beard growth which, in her opinion, made him even more attractive. When she touched his face, his attention shifted to her. His dark orbs, stormy. She attempted a smile in hopes of blowing the tempest from his face. Instead, he looked away with a more determined expression.

"Is the soaking tub prepared as I directed?"

"Aye, my lord," Fiona whispered.

It was such a delight to hear Fiona's voice that Brigette pushed off her hood and searched for her.

"Fiona," she murmured.

"My lady. I'm so happy for your return."

"Fiona, help get her undressed. Her bathing must be quick for she is already plagued with the chills."

"Ah, a washing will be very welcomed, but I'm not sure I can hold myself up. I might drown." She attempted a laugh.

"You will not drown with me by your side," Daniel encouraged.

Oh, dear. She was mortified that Fiona and Daniel would see her filthy, beaten body. With no strength left in her reserve, there was no help for it. It would, perhaps, be one of many humiliating days before she breathed her last.

Daniel and Fiona made quick work of disrobing her as if she were a porcelain doll. Fiona sucked in a quick breath when she was naked. "Oh, my lady."

She moaned as Daniel placed her into the warm water.

Fiona bathed her while her mighty husband held her head above the water. Even though every touch to her form proved painful, the sheer bliss of being clean won the battle. "Please, wash my hair."

Fiona looked at Daniel.

"That's not a good idea. Giving you a bath isn't my wisest notion, but I knew you would wish it."

"Husband, it can't hurt me. I already have the chills and will probably die within the week. I want to be clean when that happens."

Fiona gasped at her declaration while Daniel groaned. "Wife you vex me."

"Please?" she pleaded. "I would flutter my eyes at you but fluttering my one would not be as effective."

Daniel fumed as he lathered her hair, careful of her head injury. She knew he wasn't actually mad at her, just concerned which made her feel cherished. The hair washing was brief, but glorious. With the swiftness of an eagle after his prey, Daniel dried and dressed her in clean night clothes. Close to the roaring fire, he held her in his lap while he fingered her hair with gentle strokes.

After she grimaced the second time, he said, "I need to check under your hair. I want to see your injury."

He parted her hair in several spots until he uncovered her gash.

"This is an angry cut on the back of your head. I will apply my healing ointment after your hair dries."

"I knew when my head bounced against the stone floor a sore knot would form."

"It's more than a knot. 'Tis a gash. You probably needed stitching, but now 'tis too late. It's begun to heal on its own. Fiona, bring in the healer."

"Aye, my lord."

Brigette touched his arm. "Please, don't leave me."

"I'm not leaving you."

"Will you hold my hand?"

"I am here to do your biding. Whatever you need, I will supply."

She leaned into him and sighed. "Thank you. I forgot to mention there were ghastly spiders in that horrible place. They are evil," she said crossly.

"Oh, my bride, I'm sorry you had to deal with those vermin."

While they waited, Daniel continued to fluff her hair to aid in the drying. Alice assembled her potions on the table near the bed and laid out clean bandages. Once completed with her task, she nodded toward the couple.

"'Tis time. I will lay you upon the bed, and Alice will treat your injuries."

"Will it hurt?"

Daniel gazed into her face. "Ah, my Brigette. Ye have suffered and endured much. This will be of little consequence to you, my warrior bride."

She gritted her teeth numerous times as Alice prodded her cuts and puncture wounds. After a short amount of time, she began to relax and not feel the pain as acutely as before the ointments. Her husband stayed by her side holding her hand and offering encouraging words to bolster her resolve. Near the end of the examination, her eyelid became heavy. Her body still shook with the chills. Nevertheless, she drifted to sleep.

Daniel pulled Fiona away from the bed so as not to disturb his sleeping wife. "Fiona, please sit with Brigette while I speak with my men."

"Aye." Her eyes misted. "My lord, my heart is broken for all that has transpired against your lady."

"As is mine." He glanced toward the bed. "We may never know the extent of what she withstood." He turned back to Fiona. "But rest assured, her abductor will not escape a dreadful demise."

"Aye, my lord. As it should be." Fiona left Daniel by the door and pulled a plush chair close to the bedside to watch over her lady.

Daniel stole one last look before closing the door. When he stepped into the hallway, there stood Nicolas.

Chapter Thirty-Four

"I need good news, my friend," Daniel said.

"There is good news and there is disappointing news."

He grabbed Nicolas's arm and hauled him down the hallway into a vacant chamber. "Tell all."

"First, let me put your mind at ease. Brodie is dead."

"Praise the Saints above! Then what is the disappointing news?"

"I didn't get to kill him myself."

"Sit here and report the details. I want to hear its entirety."

"At first, I reasoned that burning the castle was a mistake, but it proved invaluable. The flames flushed out your enemy from his hiding place from within. He ran out screaming like an injured animal with his clothes ablaze. He died before he hit the ground. Most disappointing."

Daniel released a harsh laugh. "Mayhap his death by fire was a more tortured death than you beheading him with one slash of your sword."

"No doubt." Nicolas scoured the back of his neck. "I'm responsible for the horrid incident of Brigette's imprisonment. Even though I suspected that Brodie was senseless after our first meeting, I failed to recognize the danger he embodied. Clearly, it was my obvious blunder and my sister suffered for my error in judgment." He looked at Daniel through tormented eyes. "How

257

fares my sister?"

"Her condition is grave. I know not if she will survive it. If you want Isabelle to see her, then speed is imperative."

Nicolas bent his head and rubbed his eyes. "Might I speak with her before departing to fetch Isabelle?"

"For now, she sleeps. Gather your men in the grand hall and partake of the meal provided. I will send for you when she stirs."

"Thank you, my friend." With his face full of regret, Nicolas stood while Daniel remained seated. "I know you blame me for all that has transpired. Of this, I am deeply regretful."

Daniel allowed Nicolas to leave without voicing his own guilt in the tragedy. He had confessed to Brigette and that's the one who mattered. Pushing to his feet, he walked back toward his bedchamber. His tread was slow as if shackled to a stone. How could he face each day if she died? Two wives dead by his hand? It was more than he could fathom.

Upon reaching his room, he leaned his forehead against the door. Taking a deep breath, he sighed. He opened the door with care and walked in to find Fiona talking with Brigette. He rushed to the bedside. "Is something amiss?"

"Nay, my lord. My lady awoke and asked for some water and food. Alice permitted a small amount of each."

"Thank you, Fiona."

"Husband, I believe you might wish to take advantage of some fresh bath water," she slurred from the effects of the sleeping brew.

His face heated. "Forgive me. I'm sure my unpleasant odor is pronounced since you smell of sweet lavender." He bowed low. "I will return posthaste with an aroma more to your liking."

"Oh, no. You may not leave this room. You must bathe where I may observe," she said with a half-closed lid. "'Tis only fair, would you not agree?"

He didn't think it possible, but his face heated even more from embarrassment. Without taking his gaze from his wife, he said, "Fiona, will you ask Mungo to have servants fill the tub with fresh water. It seems I need to bathe."

"Aye, my lord."

His stomach rumbled. "And, Fiona, please send a trencher with a selection of food to satisfy a hungry soldier."

"Aye, my lord." Fiona made a rapid retreat.

"I think you have embarrassed Fiona," he said.

"I think not, but I might have made you a bit uncomfortable."

He sat in the chair Fiona had vacated. "You are a little she-devil, my wife."

"I've concluded, life is uncertain, and I need to embrace my role as a wife."

He watched as she struggled to stay awake.

"I can't wash your back, but I can talk with you while you bathe."

When steaming water filled the tub, Daniel kissed her hand he held. "If my kiss could wipe away each wound, I would kiss them all. But alas, that is not the case."

"'Tis a nice plan just the same. I'll await your kisses after you wash," she said with a crooked smile.

He wasn't sure how he felt about bathing with his wife present. Awkward would be one word. Surprised would be another. But his favorite word? Delighted.

"This is a most unusual request, but mayhap a ritual we might wish to repeat." He began unclothing while he made idle chatter only to find his little brave soldier had fallen asleep before he reached the water.

Daniel awoke with a jerk from dreaming about a burning castle. He looked upon his sleeping wife who lay beside him. After his wash and grabbing a bite to eat, he had crawled in the bed and wrapped his arm around her. She had gravitated toward his warm body. Except for her stomach, she was like bones wrapped in skin. She needed to gain body weight to fight off the fever coursing through her form. The cold compresses had reduced the swelling in her face a wee bit. He prayed she would regain total use of her damaged eye.

She groaned while in a fitful sleep.

"Brigette? Are ye awake?" He whispered in her ear. She snuggled closer and turned on her side to face him.

He rubbed her back in gentle circles. "Brigette, ye need to wake up, and eat a bite."

"Hmm?" she murmured.

With a gentle touch, he kissed her cheek and her nose. "Ye need to open your eyes," he encouraged. "Can ye do that for me? Open your eyes and behold your husband."

A frown formed between her brows. "No."

His focus fastened on her pout that demanded a caress. He imparted a feather-like kiss and waited.

Her one eye opened a slit. "You may do that again."

With tenderness, he pulled her into a loose embrace and kissed her with purpose. "Does that satisfy ye?"

More was her reply. He rested his head against hers. "The kissing must stop before I'm rendered useless. I must rise. You need to eat and drink to build up your strength to vanquish your fever." Before leaving her, he wrapped her in a sheepskin blanket. She moved to her back when he walked around to the other side of the bed where the food rested under a cloth.

He carried the tray and sat on the edge of the bed. "Can ye sit up, my dove?"

"Your charm does tempt me."

"I'll help you." He put the tray on the bed and lifted her shoulders. "Let me prop you against these downy pillows."

"I'm not very hungry."

"Just a few morsels." Daniel fed her a small bite. "Don't make that face at me," he said with good nature.

"It's not my favorite. Pastries are more to my liking."

"I'll have pastries sent up. But for now, have some berries." She opened, and Daniel placed a berry to her lips. Their eyes met and held. She sucked it from his fingers.

"Mm. That was nice."

"More?"

"Yes."

He fed her each bite until she stopped his hand. "No more." After she drank her cup of water, he dabbed her lips. She pulled his arm into her lap and weaved their fingers together before speaking. "Thank you. I am grateful for your care of me, but you and I both know it is all for naught."

He gave a gentle squeeze to her hand as he stared at her saddened face. When she didn't try to speak, he cupped her cheek. "You mustn't speak this way. You have survived much, but only God knows our future. We must trust Him."

He watched her chin tremble, and her eyes turn red. Her head sunk low with her attention on their linked hands.

"We will face each day as it comes and pray for the best. No more talk such as this. Agreed?" he pleaded.

She raised her blotchy face. "I will try."

"That is all I ask." With the cloth he dried her tears. After removing the tray from the bed, he gathered her in his arms and gently rocked. "All will be well. You will see."

When her tense body relaxed, he sat back. "I know ye are weak, but I need to ask a favor of you."

"What is it you need?"

"It's not what I need, but what you might need. I know of no other way but to be straightforward. There are people here who wish an audience with you. Do you have the endurance?"

"William?"

"Nay. I told him he could visit you on the morrow. 'Tis others."

"'Twill be acceptable, but for a short time."

He fluffed her hair that lay on her shoulders and arranged it to hide the worst of her injury.

"Ye are so beautiful," he said within inches of her lips. She awarded him a weak smile before his kiss. "Mm, you taste of sweet berries."

He rose and went to the door. "Are you sure?" he asked again.

"Yes."

Brigette sank into the soft pillows. Who would Daniel bring? She expected it was her guards who had tended to her during the trip to Fairwick castle. She needed to thank all for their watch care and reassure them that she didn't hold any responsible for her abduction.

The darkness of the sky disclosed the late hour. Why didn't her husband wait until the morrow for people to speak with her? Unless ... oh dear ... unless she really was dying. Her head jerked. He had talked as if she would be fine and to trust God, but she knew he didn't believe it.

Daniel cracked open the door. "Are ye ready?"

She wiped her clammy palms on the blanket. "Yes, send them in."

As Daniel stepped aside, there stood Nicolas behind him. He looked wretched. Her husband indicated for Nicolas to take the seat next to her bedside.

He bowed low. "Brigette, thank you for seeing me."

"Oh, me. I most certainly am dying."

Nicolas's eyes grew round. "That's not why I am here," he sputtered.

"Oh?"

He gulped a deep breath. "No. I have come to make amends. My guilt has driven me to seek your forgiveness."

She couldn't believe her ears. Her hardhearted brother wanted her forgiveness? Should she withhold it and make him squirm? *Give forgiveness for I have forgiven you.*

With his head bowed he put his elbows upon his bent knees and clasped his hands between his legs. "I know I don't deserve your pardon for all that I have put you through, but I'm petitioning you for mercy." He lifted his face. "Our Holy God and Almighty Father has convicted me of my own sins, of which are many. How can I possibly expect you to be perfect when our Lord and Savior Jesus Christ is the only perfect and Holy One?"

Seeing his ravaged face and sorrowful eyes, her heart melted. He, too, had suffered under their earthly father's tyranny. As he grew up without a mother, there was never love extended toward him except from their brother, Phillip. It was not an excuse for his treatment of her but helped her grasp why they had clashed. From his bleak expression, she sensed he had come to her in genuine humbleness.

Her left arm struggled to reach his hand. He met her halfway and placed her delicate hand in his own.

"I forgive you." She shrugged. "I was not an easy child to parent."

His eyes lit up. "Thank you, my sister. I was prepared to leave this room a broken man, but you have restored me with your forgiveness."

Daniel stepped forward. "She grows weary, and there is one more to speak with her this night."

Nicolas acknowledged Daniel. "Of course." He looked back at Brigette whose hand he still held. Placing his other hand over their clasped hands, he said, "If it pleases you, when you are stronger, I will bring Isabelle and baby William for a visit."

"That would be delightful," she said with affection.

Nicolas stood and kissed her head. "Take care, my love."

"I love you, as well, my brother." Her rapid blinking kept her eyes dry as Nicolas departed.

Daniel came to her side. "Are you able to speak with one more? I can tell them they must wait until you are stronger."

"No. One more."

He stroked her hair. "I'll be right back."

When next she looked up, there stood Thomas. Without a doubt, she was dying and probably quicker than she first imagined. He held his hands together in front of himself as he shuffled to her bedside. She was almost amused when he didn't say anything.

"Thomas?" She wasn't prepared for what happened next. He fell to his knees and buried his head in her blanket at her side.

"I'm so sorry. Please forgive me," he cried.

263

His sobs were her undoing. She placed her hand on his bent head and slid it around to cup his chin. With reluctance, he raised his head.

"Of course, I forgive you." Her own eyes burned with unshed tears.

Still on his knees, he grabbed her hand and clutched it to his heart. "My heart has been heavy with my guilt ever since your wedding day. And then when you were captured and tortured, I feared I would lose my mind from grief … and guilt." He kissed her hand. "I deserved my misery, but you didn't merit what Brodie did to you."

"That's enough, Thomas," Daniel interrupted. "Your sister is drained and needs her rest."

She had to smile at Thomas's behavior. Leave it to him to mention her horrific ordeal. He had much to learn about how to converse with a woman, but now was not the time to lesson him. "You are forgiven. Go in peace." Her hand slipped from his grasp when he stood.

He gave her a chaste kiss on the cheek and left with a bounce in his step—so different from when he first came into the room. As she watched him leave, she understood that her maturity had surpassed her brother's. Sharing the wedding bed with a husband and being beaten by a crazy man had sped up her development both emotionally and spiritually.

After Daniel closed the door for the last time, he came to her side. "You are a merciful and loving sister."

"When I saw them tonight, it made me recognize how much I do love them."

He sat on the edge of the bed and bracketed her body with his arms. "You are also an amazing mother to William … and … a breathtakingly beautiful wife to me. One who continues to amaze me with every word she speaks."

She soaked in his praise. Was he truly happy that he wed her? Did he no longer ponder her sinful past? She prayed so. If she was not long for this world, then she wanted her last days to be spent with her husband and her son, who brought her delight.

Her hands crawled up his chest and around his neck. "I might be weak and weary, but I'm not dead yet. Kiss me."

"Of this, I concur."

He kissed her long and well.

Chapter Thirty-Five

"I can't take another bite," Brigette whined.

"Ye must increase your strength, and for that to happen, nourishment is what is needed," Daniel persisted.

As he tried to coax another spoonful of porridge through her lips, she gagged. "Hurry get a pan," she pleaded.

Daniel wasn't fast enough as she retched over the side of the bed. In between breaths, she cried, "I'm sorry."

Her husband held her hair back until she finished. He grabbed the cloth off the near-by table and allowed her to wipe her face before giving her a sip of water to rinse her mouth.

He sat on the edge of the bed. "Are ye done?"

Closing her eyes, she plopped back against her pillows and sank deep into their softness. "Aye. I've emptied out all that you put into me this morn."

"I'll return straight away." He went to the door and called for a maid to come to clean the floor and then came back to her. He dipped a clean cloth into some cool water and bathed her face and neck.

"Forgive me for encouraging you to continue eating when 'tis clear you were too queasy. I anticipated you might feel better if you ate something."

"'Tis not of your making. I place the blame on that worthless Brodie Elliot."

"Well, ye need not concern yourself with him anymore."

Her eyes popped wide. "Is he dead?"

"Aye."

"Did Nicolas kill him?"

"Nay. His blood is on my hands."

"Your hands? You told Nicolas to see to his demise before we pulled out of the gate."

Daniel rubbed his chin. "Was there nothing ye didn't hear me say?"

"Not much," she said with a crooked grin.

Daniel rose at the knocking at the door. When he opened it, in rushed Fiona with a young girl. Fiona gripped Brigette's hand, "Was the food not to yer liking?"

"Nay, Fiona. I'm not up to eating this morn."

"Have no fear, we'll get ye cleaned up."

Fiona and the young girl made quick work of the floor and cleared away the remaining food. "No need for ye to smell the offending porridge." With a delicate touch, Fiona brushed a wisp of hair from Brigette's face. "We'll leave ye to rest, praying ye feel more the thing soon."

Brigette reached over and touched Fiona's hand. "Thank you, sweet friend."

"Yes, m' lady." She bobbed a curtsey and left with the young girl in her wake.

"Husband come away from the door. All is well."

Daniel walked over to the opposite side of the bed and crawled in close to her. "Do ye think ye can rest?"

She pulled his arm across her body and held it fast. "Now I might be able too. But only if you tell me of Brodie's end."

"Now, wife, that's not a good bedtime tale."

Her brow arched. "Now."

"Aye," he agreed on a sigh. "From Nicolas's account, Brodie had been hiding within the castle when it was put ablaze. The fire and smoke flushed him out into the courtyard, his body already on fire. Nicolas said he died before he fell to the ground."

"Oh, I see. I'm sure Nicolas was most displeased that Brodie died before he had a chance to end his miserable life with the sword."

"Ye know your brother well."

Just hearing the recounting of Brodie's demise reminded her of life's uncertainty. "How late is the hour?"

"'Tis midday."

"I'm wasting away in this room."

"Nay, sweet wife. Ye are healing. Your eye is much improved from the cool compresses and ointments Alice applied." His hand caressed her arm. "It takes time to recover after what you have endured."

Before she had time to respond, a loud knock rattled the door. "I believe Mungo needs you," she said dryly. "He's not known for his soft touch."

Daniel chuckled as he rose to answer the door. She frowned when he stepped into the hallway, and she couldn't hear the conversation. One day she would hear Mungo speak. Well, if she lived. When Daniel came back inside, he wore a wide grin.

"Ye have a special visitor. Are ye up to receiving?"

Her shoulders slumped. "Now, who?"

"I didn't want to ruin the surprise, but 'tis Isabelle."

"Isabelle is here?" she asked with disbelief.

"Aye. I'll be back post haste."

He dashed from the room leaving her with dreary imaginings. She was a little alarmed when Nicolas and Thomas came to see her immediately after her rescue. It made her speculate that she might be dying. Now ... now, with Isabelle's arrival ... her days were short in number.

She gulped several deep breaths and blinked fast. No need to be a crying babe when Isabelle reached her room since her time on earth was sorely limited. Isabelle's words came to mind. *God has a plan, and it's for your good.* "Unlikely," she said.

She didn't have to wait long.

Isabelle burst into the room. "Brigette, my sweet girl." She hurried to reach her. Gathering her into her arms, Isabelle's tears flowed which caused Brigette to weep. She didn't know how long they embraced, except they held tight until their eyes ran dry. Leaning back, Isabelle laced their fingers together and gazed at her.

"How fare you, my love?"

"It doesn't go well. I'm sure I'm dying." She sniffled.

"You know, there was a time when I believed my end was near, but God brought me through. His plans for me were not complete. I have a hard time believing God is bringing your earthly journey to an end."

"I had hoped that once I was rescued, my life would take a turn for the better, but this morning I spewed my meal on the floor. Even the smell of food caused my stomach to rumble." Shaking her head, "It was most foul."

Isabelle sat quiet for a moment. "If it's agreeable with you, I would like to examine your wounds and see for myself. What say you?"

Brigette sighed. "I don't see how it will help, but you may do as you wish."

Daniel stood with his back against the door watching the two women hold each other as if one might vanish if their grasp was broken. In his view, a touching moment for sure since he held tenderness for both. One through friendship while the other born from a passion that grew deeper with each passing moment. Oh, how he wished he could change his poor decisions and turn back the sun. If only...

Daniel aroused from his woolgathering when Isabelle said she wanted to examine Brigette. He realized his presence would cause more harm than good. She was safe in Isabelle's competent hands.

"I will leave you two alone if that is acceptable."

Isabelle jerked her head around to glare at Daniel as if he were an interloper. "Have you been here the entire time?"

He threw his hands up in surrender. "Aye. I don't leave my

wife's side unless there's a crisis. "

"You are not needed," Isabelle emphasized.

"Tell Mungo where you will be, my husband, and I'll send for you when Isabelle has concluded." Brigette winked.

"As you wish." Daniel bowed and closed the door with a click.

He found faithful Mungo outside their closed door. "I'm going to stretch my legs. I'll head toward the back of the castle."

Mungo nodded in acknowledgement.

He had nowhere in particular to go but gravitated toward the abandoned wing of the castle. The closer he came to the uninhabited area, the colder the air became. It was no wonder. The hearths had been chillingly silent for years. Even though it was midmorning, the passageway became gloomier the farther he walked. At one point, he retraced his steps and retrieved a torch from the wall.

When he reached the entrance to one hallway, he froze in place. Bewildered. Near the end of the hallway glowed a lighted torch. Without venturing farther, he knew it was outside the room he had shared with Anna. Who had dared to walk these halls?

Anger gave fuel to his steps as he marched toward the light. After Anna's death, he had forbidden anyone from gracing these halls ... ever! The doors had been sealed and the rooms left untouched. His breathing escalated the closer he came to his old bedchamber.

When he reached the closed portal, he halted. Staring at the door, he broke out in a cold sweat. His hands shook and his heart pounded as he placed the torch on the wall. Theories bounced around in his mind. If he passed through that door, he would pay a price. Deep within his spirit, he knew he needed to face his past if he was ever to have a future with Brigette.

With his hand on the latch, he inhaled a steadying breath and pushed. He stepped over the threshold and stiffened. The smell raced up his nose and memories flooded his mind weakening his knees. With feet of stone, he allowed his eyes to roam the room.

To his left sat the fireplace that Anna had insisted be ornate and grand. Now cobwebs covered the ornamental mantle and the candle sticks that rested upon it. On his right was their wardrobe. It had been hand carved to Anna's specifications. If he opened it, he would find elaborate moth-eaten dresses on the hooks. No doubt mice had taken up residence inside. Then his gaze gravitated to the lavish platform bed with thick tattered curtains.

His eyes closed on a groan from deep within. The blunders he had made rushed back to his memory—Anna with excruciating pains from labor were vivid. In his mind's eye, he could see Alice scurrying about to help ease the new babe into the world … but something wasn't right. Alice's face showed fear. No, it was terror!

Daniel had fled the room, unable to handle Anna's screams and Alice's panic. He had had no training of which he could draw to offer aid in the situation. Instead, he ran to the grand hall where he drank his fill of ale to dull his awareness. In short time, he had passed out and slept through his wife's death. Inconceivable!

His burning eyes opened to the reality. If he had been in this room on that fateful night, his wife might have lived. Wandering farther into the room, he noticed an easel covered with a large white cloth. Standing before it, his shaking hand pinched a corner of the cloth. With a slight tug, the fabric fluttered to the floor.

On a quick intake of breath, he stared. Awestruck. There before him rested a portrait of William, Brigette, and himself. Who painted this? Brigette? No other would have dared to go against his directive concerning this room. He cocked his head and regarded the remarkable resemblance of William. She had captured his adoration as he looked upon his new mother. Even her own expression was a caring mother with tender eyes fixed on William.

The positioning appeared similar to the painting with Anna. His head swiveled to look over the fireplace … and there it was … the original portrait of Anna, William, and himself. Someone had removed it from his current chamber and hung it back in its rightful place.

"Brigette," he whispered.

He edged toward the fireplace for a closer look. As he looked at the expression of his first wife, he came to a realization. He had loved her as a young man with his first love. Her beauty had drawn him like a bee to honey causing him to disregard her flaws. Now, as a man full grown, her weaknesses came into focus.

So deliriously in love, he had fed her penchant toward self-centeredness and overindulgence. "I denied you nothing. You, in turn, obeyed me without question. A perfect pair until we lost the ability to put others first." His jaw clinched. "I turned you into a pampered princess while I became the arrogant fool. Why did I allow it to happen?"

His head swiveled toward the new painting—starkly different from the one with Anna. Even though a young bride, Brigette had changed or perhaps his view of her had altered.

"You are no longer a child but a strong woman withstanding collisions of the worst sort ... one who loves my son without question ... one who laid siege to my heart ... and won." He shook his head in wonder. "I love my wife!" Upon his revelation, he felt compelled to confess all to her. He wanted nothing to impede their future together.

"I love my wife." Even with the admittance of his affection, tears cascaded over their boundaries. He fell to his knees in anguish of heart. She would most likely die in a short time, and he was to blame.

Looking heavenward, he cried out. "Almighty God and Father, I am a wretched man. A man whose arrogance has endangered the ones I love the most. Forgive me, Father," he cried. "Forgive my sins against You and against Brigette." His head sank to his chest. "I have made so many mistakes ... so many."

The weight of his guilt pinned him to the floor. "Holy Father if You would but punish me and not Brigette. Let Your condemnation fall on me. Spare her life, I pray You," he pleaded.

While wallowing in despair, Mungo exploded into the room. "My lord come quickly. 'Tis your lady. She is wailing and in great need."

Daniel rushed from the room and sprinted down the dark

passageway praying God's protection on his wife. He ran into their room and skidded to an abrupt stop near the bed. His pounding heart accelerated when he found Brigette alone and weeping. Anxiety filled him.

"What is amiss?"

Through her tears, a beaming smile broke forth. "I'm not dying! God has spared my life and the life of our babe!"

"Truly?" he asked shocked at her words.

Her cheeks glistened. "Aye."

Daniel scooped her into his arms and snuggled her close. "Oh, my wife. What a joyous wonder! I am blessed beyond what I deserve."

She grasped his face between her hands. "God has worked another miracle. I desire this babe with all my heart," she said with awe in her voice. "I didn't think it possible."

Holding his wife, he sat on the edge of the bed trying to grasp all that had happened. Their heads touched as his eyes closed. "God our Father, our Prince of Peace, and our Healer, we praise You for Your provision. We praise You for sustaining us through our greatest trial and sparing the life of Brigette and our child. May we never forget to give You praise as You continue to hold us in Your embrace." Amen and Amen.

Epilogue

Fifteen years later . . .

She breathed deep. "I'm not ready to go back."

Nestled in her husband's embrace, Brigette's head rested against his shoulder. The view from the hillside—spectacular. The clear sky was deceptive as a biting wind swirled around them. Off in the distance, sheep grazed at the bottom of the snowcapped mountains presenting a picturesque backdrop. She shivered as a chill overtook her.

"Are you cold?" Daniel asked as he wrapped his cloak to encompass her whole body. He rested the flat of his hand on her small, rounded stomach.

She gazed into his loving eyes and warmth pooled in her belly. "No, all is well. You are as warm as a roaring fire in the winter days. I but dread traveling without you." She pouted.

"Those puckered lips demand a kiss." Daniel hauled her into his lap and kissed her with fervor.

"You do have a splendid way of taking my mind from my troubles."

"We mustn't linger. The children will be dismantling the castle if left unsupervised overlong."

"I thought William had them under control?"

"Emilia follows his every command. I believe she would wed him if I allowed it. But the twins ... they presume they were created to annoy each person who crosses their paths."

She stroked his bearded cheeks. "Now, my husband, Helen and Gillian are sweet ten-year-old girls that love their older brother." She batted her lashes. "They just delight in tactics that exasperate him."

He tweaked her nose. "They learned it from their mother."

Her brows raised. "And what about James? He will be the one to turn my hair gray."

Daniel gasped with his hand to his heart. "I take offense to that statement. How can you say such about our seven-year-old baby?"

"He won't be the baby much longer," she said as she rubbed her tummy.

Daniel leaned down and spoke to her protruding stomach. "We need another boy to even out the home forces. Do you hear me?"

With a gentle touch, she pulled his hair to bring his face back up to her. "Stop that. We will be happy with another girl if that's who God has in store for our growing family."

With one final kiss, Daniel set her aside and stood. He reached his hand to assist her to her feet. "Come, my wife. You must have adequate rest before your journey on the morrow."

"As you wish." She brushed off the back of her cloak that had protected her from the cold ground. "I don't relish journeying while you finish the castle wall. 'Twould be no trouble to wait until you have completed the task."

With his arm around her shoulders, he guided her down the slope toward home. "We've been over this before. It's too dangerous to wait for me to oversee the completion of the wall repair. The weather could turn angry with ice and snow. I won't chance the safety of my family ever again. William can direct the mighty men who will accompany you and the children to see Isabelle. I am regretful that you must sleep under the stars for one night since the Fairwicks moved to the coast."

"From her letters, Sanddown Castle has a beautiful location overlooking the ocean. I do look forward to wintering there."

When within sight of their home, Daniel reassured her. "Have no fears. I'm sending Niall, Iain, and Mungo with your party. All will be as it should."

On a quick stop, she pivoted to face her husband with her hand upon his chest. "You mustn't send your three best warriors with me. Who will accompany you when you join us on the coast?"

Covering her hand with his own, he smiled. "Wife, ye wound me with that question. I will travel with a small contingency of men so that I might reach you with speed. And remember, I'm not a warrior in my dotage."

With a quick hug around his waist, she peered into his sparkling eyes. "No, you are not. You're my most valiant warrior husband." Remaining in his embrace, she became serious. "I never dared to dream it possible, but I care for you with a fierce kind of adoration—an all-consuming love."

With his eyes riveted on her face, his arms tightened. "Aww, my dove, I am undone. Your selfless love has vanquished me. If we were ensconced in our room, I would let down your hair and kiss you properly." Instead, he smoothed back her hair that blew in the wind. "I'm hopelessly devoted to you, my love. You arrived at my point of need, upended my life and captivated my heart. My love belongs to you," he said before planting a soft kiss.

His words of praise were a soothing balm to her once wounded soul. She was so thankful for all that God had provided through her husband. He loved her with abandon, provided protection, supported her endeavors, and gave her precious children. However, the greatest gift was his spiritual leadership in their home. He made it known that with God as the Lord of their lives, all would be well … not perfect, but joyous.

Hand in hand they walked toward home and their next adventure.

DICSUSSION QUESTIONS

1. What was at the heart of Brigette's decision to remain unmarried?

2. How were women affected when they had no voice in their futures?

3. What was Daniel's motivation to marry Brigette?

4. What knowledge about marriage did Brigette lack when she entered the marital contract with Daniel?

5. What was the main issue that kept Brigette from being reconciled with her brother, Nicolas?

6. Was it a wise decision for Daniel to travel with the king? Why or why not?

7. What words of wisdom did Isabelle give Brigette?

8. Who was Tancred and what was his purpose?

9. What life lessons did Daniel learn from God?

10. What was God's purpose in allowing Brigette's abduction?

11. What can be gained from confession to God and to others?

12. What are the advantages of following God's plan?

Author's
Note

King James VI of Scotland and King James I of England and Ireland were the same person. In 1603, James and Anne, his wife, were crowned at Westminster Abbey. The kingdoms of England and Scotland were united under one crown; yet, remained individual sovereign states, with their own parliaments, judiciary, and laws. He continued to reign in all three kingdoms for 22 years, a period known as the Jacobean era, until he died in March 1625.

Not only was King James the first monarch to unite Scotland, England, and Ireland into Great Britain (as he liked to call it), but he ordered the translation of the Authorized Version of 1611 of the Bible. We know it as the Authorized King James Bible. King James gave his subjects the greatest gift possible—the Bible—so they could read it and come to salvation through Jesus Christ.

Having access to a Bible was paramount for my story. Therefore, I used facts about King James and weaved a story of what could have been.

Did you find yourself identifying with Brigette's predicaments? One sizeable crisis was of her own making—a ruined reputation. It's not uncommon for each of us to make poor decisions based on our anger, jealousy, or bitterness. Just as Brigette experienced, when we step outside of God's will for our lives, it can have forever consequences.

However, there are times when we are in the middle of a violent storm not caused from a bad decision. At the time of Brigette's kidnapping, she had decided to follow God's instructions about marriage and apply them to her situation. So, if she was following God, why did she encounter such a horrible calamity?

In the life of a Christian there will be times when God allows painful events to occur. Often, we question God's wisdom in permitting these terrible episodes to invade our lives—cancer, loss of a job, death of a child, unfaithfulness of a spouse. It doesn't make sense to us.

As you study the Bible, you will find that God has a purpose for your pain. This pain will remain only long enough for God to accomplish His purpose in your situation. Since God's highest priority is for you to know Him intimately, He oftentimes will give you more than you can handle. Why? So, you will depend on Him for guidance, advice, wisdom, and strength.

Isaiah 41:10 says: *Fear not, for I am with you;*
Be not dismayed, for I am your God.
I will strengthen you, Yes I will help you,
I will uphold you with my righteous right hand.

Therefore, when you find yourself in a "Brigette-size" storm, don't run screaming from the room. Instead, turn to Jesus Christ, our Lord and Savior. He knows the outcome of your situation and is ready to walk through the fire with you. Take His hand and let Him lead. He can take your messy life and turn it into something beautiful. Try Him. You will not be disappointed.

"For I know the thoughts that I think toward you,
says the Lord, thoughts of peace and not of evil,
to give you a future and a hope."
Jeremiah 29:11

Teresa Smyser lives in Northern Alabama with her minister husband and their deaf cat, Spock. They have two married children, two grandsons and two granddaughters. She graduated from Eastern Kentucky University and now works as an accountant and divides the rest of her time between family, friends, church activities and writing. Teresa's prayer is that not only will her novels entertain, but they will point people to the love and the hope found in her Lord and Savior, Jesus Christ.

For more information about Teresa and her books, visit her at www.teresasmyser.com or www.facebook.com/teresasmyser

She loves hearing from her readers. Send questions or comments to authorsmys@gmail.com

Thank you for reading the second book in the Warrior Bride Series. If you enjoyed it, please take a moment and leave a review on Goodreads or amazon. It would be greatly appreciated.

If you enjoyed

IN HIS EMBRACE

then read:

Warrior Bride Series: Book 3
Find out what happens to William

COMING SOON!

Made in the USA
Columbia, SC
14 November 2021